## About the Author

James William Ring grew up and lives in Kent, England. He
spent many years working and volunteering abroad in Israel,
India and many other countries. He has always been
interested in writing.

# Seconds From Death

# James William Ring

# Seconds From Death

Olympia Publishers
*London*

**www.olympiapublishers.com**
OLYMPIA PAPERBACK EDITION

A CIP catalogue record for this title is
available from the British Library.

ISBN: 978-1-80074-254-3

This is a work of fiction.
Names, characters, places and incidents originate from the writer's
imagination. Any resemblance to actual persons, living or dead, is
purely coincidental.

First Published in 2022

Olympia Publishers
Tallis House
2 Tallis Street
London
EC4Y 0AB

Printed in Great Britain

# Dedication

For my mother and father

# 1

Gavish Molcho stood, crunching the cool night sand between his toes. He was looking out over the Mediterranean, his shoes in one hand and his trousers rolled up to his knees. A wave rolled in from the darkness and he stepped backwards to avoid getting his feet wet. Off to his left came the cries of laughter, as a young man chased a girl.

Would they take the mission? They would he thought. They would do it for Adar. Gavish turned and started back up the beach to the promenade, letting his feet sink into the cool, golden sand that still glowed in the moonlit night. Overhead a plane flew in low, passing over the big hotels, heading to Ben Gurion airport. Glancing right towards the lifeguard tower, Gavish noticed a couple making out. He smiled. It was one of those nights, the stars, the beach, summer, and somewhere, in another part of the world there was a maniac on the loose, killing agents.

Gavish sat down on the sandy wall, that ran the promenade, and smacked the sand off his feet with his hands, knowing it would be impossible to get them completely clean. He took his socks out of his shoes and pulled them on, then slipped his shoes on, rolled his trousers down and stood up and dusted the sand of his backside. It was near midnight, but the city was just waking up. Lovers walked hand in hand, families coming out for a midnight feast, dog walkers, joggers, roller skaters and skateboarders all lined the promenade. He crossed the road, still hearing the echo the waves made as they crashed in on the shore. The sea always sounds different at night, he thought. A short walk up the block and he was at, Ben Yehuda Street. When Gavish got to his car he sat for a while, smoking, pondering and listening to the easy music playing on the radio. He knew where the two men were. He had had them followed all day and night. He just hoped that they would not be too shit faced by the time he arrived. They both had their flaws, one of them more so than the other. He might even be insane, but they came as a pair, and by God they were good at their job.

Gavish turned right on to Sderot Ben Gurion Street. He cruised slowly with the car window wound down. Marvin Gaye and Tammi Terrell had just started to sing, about how good loving ain't easy to come by and Gavish thought he could feel the sexual energy between them in that song. It was a short distance up the road. He turned on to Shlomo Hamelech Street, just as the song started to fade, parked and got out. He could still smell the sea and the sweet summer air, as he walked towards the bar.

Foster was the name of the bar, and from the outside Gavish thought it looked abandoned. A few motor scooters and a bicycle were parked up outside, but that was all, no one was waiting outside to go in, and he could hear no music playing, but this was the place he was told they would be. Suddenly the sound from inside the bar filled the quiet neighbourhood. Two tall beauties came out the glass door, their arms linked, staggering and giggling. The glass door swung shut behind them and then there was quiet again.

Gavish entered the bar and was hit straight away by the muffled sound of a dozen conversations all happening at once. The two men he was after were sat on stools at the bar. They stood out from the rest of the crowd, who were mostly smartly dressed, attractive twenty somethings. These two looked like they were going through a midlife crisis, with their flip-flops and Hawaiian shirts.

Ron Yaffe and Netzer Akerman liked this bar. Foster was a good place to drink. Both men were thirty-seven now and starting to feel it, but this place made them feel young again. Good music, not the same shit they were playing everywhere else around Tel Aviv. Youngsters drinking and smoking the night away. The smoke in Foster was four-tenths cigarette and six-tenths hash.

Ron grew up on a kibbutz in northern Israel, a few miles and a stone's throw away from the Lebanese border. The border was so close to kibbutz Yiftah, that he could hear the prayers from the mosques that played on loudspeakers. Unlike a lot of his friends and fellow kibbutzniks, Ron liked the sound of the prayers, particularly in the early morning, when he would look out his bedroom window and see the sun rising over the orchards.

Ron had a happy childhood, like nearly all the children on the kibbutz. To him the other children on the kibbutz were not merely friends, they were his brothers and sisters. They grew up together, learned together, some even eventually married and got divorced. They celebrated the holidays not just as a community, but as one big family. No doors on the kibbutz were ever locked and you were always welcome in your neighbours' home and treated like a member of the family. As teenagers they worked on the kibbutz, partied and smoked their first joints together.

It wasn't really until Ron did his service in the IDF, that he made his first friends from outside the kibbutz. He enjoyed his service and excelled in training, quickly becoming someone others looked up to. Most of the youngsters resented having to spend the best part of three years in the IDF, at an age when they would rather be going to college and partying or backpacking the world. Ron didn't, he saw it as his duty and a great way to meet people from all over Israel. One person he met was a young man named Netzer Akerman.

Like Ron, Netzer was also born and raised on a kibbutz. Kibbutz Lahav in southern Israel is twenty kilometres north from Beersheba and about ninety kilometres south of Jerusalem. Growing up, Netzer kept himself to himself. At the age of seven, his mother, his world, died of cancer. He took comfort in books and food, reading and eating everything he could get his hands on. By the age of thirteen, Netzer was fluent in English, Spanish, Italian, French and German. He had picked up different languages, hanging around with the kibbutz volunteers who had travelled from all over the world to spend some time on a kibbutz and work the land and party. The one thing the volunteers loved most of all, was to get high. Netzer had a cousin, Elad, who was twenty-three and from Beersheba. Elad was just starting out as a dealer after failing at everything else. Elad saw the benefits of his younger cousin being friends with the foreigners, who loved to smoke, so he exploited the opportunity. Selling hash to the volunteers was easy and it made Elad and Netzer a lot of money. Not exactly fifty-fifty, more like eighty-twenty, but still a good amount of money for a kid Netzer's age. Everything was good, until everything wasn't. Elad got pinched one night in a bar, sealing a deal to sell a large quantity of LSD, he had just got his hands on, as a one off, to two undercover narcotics agents. Elad went to prison for three years, never mentioning Netzer's name to the police. A year after his release, Elad was dead. He was found alone with a needle stuck in his arm in some run down flat in Tel Aviv.

At fifteen, Netzer decided enough was enough. He wanted a body to match his brain. Every morning he would get up at the crack of dawn, before school, and go running around the surrounding Lahav forest. After the run, press ups, pull ups and sit ups, and they would increase every five days. After one-month Netzer could see his feet, and after three months Netzer was not only slimmer, but he also found he was toning up and maybe getting a little taller as well. Good habits followed, ditching chocolate for nuts and fizzy drinks for water and black coffee.

When it was time for Netzer to do his time in the IDF, he was in fabulous shape. He quickly became friends with a young man named Ron Yaffe who, like Netzer, had a superior IQ.

The two youngsters were quickly noticed by their senior commanders and invited to try out for Sayeret Matkal on Special Forces Day. Only the absolute elite are chosen. Hundreds of willing candidates participate in the rigorous try-outs, with only a handful passing the first phase of training. Ron and Netzer both recorded excellent intelligence scores and showed great mental and physical endurance skills. At the end of extensive training, only the best, were left. Fitter people than Ron and Netzer were not selected because they could not handle the emotional strain. Psychologically, the stress of little to no sleep, extensive training and problem solving all repeated again, and again over continuous weeks destroyed some of the candidates.

Within two years and after a daring rescue mission into the heart of Beirut, both men had been hand-picked by Yossi Ben Hadar to join a special team he was putting together. Yossi Ben Hadar, a hero of the Yom Kippur war, took to Ron and Netzer immediately and they to him. Over the next ten years Ron and Netzer travelled all over the globe using numerous forged passports. Their identities and appearances changed from mission to mission. They were priests from Italy, businessmen from Germany, brothers, lovers and skin heads. Everywhere they went they gathered intelligence, followed suspects, money launderers with connections to Iran and Egypt. When they had gathered all the facts, and they had been given the green light, only then they would act. It was sometimes a small explosion, a gas leak, or faulty wiring. Occasionally a bullet, or knife wound — a mugging gone wrong. But most of the time it was just everyday unlucky stuff, like a car accident, a fall, a heart attack, or an electrical mishap. Rarely an act that would make the news, or make the world take notice.

For ten years they had dealt out justice, and the powers that be in Jerusalem had supported them unconditionally. The last few years however had been hard. Promotions had put different people in power. Less power to people like Ron and Netzer. Their old mentor, Yossi Ben Hadar was decommissioned, retired. The world had started to think of Israel as an enemy to peace now. A new look was needed. A woman was sent in. Ayala Grazit was now their boss. More new school than old school, sent in by the government to help

Mossad, to educate them. She was a political tool. Words were to be the new weapon, the retaliation now.

'You should enjoy the remaining years you have with your grandchildren,' Ayala Gazit told Yossi Ben Hadar, the day she replaced him, sitting in his old chair in the office he had occupied for more than twenty years.

'My dear,' Yossi Ben Hadar said, turning from the window that he was looking out of for the last time. 'All that's happened today, is that our country has been made weaker.'

'Really?' Ayala said, looking up at him from her notes, with an amused smile.

'Really,' Yossi said, walking back to the desk. 'I've seen people like you come and go before. You may think you can get along without motherfuckers like me and the boys, but the sad reality is, you cannot. The truth is, you'll need them tomorrow.'

'That's a lovely sentiment. You will always be thought of in high regard here.' Ayala said, smiling up at him, then turning away to look down at her paperwork.

'I never want that. All I want is for you to unfuck yourself.' He said this as calmly and as pleasantly, as an old man asking a waitress for slice of his favourite pecan pie.

Ignoring this, focusing now on her computer, Ayala continued. 'I'm also going to need Ron and Netzer to stop whatever shady shit they're currently doing. I want all documents I don't have on those two loose cannons on my table, as soon as.'

Yossi Ben Hadar hated Ayala more than he had ever hated anyone, ever, at this moment. He felt a rage he hadn't felt since he was a young man. Who was this kid? She couldn't even be thirty and she was giving him orders. Yossi slammed his fists down hard on the desk making the computer monitor shake and Ayala jump. She looked up at him and he saw the scared little girl behind the tough exposure. He felt momentary remorse, but knew he had to continue. 'Those two loose cannons might just save your job one day. You want those documents? Look for them yourself. I seem to have forgotten where I put them. Must be my old age catching up with me,' Yossi had one hand on the door handle and was about to leave, when he turned. 'Your grandmother, she survived the holocaust?'

'She did, I guess we wouldn't be having this conversation if she hadn't.'

'Was she in a camp?'

'She was.'

'Which camp?' Yossi asked, his head down, seeming to examine the floor of his old office.

'Auschwitz,' she replied, staring up at him uneasily, not sure where he was going with this.

'You ever been to Argentina?'

'What?' Ayala shouted. She was confused and annoyed now.

'I have,' Yossi continued. He was looking out the window again, looking far away, remembering. 'In nineteen sixty-five. I was a lot younger then, and I didn't have this gut,' he said patting his stomach. 'I went on a French passport and found Carl Hess. You've probably not heard the name. He was a young doctor who worked with the angel of death himself, Josef Mengele at Auschwitz. It just so happened that Carl Hess had a fondness for the young children he experimented on,' Yossi turned to Ayala. 'Would you like to know what he did to the children?'

16

Ayala shook her head slowly. Her complexion was grey now. 'I would rather not.'

'Oh, but you must,' Yossi insisted. 'You must.'

The hairs on the back of Ayala's neck stood on end. His glaring eyes scared her, and she suddenly knew all the stories she had heard about this man were true. But it was his smile, the smile of a madman, that made her want to get up and run for the door, run for the door, open it and scream, scream for help. She sat still.

Yossi continued. 'Young boys were his favourite, but sometimes he used little girls. After he had raped a child, acting out all his wicked fantasies, he would experiment on that child. Lethal germs were his favourite. He loved to watch the changes in the subject, he liked to watch the children go crazy. There are other reports of slow cooking in an oven, seeing how long a child could stay alive, whilst being cooked. Freezing them, then trying to bring them back to life, and so on. A real-life Frankenstein,' Yossi paused for a second, taking in a deep breath, then sat down on the edge of his old desk, one hand in his pocket jangling his loose change. 'Anyway, I found this nice, polite man in a sleepy town called El Calafate, down in the region of Patagonia. Have you by chance heard of it?'

'I have not.' Ayala replied.

'Cold place. There were five of us in the town of Bariloche, a Mini Third Reich capital near the Andes. We had reliable intelligence to believe that Klaus Barbie was living there. And he was, but he had just left. Barbie was like a ghost, every time we got close to him, he would vanish. And guess who was always in the area?'

'I don't know, but I'm sure you're going to tell me.'

'The CIA. I still believe to this day, no matter what anyone else says. They recruited him. The fucking butcher of Lyon and the CIA in bed together. I'm going off-course again. So, we got a tip, along with a few photos of this man, believed to be Hess. So, I said I'll go check it out, the others stayed in Bariloche and I took a two day drive down to El Calafate, reading Hess's file on the way. I found him working as the town doctor, using the name Peter Müller, a well-respected member of the community. The townsfolk loved him. He had a beautiful wife and two children, a real family man. I watched him for three weeks. I was certain it was him, apart from a bit more weight and some grey hairs, he was exactly the same. My job was to make certain it was him, then call in the team for a possible extraction, so we could take him back Israel. Problem was after Eichmann, getting anybody out alive would be dangerous and unlike Barbie, Hess wasn't seen as so important. I got the message to leave and come back to Bariloche. A problem occurred the night before I was to leave. I had read his file. I knew all about the children he experimented on and raped. I saw him living a peaceful, tranquil life with his perfect family after he had destroyed thousands of families. I acknowledged the order. I also followed him the next morning on one of his walks through the forest. I walked right up to him and asked for a lighter. He took out a lighter from his coat pocket and smiled at me, and it was a warm smile. It was a trusting smile. I wondered, if that was the same gentle smile he gave the children, before raping them and injecting their little bodies with lethal germs.

"Certainly, young man."

I was face to face with him. He pressed the lighter in my hand, his eyes never left mine. His smile was disguised and fatherly, but he couldn't hide the truth in those eyes. They were pits of evil. Black and soulless.

"Where are you from, if you don't mind me asking? It's just that I haven't seen you around before, and I know nearly everyone in town."

"I'm from nowhere. My family was wiped out in the holocaust." That fake smile melted away from his face then, and he knew, I knew. "Still pretending to be a doctor are we, Hess?"

His polite manner vanished at that, and I saw the true face of evil before me. "I am a doctor," he said proudly, straightening up, and I could picture him then, there in his SS uniform.

I laughed in his face. "No, a doctor saves people. You raped and murdered them." I pulled out a pistol, a Ballester-Molina. A very reliable pistol with a comfortable grip and pointed it at his face.

"My dear boy, the war ended a long time ago."

"Not for me."

"I was just following orders," he said, shakily, and with lips trembling.

I shot him in his right eye, and his head flung back, a red mist engulfed the air. I watched him fall backwards on to the ground. He twitched for a few seconds, shaking on the floor, his brain not fully comprehending what had just happened. His right leg bounced up and down, still trying to live. I hate it when that happens, it leaves a lasting impression on you. I dragged the corpse into the woods, then rolled it down a bank, and drove back to Bariloche.'

'Why did you tell me this story?' Ayala asked.

'I just want to know how you plan to stop monsters, when you're hiding behind that desk?' Yossi Ben Hadar turned and walked out.

He was right. She needed them now. The shit had hit the fan. Someone was killing her agents and needed to be stopped. Ayala was out of options.

'Can I buy you bums a drink?' a familiar voice asked, from behind where Ron and Netzer were seated drinking in Foster, and singing along badly to Goodbye Stranger by Supertramp.

Ron and Netzer both twisted round. 'I see you standing there, but I don't believe it.' Ron said, shaking hands with his old friend that he had not seen in years.

'What brings you here?' Netzer asked, not smiling and getting straight to the point.

'Don't you believe I've just come out for a friendly beer and bumped into some old friends?'

'Where are they?' Netzer asked, turning back to the bar and lighting a cigarette.

'Who?' Gavish asked, laughing and putting a hand on Netzer's shoulder.

'Your friends?' Netzer asked, blowing a cloud of smoke up into the air.

'All right, play nice,' Ron said. 'You still working for that bitch?' Ron asked, looking at Gavish, who was feeling a little uncomfortable now.

These men were blunt, but what had he expected after all these years. It wasn't important for them to like him. What was important, was that they were still as smart and ruthless as he remembered. They weren't going to kiss your ass and call it ice cream. That's why he had convinced Ayala, that they were the only ones for this mission. They were the best.

'I am. Listen Ron. That is why I'm here.' Gavish said,

sounding serious now.

Netzer spun back around with the cigarette in his mouth. 'Is the witch dying? Has she got cancer of the cunt?' Gavish noticed the barmaid, who was pulling a pint of Guinness, look at Netzer with disgust. 'We should make it a national fucking holiday. I'll drink to that.' Netzer said, with imitation joy, but really, he was angry. Netzer turned to the barmaid and held up three fingers. 'Hey, three shots of tequila over here.'

'How the hell did you find us?' Ron asked, knowing full well Gavish had had them followed.

'You're not that hard to find these days. You're both quite predictable.'

'Of all the gin joints in all the towns in all the world, and you had to walk into ours.' Ron said, doing his best Humphrey Bogart impression from the movie, Casablanca.

Netzer passed Ron and Gavish a shot each. 'Here's to whatever poor, horrible, fucking disease that has had to infiltrate her clap-happy body.'

'It's fair to say Netzer still isn't too keen on Ayala. She is, after all, solely responsible for the dismemberment of our unit,' Ron said.

'Actually, Ayala is still very much alive,' Gavish said, still grimacing from the tequila shot.

'Fuck,' Netzer said, disappointed.

'What do you want from us?' Ron asked.

'Can we go for a walk?' Gavish asked them.

Ron and Netzer looked at each other and shrugged. 'Why not.' Ron said.

The three of them walked the short distance to Rabin Square.

'We have a mission for you,' Gavish said, lighting a

cigarette.

'Unbelievable. She's something special, that witch. Cuts our balls off, locks us in a cupboard and now she wants to let us out to play!' Netzer exclaimed.

'Not Ayala. You guys are my idea. Ayala didn't want to use you. It took a lot of convincing on my part.'

'Don't do us any favours, buddy. You can stick her broomstick back up her ass,' Netzer said, pointing a finger at Gavish.

Gavish turned to Ron. He knew Ron was calmer, a deeper thinker and would hear him out. 'I told her we needed the best.'

Ron studied his old friend for a moment, while Netzer continued to pace about swearing and punching the air. They were good friends once. All three of them had been part of Yossi Ben Hadar's elite unit along with Adar Greenberg, who had decided to get out and move to America after he had been given a desk job. When Yossi was retired, Ron and Netzer were thrown in the cupboard and forced to trade in their guns for pencils and made to follow low level leads that you wouldn't give a rookie. Gavish caved in and joined Ayala in reforming Mossad. Yossi had not held this against Gavish, but Ron and Netzer saw it as a betrayal, especially Netzer, who could bear a grudge against the weatherman if he fucked up the forecast. Ron was a master at reading people, and he thought he knew why Gavish had joined with Ayala and kept his high status. It was his father. Gavish's father was a hero within Mossad and Gavish was always trying to live up to his father's reputation and show his worth. It made Gavish an excellent agent, fearless and relentless. It also made him loyal to Mossad, before everything else.

'What's the mission? And what do we have to do?' Ron

asked, lighting a cigarette, looking from Gavish to Netzer, then back to Gavish.

'Yes, do tell, arouse our curiosity,' Netzer said. He knew they would take the mission. He knew it when he had heard Gavish's voice at the bar. In truth he was praying for it.

Gavish walked over to a bench and sat down, running his thumb along his bushy moustache. 'Two months ago, we lost a young agent in Melbourne.'

'Like a penny,' Netzer interrupter.

'Netzer, please. Two early morning runners found the kid leaning against a tree by the Yarra River. A week later we lost another agent in Lyon. His body was found next to a dumpster behind a strip club. Two days ago,' Gavish paused for a moment, taking in deep breath. 'Adar Greenberg's decomposed body was found with his wife's, in their Florida home.'

'Adar,' Netzer said softly, running his hands through his curly, dark blonde hair.

'Do we know who is doing this?' Ron asked, showing little emotion.

'We've got very little to go on,' Gavish said, still playing with his moustache and looking out across Rabin Square.

'Well, what do we have?' Ron asked calmly.

'Only that it's the same person doing it. We think it's probably a man.'

'What's the M.O?' Ron asked.

'He,' Gavish paused, looking up at Ron. 'He takes their eyes.'

'What's the connection with the agents?' Ron asked unflinching.

'We can't find one. They've never worked together, and

23

they've never met. We believe it's the work of a single person.'

'Three agents dead and we have nothing,' Netzer said.

'No witnesses, no hair fibre, no finger-prints. We have nothing. That's why we need you. We need the best.'

'Sounds like we're after a fucking phantom,' Netzer said, lighting another cigarette.

Gavish stood up. 'I've got you booked on a flight to Miami with United Airlines.'

'What time?' Ron asked.

'4:50 a.m.'

'Not coming with us?' Netzer asked.

'I'm too old and slow for all that shenanigans now,' Gavish said.

'A desk man. Who would have thought? Gavish, the desk man. Mr Pencil Pusher,' Netzer teased.

'I like the view from my window, also I have some internal business to take care of here, but this mission takes priority. I'll be here at the controls, anything you need, just contact me.'

'We'll be fine,' Ron said.

'I know, but I would like someone to tag along with you. Get some experience. Learn from the masters.'

'I don't like the sound of this,' Netzer said.

'I already have someone in mind for you. We can drive to her apartment now. It's not five minutes away.'

'A girl?' Netzer said disapprovingly. 'It's not Ayala, is it? If so, maybe we can throw her out the plane and into the Atlantic on the way over. Oh, wait that wouldn't work, silly me, I forgot shit floats,' Netzer said, slapping his forehead.

'She any good?' Ron asked.

'She's a killer. Born in Kenya. She'll go below the radar.'

'Is she black?' Netzer asked.

'Do you know many white Kenyans?' Gavish replied.

'I don't know any Kenyan's, period,' Netzer said.

'How old is she?' Ron asked.

'Malia is twenty-three and this ain't her first mission.'

Netzer sniggered. 'What's she done, bust some poachers smuggling ivory?'

'Last month, in Nairobi, she assassinated two Kenyan government ministers that we suspected were passing on information to a certain Islamic terrorist group. Trust me when I say she's good. I picked her personally.'

'Good, coz I ain't no babysitter,' Netzer said.

Ron threw his cigarette on the floor, stamped it out, then looked up at Gavish. 'Let's go meet this killer of yours.'

# 2

Friday June 2nd 2017
Old Jaffa, Tel Aviv 00:55

Malia Kimani was leaning back in her chair, feet up on the table, looking at her landscape canvas with a feeling of disdain. She hated the heavy-handed brushwork and wished her strokes were not so apprehensive, but she also knew she was slowly improving. The apartment was on the third floor; small, basic, nothing special, better than a hut. On the table was a scattering of several fashion magazines and a glass vase with wilted flowers that once stood tall and beautiful. The walls were bare, apart from an old dreamcatcher left behind by the previous tenants. A tattered rug lay on the floor, that may have once been something to look at and admire. A couple of small windows, a pokey bedroom, a shower. It's winning feature though was the kitchen area, big with all the mod cons, but sometimes unworldly sounds would come from the sink, and she would be reminded of Stephen King's, IT.

When the knock came at the door, Malia instinctively snatched for the palette knife that she had used to mix red and orange together with in order to create the sunset she now thought sucked. She pushed the blunt steel blade up her pyjama sleeve and quickly surveyed the room. Her training had taught her to kill with many everyday household objects, but the palette knife would be her first port of call. Malia approached the door and stood against the side wall.

'Who's there?'

'Malia, it's me, Gavish. I've brought some friends for a chat.'

Malia relaxed a little and unlocked the door. She saw her mentor standing beside two men who were leaning against the railing of the stairs.

'It's late,' Malia said, looking from Gavish to his friends, then back to Gavish.

'Actually, it's early,' Netzer said, glancing at his watch.

'Can we come in? It's important,' Gavish asked, with his trademark sombre expression.

She had come to know him quite well these past years in training, but she couldn't read him, that poker-face of his, and yet she was generally good at reading people. Even if he had just had the best sex of his life, she reckoned he would still be able to carry that sombre expression.

'Okay.'

'Not in here,' Ron said, poking his head inside Malia's apartment. 'Get changed. Let's go for a walk.'

Malia went to her bedroom and Netzer looked at Ron and grinned. 'She's pretty,' Netzer remarked. 'You fucking her?' Netzer teased and winked at Gavish.

'I'm married. You know that,' Gavish said, feeling embarrassed, his face turning red.

'He's definitely screwing her,' Netzer returned.

'Please Netzer, lower your voice,' Gavish said.

Malia came back and she noticed there was tension in the air. They've been talking about me, she thought. She wore clogs, comfortable, but never attractive, joggers and a white T-shirt. Her hair was tied back, and Ron was impressed by her beauty. He wondered how a stunner like this could ever become a cold-blooded killer.

The four of them walked out of the historical old city of Jaffa, passing the Jaffa clock tower and a cafe where Arab men were sitting outside smoking shisha, and blowing huge smoke clouds into the night air. They passed the port, where the small fishing boats were gently knocking into one another and rocking back and forth on the water. Cats lined the harbour, alert and hypnotised by the fishy smell. From this end of the promenade, they could see all the big hotels that lit up the skyline that ran along the seashore.

'I love this place at night,' Ron said, looking out at the sea.

'You paint?' Netzer asked Malia, pointing at her fingers.

'I'm no Van Gogh, but I try,' she said, studying her finger tips that were a mixture of colours. 'Why are we out walking at silly o'clock?' she sighed.

Ron stopped and offered her a cigarette. 'Smoke?'

'No thanks.'

'Good, these things will kill you.' He lit himself a Noblesse cigarette.

'I only thought the kids in the army smoked Noblesse,' Malia said.

Ron smiled, 'I like the colour of the packet, and I'm sentimental.'

Malia smiled back. She liked Ron. She had a good feeling about this one but wouldn't trust him just yet.

'We're in a spot of bother. Someone is killing our agents and we need to find out who's doing it,' Gavish said. 'You will have to leave toni—'

'It's a mission,' Ron interrupted. 'Before we tell you any

more, are you in, or are you out? If you're out, you can go back to painting pretty pictures.'

'I'm in,' Malia said, without any hesitation.

Ron gave her an approving nod. A warm breeze had picked up, and under the moonlight Ron thought she looked truly beautiful.

'Have you had much sleep?' Gavish asked.

'I don't sleep much.'

'You can sleep on the plane,' Gavish said.

'Plane? Where are we going?' She asked, trying to hide her excitement. Despite being twenty-three years old, Malia still loved flying in an aeroplane.

'The three of you will be flying out to Miami,' Gavish said.

'You're not coming?' Malia asked, looking at Gavish.

'I have business here.'

'Don't worry kid. Uncle Netzer is here to look after you,' Netzer said, grinning.

A look of disgust ran across Malia's face. 'Yuck.' She didn't have the same good feeling about this one.

'You'll get used to Netzer,' Gavish said.

'Get Malia everything we have on the three dead agents, and I mean everything. I want her to know them personally by the time we land in Miami,' Ron said.

'Dossiers will be waiting for her on the plane,' Gavish promised.

'When we get there, Netzer will look into all aspects of Adar's life in Florida, his neighbours, his hobbies, his wife, mistresses, if he had any,' Ron said.

'Knowing Adar, I'll probably be chasing down half the women in Florida.' Netzer said, reminiscing.

'You knew one of the agents?' Malia asked, a little surprised.

'Adar, yes. He was our friend,' Netzer said.

'And by the time you've studied his dossier you will also know him very well,' Ron said.

'It's dead on half one now,' Gavish said, looking at his watch. 'You fly in just over three hours.'

'I suppose they know we're coming?' Ron asked.

'Tim Baines is the special agent in charge of the Miami field office. He'll be waiting for you when you step off the plane.'

'Good. Good,' Ron said.

'What are you thinking?' Gavish asked.

'If we can get the names, flights and photos of all the people who have applied for short stay visas to the US from within Europe in the last three months, and then cross reference that with people who applied for an Australian visa in the last year, then we are very likely to come across the same name and face,' Ron said.

'The FBI are going to give you some space when you get over there. That they promise, but they made it clear that they are in charge, and they want no secrets. You are there as representatives of Israel. You will liaise with them and be good guests.'

'So, we're going over there with our thumbs up are arse,' Netzer said.

'Not at all,' Gavish replied.

'Weapons?' Netzer asked, already shaking his head, knowing the answer.

'Afraid not. It's on you to be professional, there is to be minimal violence, no blood baths. Netzer, are you understanding this?' Gavish had a flashback to seven years ago, when Netzer had been over-zealous with the amount of plastic explosive he used. The bomb that was detonated that day in Iran was only meant to take out one car, not the whole convoy. They were all bad guys, but it was meant to look low key. Instead in turned into a cluster fuck. One of the body-guards who died in that convoy, that day in Iran, was third cousin to the Iranian Prime Minister's wife. Netzer claimed he had simply made a mistake when calculating how much explosive to use. Gavish knew that Netzer was somebody you would want on your side, when you had your back against the wall. Killing was part of their job. Gavish and Ron killed because it had to be done, Netzer as well, but Netzer loved his job a bit too much for Gavish's taste.

'Crystal,' Netzer replied with a fuck you smile.

# 3

Thursday August 14<sup>th</sup> 2014
Sidon, Lebanon 21:02

Mustafa Khoury's life is about to change forever. A distinguished young doctor at only 33 years of age, with an exemplary military background. Admired by all who know him. Loved by his family. His wife Adeline and two young daughters worship the ground he walks on. It would be a hard push to find a happier man.

Mustafa Khoury started his life from humble beginnings. The third of seven children to two hard working parents, with no education. Michel and Saada Khoury both worked long shifts in a textile factory. They suffered hardships throughout the civil war, but always kept their dignity. They made sure all their children ate and got an education, so they would be the best that they could be. Mustafa was naturally gifted, nothing fazed him. He would read every book he could get his hands on. He excelled at school and later joined the army, where in 2006 he saved the life of General Fouad Aoun.

An Israeli tank shell had hit a fuel tanker next to the building where General Aoun had set up a communications room. The four-storey building collapsed within seconds. Mustafa's regiment, who were resting up in an abandoned barn, less than a mile away, were the first on the scene and it was Mustafa who climbed under the rubble, ignoring his Captain's orders to stay out. The smell of gas lingered in the air stinging his eyes and it grew stronger the deeper he went. Mustafa knew he was crawling and squeezing his way along and down a ticking time bomb. Still, he went on looking and calling for survivors without any regard for his own life. No one answered back. He only heard his own soft scared voice and the horrible surround sound of concrete grinding and metals bending in the darkness. I'm crawling right to hell he thought. I should have listened to the captain. He was almost at the point of giving up, turning around and hopefully finding a way back out of the nightmare he now found himself in, when he saw a beautiful light. A ray of sunlight shown through a gap in the rubble and Mustafa thought how magnificent it was to see his own hands again. And something else, not a cry, but a groan. It was coming from the same area as the light.

'Hello,' Mustafa cried.

'Cigarette,' a faint voice called back.

'Did you say cigarette?' Mustafa replied, laughing, unable to help himself.

'Yes, you know the nasty things you put in your mouth,' the voice called back.

'I know,' Mustafa replied crawling slowly and carefully towards the voice over jagged concrete. 'But you should know something.'

'What?'

'They're really bad for your health.' Mustafa answered looking down at the man, who was sitting upright in a small crawl space. The man's clothes had been blown off and only a pair of green pants remained to hide his dignity. The man was General Aoun, bloodied and dazed. Mustafa recognised him immediately. The general had inspected his unit only a week before. His right leg looked broken in at least five places, but thankfully the femur looked like it was okay. An iron rod had pierced his stomach and the colour around the wound did not look good. He was only alive thanks to a concrete pillar that was holding the rubble from collapsing on top of him.

'What I wouldn't give for a cigarette,' the general said. 'Be a good boy and check his pockets for a smoke?' The general asked, nodding upwards above Mustafa's head.

Mustafa turned his head and gasped. Above him, the dangling blood-soaked legs of a soldier, minus the rest of his body. Mustafa quickly turned his head back around, putting his hands to his mouth. For a second, he thought he may throw up over the general, but after a few deep breaths he composed himself. 'If you light a cigarette up in here, we will be blown up in to a thousand pieces. Can't you smell the gas?'

'I seem to have lost my sense of smell,' said the general.

'I will get you out of here general.' Mustafa said, climbing down into the crawl space.

'You recognise me?'

'You inspected my unit, but you were wearing clothes when I saw you last time.' With this both men started laughing.

'Oh, it hurts to laugh,' the general said. The building moved and vibrated. The rubble above was slowly crushing down on them. 'You must leave me now boy and get out whilst you still can. I'm at the mercy of God now.'

'I'm afraid we are in this together. We will both live or die today.'

'I admire your bravery. I really do but…'

'But nothing. You still have pages to write general,' Mustafa said, studying the iron rod that had pierced his stomach. 'And you forget…'

'What, what do I forget?'

Mustafa smiled at the general. 'God is great.'

'I guess that slipped my mind.' The general said, looking up at the legs of a soldier that were once connected to a torso.

'Your right leg is smashed, and you are bleeding badly. I'm going to set it now as best I can, then move the rod out from your stomach.'

'Are you a medic?'

'I'm a soldier, however I dream of one day becoming a doctor. I have attended to many who have been wounded in this damn war.' Mustafa had saved two lives the week before. He had taken on the responsibility of dressing wounds and setting fractures after the medic in his unit was killed by an Israeli sniper. One of the men he had saved only survived because Mustafa had improvised using an old bicycle inner tube as a tourniquet to stop the man's severed arm from bleeding out. He had also cut a small hole in another young soldier's neck, putting a small ball valve in his airways so that he could breathe, after being shot multiple times. All this from medical books and watching and assisting army medics whenever he could. Being poor made it hard, almost impossible to become a doctor, but Mustafa was a natural, just like Mohammad Ali was at boxing and Marlon Brando was at acting.

Mustafa set the leg as best he could by tying two rags to each end of a wooden chair leg. He placed the chair leg at the bottom of the old man's foot, then pressed down on the broken leg with one hand whilst simultaneously pulling the rags up with the other hand. The general screamed and bit down hard on his hand as his smashed leg clicked and cracked back into place.

'That should do it,' Mustafa said, patting the general's chest.

'You are not my favourite person,' the general said, holding Mustafa's hand.

'That was the easy part.'

'It wasn't easy for me,' the general groaned.

'The rod has pierced your abdomen, just to the left of your bellybutton. What I'm about to do will feel horrible, but necessary.'

The general squeezed his young friend's hand. 'There is no lying with you is there. If we get out of this hole…'

'That's a big if,' Mustafa interrupted. 'Stay still now,' Mustafa put a finger into the wound and the general screamed for him to stop, but Mustafa paid no attention to the old man. 'The good news is the rod has missed the kidney. The bad news is, it's deeper than I first thought.'

'I swear if you do that again, I will have you shot. Twice!' the general said. He was almost at the point of passing out.

Mustafa saw that there was no leeway under the old man and decided he would have to push the concrete pillar that the iron rod was attached to upwards. The danger in doing this was real and Mustafa knew it was the only option. Never did it cross his mind to leave the old man. A life, be that of a general, or a peasant farmer was just the same to him. His belief in God and humanity was great. War had not dented his spirit.

'I'm going to try and push the concrete up. When I do this, you are going to have to try and move out yourself. Can you do this?' Mustafa asked, wiping the blood and dust away from the old man's eyes.

'Haven't you tortured me enough? We should have you

interrogating enemy soldiers.'

Mustafa pushed upwards with his back and the concrete pillar gave a little and the rod moved out from the old man's abdomen about two inches. Mustafa prayed the rubble would not come down and crush them. The general wiggled a little to the left, but a good portion of the rod was still embedded in his stomach.

'Don't give up,' Mustafa screamed and pushed up with all his might. His legs started to shake and for a brief moment he went somewhere far away. Somewhere beyond what is believed to be normal. The concrete pillar above him started to move upwards. This display of superhuman strength did not go unnoticed by the general, who watched, screaming, with tears running down his face, as the end of the bloody rod rose from out of his stomach. The general wiggled free and rolled over, hurting the leg Mustafa had set. Mustafa set the concrete pillar back down and felt his back spasm. He fell on to his elbows and vomited onto the floor. He wiped his mouth and crawled over towards the general. Wasting no time, ignoring his own pain, Mustafa started to drag and lift the old man through the rubble. It was a slow, painful process and the general felt every bump. Just before they reached an opening the general passed out. Mustafa fell to his knees, as fresh air engulfed his lungs like a drug, and the ground around him started to sway. He fell down like a drunk next to the general and passed out. Both men were covered in dust, blood and sweat and bonded by it. Mustafa came back around a few minutes later, dazed and confused. He checked the old man's vitals. The general was still alive but only just. Mustafa got to his feet and carried the general back around to the other side of rubble where the rest of his unit were waiting for him to re-emerge.

The captain saw Mustafa carrying the old man and ran over to help. They put him down next to a stream where an old bridge crossed and had stood for over a hundred years and led into a forest that had no military importance.

'This is General Aoun.' One shocked soldier said, washing the old man's face with a wet towel.

Mustafa looked out at the setting sun. A purple haze had covered the skyline and the trees way off in the distance looked magical.

'Where is my young friend?' These were the first words that General Aoun spoke when he awoke from his hospital bed in Beirut.

A day later, on the eve of the end of the 2006 Israel-Hezbollah War, also known as the July War, an army truck pulled up on the bank of the Litani River. Two young soldiers jumped out with orders for Captain Rashad Haddad. They found the captain sitting by a tree, drinking coffee and looking out over the lake. Haddad had made a promise to himself, that if he ever got out of this war alive, he would ask the young woman who comes to his mother's bakery each morning out on a date. He looked out on the lake and dreamt about taking her here. He imagined they would have a picnic and she would smile at him, and they would make love. War has a wonderful way of effecting people he thought.

'Captain Haddad?' one of the young soldiers asked.

Captain Haddad was young himself, only twenty-five, but when he turned to look at these two young boys, still with acne on their faces he felt a hundred years old.

'Yes. What can I do for you fine young men?'

'We have orders from the war ministry on behalf of

General Aoun to take with us the soldier who saved General Aoun's life.' One of the soldiers said, holding out a letter for the captain to read.

Captain Haddad emptied the remains of his coffee in the grass and took the letter, reading it quickly and looking amused. He ran a hand through his short oily hair, folded up the letter and put it in his shirt pocket.

'Let's go find Mustafa. Follow me.' The two soldiers followed Captain Haddad, who was walking with his hands in his trouser pockets, strolling like a man without a care in the world. At one point he stopped, picked up a stone and skimmed it on the lake that was calm. They found Mustafa sitting on a boulder polishing his boots outside his tent. Some men were singing, some laughing, everyone could sense the end of the war was near.

'Mustafa,' the captain called out walking towards him.

Mustafa put his boots down, jumped up and ran over towards his captain. Mustafa had a lot of respect for Captain Haddad, whom he thought was a good man. The feeling was mutual.

'At ease Mustafa. You have orders to go to Beirut with these two young men.'

'Beirut?' Mustafa asked, puzzled.

'General Fouad Aoun has called for you and you must go.'

'But we have no medic, and I'm the only one who can attend to the men if they get wounded.'

'The war is as good as over,' Captain Haddad said, putting a hand on his friend's arm. 'And the rest of your life awaits you in Beirut.'

Mustafa grabbed his gear from his tent, then went to salute the captain, but the captain held out his hand. The two men shook hands. 'I'm going to miss beating you at chess, Rashad.'

'Go on, get out of here.'

Mustafa got in the truck, and it pulled away. The captain watched the truck bounce along the dirt track, and then turn right and go up a steep bank and disappear.

The general had his own room with a big window and a television. Mustafa was looking in on the general who was sitting up reading some papers. Mustafa thought it vulgar that one man should have all this, when wounded civilians and soldiers lined the corridors on beds and makeshift stretchers. One of the two young soldiers who had brought him to the hospital knocked on the door and announced that Private Mustafa Khoury was here.

The general put aside his papers and clasped his hands together. 'Show him in.'

Mustafa stood by the doorway and waved at the general. The general held his arms out open for Mustafa to embrace him. 'Come here my dear boy,' Mustafa approached slowly. 'You do remember me don't you, the man whose life you saved?' The general asked, bemused by this shy boy in front of him, who in the rubble was full of life.

'I do general,' Mustafa said, sounding slightly nervous, and then a bit livelier. 'And I must say you look like you've made a remarkable recovery.' And the two of them embraced.

'Only thanks to you.'

'No, no. God.' Mustafa said.

The General waved this notion away. 'Sit, sit,' the general said, patting the edge of his bed. 'And call me Fouad.'

'Okay.'

'Tell me, my boy, what will you do now?'

'Now?' Mustafa asked, confused by the question.

'Yes, now the war is over. What will you do for work?'

'I will go back home and support my family so my younger brothers and sister can have an education.'

'And where is home for Mustafa?' The general asked this question, even though he already knew. He had read his file. The general knew all there was to know about this young man sitting on the edge of his bed.

'Sidon.'

'Sidon. A beautiful place it is. And do you have a woman waiting for you?'

Mustafa smiled. 'Adeline. She smells of Jasmine,' Mustafa spoke dreamily. 'We hope someday to be married and start a family.'

'And what will you do for work in Sidon?'

'I will work in the local textile factory and hopefully in a few years become a supervisor.'

'Not a doctor?' The general asked.

Mustafa laughed at this impossibility, expecting the general to join in at the joke. Mustafa stopped laughing when he noticed the general's flat expression. Mustafa feeling embarrassed and a little ashamed explained. 'That is a dream. I am poor and have little education.'

It was General Fouad Aoun who laughed this time. Fouad slapped Mustafa on the hand. 'You are a natural and I am a dream maker. I have already set your future in motion.' He seized Mustafa hands and held them tight in his. 'These hands will never work in a factory. I have great expectations for you, my boy. You are, as from today, enrolled as a medical student here in Beirut.'

Suddenly Mustafa looked like he should be the one in the hospital bed. His face showed a blank, dumb expression, his lips tried to move, but he was lost for words. What cruel joke is this he thought? Mustafa knelt beside the bed still holding onto the general's hands. The general smiled at him. All his dreams had come true. 'How can I ever repay you?' Tears had started to roll down his cheeks.

'You already have. Don't worry about your brothers and sister, we will make sure they get a first-class education.' Fouad took an envelope that was on his bedside table and passed it to Mustafa. 'This is for you.'

Mustafa opened the envelope. Inside was a single key. He held it in his fingers. 'What is this for?'

'You now have an apartment here in the city. So, I suggest you call, Adeline, is it?'

'Yes.' Mustafa said, sounding far away, still in a state of shock. If this is a dream, I hope I may never wake from it, he thought.

'Yes, Adeline. Better tell her to pack her bags.'

Mustafa and Adeline spent four years in Beirut, four happy years. They were married and had a daughter, Amal. After four years and halfway through his training they moved back to Sidon. In Sidon, Mustafa's reputation as a doctor and surgeon grew. His steady hands and sharp thinking got him the respect of his peers. Although still a junior doctor he was performing operations like it was second nature to him. By the time his seven years of training was up, Mustafa Khoury was already a renowned doctor and surgeon. Mustafa and Adeline had a second daughter, Dasia and life was good.

It was a warm, sticky evening in August when Doctor Mustafa Khoury walked through the front door of the apartment where he lived with his young family. The normally pleasant two mile walk home from the hospital had been uncomfortable in the heat and he really wanted a good rest. Unfortunately for the good doctor there would be no rest. He was greeted the same way that he was greeted the night before. Two young Indians ambushed him with bow and arrows as he walked in. But he was ready for them tonight. On his short lunch break he had brought two toy hand-guns and a cowboy hat. He fired imaginary bullets at the Indians, as an onslaught of arrows hit him from two different directions. He staggered into the living room, groaning and holding his chest and then fell to the floor. He had lost the battle. Adeline was crying with laughter and the two Indians were jumping up and down, celebrating their victory.

'Don't worry daddy, it's just us.' Amal, his eldest daughter said, as the two Indians climbed on top of him.

Suddenly Mustafa burst into life and sprung to his feet. He picked the two Indians up, one in each arm and ran around the room with them both giggling. He slung them both on the sofa and started to tickle them.

'I've got you now.' Mustafa said, tickling his children who were wiggling and screaming uncontrollably.

'Enough, enough,' Adeline said, and slapped her husband's back with a tea towel. 'The neighbours will think we are killing them.'

Mustafa turned to look at his wife. 'I am. I'm tickling them to death and when I've finished, I'm gonna tickle you to death too.' Mustafa proceeded to walk slowly towards Adeline, wiggling his fingers.

'Don't you even try.' Adeline said, backing away from him.

'What do you think?' Mustafa said, turning to his children, who were still laughing on the sofa. 'Should I tickle mommy?'

'Yeah,' Amal and Dasia both screamed together. 'Get her, daddy.'

'There you go, the votes are in, and the majority have voted in favour of tickling.'

'Don't you… dare.' Adeline said, struggling not to grin and swinging the tea towel at him.

'It wouldn't be democratic if I didn't.' Mustafa declared and started to tickle his wife. Adeline cheeks went red and she stared to giggle. She fell down to the floor and Amal and Dasia ran over to join in.

'Stop, please stop,' Adeline said, smiling.

'Okay. I think mommy has had enough.' Mustafa said and helped his wife to her feet. She looked at him, still smiling, eyes bright, hair in her face, cheeks flushed. He thought she was the most beautiful woman in the world, and never more so than at that moment.

Adeline kissed him. 'Go take a shower, dinner is almost ready.'

'It smells wonderful, what is it?' Mustafa asked, looking towards the kitchen.

'Chicken. Now go take a shower, you smell,' she said and pushed him away.

'Daddy smells,' Dasia said giggling.

Mustafa walked on down the hall towards the shower. He could still hear the innocent giggling of his children as he closed the door. They adored him and they were the centre of his world. They were the last memories he had of them. He stepped into the shower and then everything went black.

The bomb that tore open his apartment block killed seventeen people, including his wife and two children. By some miracle Mustafa survived. He woke up a week later from a coma to find General Fouad Aoun asleep in a chair next to his hospital bed.

'Adeline, Adeline?' he murmured, looking glassy eyed at all the tubes sticking out of him.

His old friend awoke in his chair and sat up startled. 'Nurse, nurse?'

'What is going on?' Mustafa murmured. The room was spinning out of control, and he felt like he was suffering from the most horrible of headaches. Most of all, he was scared. Worryingly worse he was scared that something bad had happened to his family.

'Mustafa? I'm right here.' His old friend said, leaning in and holding his hand.

'Adeline?' he asked dazedly, and then passed out.

When he came around again there was a doctor and two nurses in the room who looked sorrowfully at him when he caught their eyes.

'My Adeline, where is my Adeline?'

One of the nurses scurried out of the room in tears. He recognised her. He recognised all of them but couldn't remember their names. 'The general will be here soon. He will explain to you,' the doctor told him.

An hour later the old general entered the room.

'My family?' he asked, somehow knowing something bad had happened, but unable to remember what.

Fouad Aoun looked at his young friend for what seemed to Mustafa an eternity and shook his head. 'No.'

Mustafa closed his eyes and tears began to run down his face. 'My girls,' he said, sobbing.

'We buried them two days ago,' Fouad Aoun said, hanging

his head.

It was the general himself who identified the remains of Adeline and the girls. He was their godfather after all and it was the hardest thing he had ever had to do in his life.

Mustafa would later find out that the explosion that ripped his world apart, killing his young family, was from a satellite guided bomb that was intended for a Hezbollah strong hold.

'Who did this?' Mustafa asked from his hospital bed, as Fouad peeled him an orange.

'It was the Israelis. We know this because they are the only ones that manufacture the Spice Bomb.'

'Spice Bomb?' Mustafa frowned, putting his bruised hands to his aged face. It was like some terrible culinary joke. It was a living nightmare.

'They are normally very accurate,' Fouad said, passing Mustafa a segment of orange and taking one for himself. 'Our Israeli friends,' Fouad sighed. 'They are keeping very quiet and the world as usual doesn't seem to care.'

Mustafa stared down at his legs. His left was in traction. It had been smashed to bits. The doctors had considered amputating the leg from the knee down, but after hours of surgery had saved it. His right leg had fared slightly better. No breaks, but the Achilles heel had been torn.

Fouad followed his young friend's stare. 'I don't think you'll be doing the one-hundred-meter hurdles any time soon.'

Mustafa let out a small despairing laugh, that was bordering on a cry. 'I was hoping to do the triple jump.'

'Brave boy.' Fouad said and grabbed his friend's hand. He was sure Mustafa would overcome the physical pain, but the mental pain, he was not so sure about.

'I want to die,' Mustafa cried. 'I want my girls. Adeline!'

He screamed in anguish, rolling his head on the pillow.

'I know, my boy, I know.'

'I didn't even get to bury my girls! I didn't get to say goodbye! Adeline! I want to die!'

'You will see them again, but not yet. You still have pages to write.'

Mustafa's cries echoed down the hospital corridor. Two nurses rushed in and told Fouad he must leave.

The old general stumbled out of the hospital. He opened the door to his car, sat for a moment, putting both hands on the steering wheel and then started to cry.

# 4

Friday June 2nd 2017
FBI Office Miramar, Florida 07:41

Agent Sally Anderson opened her desk drawer and looked down at the assortment of candy bars there with a feeling of loathing. She decided on a Hershey bar. In recent weeks the candy bars had replaced warm meals. Today a Hershey bar and a cup of strong black coffee from the vending machine would be her morning breakfast.

She had been with the bureau a little over a year. In that time, she had left her boyfriend and moved back in with her mother, who kept six cats. She had walked in on her boyfriend screwing some girl he had met at the supermarket. Screwing and screaming the apartment down, and on the rug her mother had given them as a moving in gift. The rug had been a family heirloom, passed down through the generations. It was an item her mother truly treasured. Since moving back home, her mother would ask her almost daily, when she would be getting the rug back. 'It's an heirloom, it belongs in our family. I have many fond memories of that rug.' Her mother would say. Fuck the rug and fuck the memories, Sally felt like telling her.

Sally had also realised that being a woman in the FBI was hard work. She was still the rookie. She wasn't what you might call pretty, which is and always will be an obvious advantage around men. She had a bob haircut and a scar above her top lip. She was born with a cleft palate, but now hardly noticeable. The surgery she had when she was young had been very successful. She went through years of speech therapy growing up and was bullied religiously, mainly by other girls her age. This just made Sally more determined to be the best she could be. She took up Judo and swam the 200-meter freestyle for her school and then state. Her grandmother had taught her how to shoot and Sally loved nothing more than to go to the range with her and fire off a few rounds. Sally became so good that she started competing in shooting divisions. She graduated college with a degree in law and then joined the Miami-Dade police department. After three years she applied to join the FBI and finished top her class.

Now Agent Anderson sat at her desk, sipping her coffee, looking at the file of Adar and Tal Greenberg. Agent Anderson was the first FBI agent on the scene. She grimaced as she recalled the smell of the decomposing bodies of the husband and wife. And so far, there was nothing to go on. No forced entry, no witnesses, no prints, no signs of a struggle, no nothing. It was as if the Greenberg's were killed by a phantom. The photos inside fell out as she opened the file and she quickly looked away and then took a deep breath, composed herself and then studied them. How the hell was there no struggle? She wondered with horror. Who could endure that and not? Agent Anderson remembered the neighbours, the Dorans, an elderly couple who had reported the smell, saying how the Greenberg's were a nice couple. They would regularly be seen out jogging together and would always stop for a chat. 'Everyone loved the Greenberg's,' Joyce Dorans said. Not everyone Joyce, my dear, not everyone. It would appear that the Greenberg's were not everyone's cup of tea, Agent Anderson thought.

The only fingerprints at the scene were those of the two police officers who were first on the scene and who gained entry to the house. One of them, Officer Aaron Ellis, with more than ten years on the beat had to run outside and vomit over the Greenberg's red Chevrolet that was parked on the drive when he saw the flies and maggots on the dead bodies of the husband and wife. 'Never in my time on the... I mean I've seen lots but... never like that.' Officer Ellis said, shaking and smoking a cigarette while leaning against the hood of the patrol car.

The police called in the FBI because of the violent nature of the crime and possibility that it might be a serial killer. It was the case Agent Anderson was waiting for. Up until now she thought she was being overlooked and undermined. She had worked with the linguistics department and counter terrorism unit, but nothing more than as a tag along, look and learn. Sally had made her feelings known to her boss — Special Agent Tim Baines, and now he was giving her something. She suspected it was only because everyone already had their hands full, and that Tim Baines was getting sick of her relentless door knocking.

She applied the menthol gel around her nose before she got to the door. She remembered her training and she was excited as well. She had seen numerous bodies in different states of decomposition, but there was nothing to ready her nerves for what her eyes were about to fall upon. She gasped in a sudden and intense terror, she felt her body stiffen, and a chill ran right through her bones. In front of Agent Anderson, sitting together on the sofa, as if they were waiting to go into a meeting, were the decomposing bodies of the Greenberg's. Mrs Greenberg's left wrist had been cut open and she was sitting upright in a pool of solidified blood that had covered the glass coffee table in front of the sofa. The blood had sprayed upwards and out about three feet. Her once neat, short brown hair was covered with her congealed blood, and it looked like a horror show. Agent Anderson knew by the colour of the victims and the size of the flies she was seeing that the victims had been like this for a period of between five and seven days. The Greenberg's bloated corpses were turning from green to a reddish colour. Bloody foam was leaking from their nostrils and mouth. Mr Greenberg's death was far more gruesome. He was sitting next to his wife and both his eyes were missing. They had been removed, cut out. Blood had run down from those empty holes and was now dry on the deceased's face. He had a look of total fright on his bloody, bloated face. 'My god, you were still alive,' Agent Anderson said softly. She took out her voice recorder and walked the room, and then the rest of the house. Even in the upstairs bathroom she could still smell that rotten blood odour. She thought that if there was a hell it would smell something like this. The Greenberg's looked like a very handsome couple in their photos. The sound of the sirens from an ambulance were nearing, coming down the street. She had called in the forensics and more police were on their way. Pretty soon this quiet, low crime neighbourhood would look like the circus had come to town. There was no evidence of the victims having any pets or children, Sally found that a small relief. No one would want to identify a loved one who looked the way they did. Agent Anderson put a couple of mints in her mouth and made her way back downstairs to greet the cavalry. It frightened her to look at Adar Greenberg, staring back at her with those black pits. What did you do to deserve this, she wondered? It looked like the Manson family had popped over for a visit. There was no sign of forced entry. Someone they knew? Someone they trusted maybe?

The police questioned all the neighbours and checked all the CCTV cameras in the area. They found nothing. There were some phone calls made around the time of their death, but nothing unusual. One call to a local sports centre for the booking of a squash court that the deceased never got to go to. An international call to Tel Aviv, Israel that Tal Greenberg, made back home to her sister — this was a weekly call.

Agent Anderson took another Hershey bar from her desk drawer and drove down to the pathologists. The toxicology results were in.

'The male and female victims both had vast amounts of succinylcholine in their bodies.' said Brenda Hu, showing Agent Anderson the results on the computer screen.

'What is succinylcholine exactly?'

'It's used during surgery to calm the muscles. Given in high doses it can be catastrophic. The female victim had been given double the amount of succinylcholine used in normal surgeries. It was injected into her neck from behind,' said Brenda Hu, showing Agent Anderson a photo of the puncture wound. 'The needle made quite a mark.'

'Forced in, like in a stabbing motion?' Sally asked.

'Exactly. Must have been a nasty shock. No signs of a struggle. Totally unexpected.'

'What about the male?'

Brenda passed Sally another photo. 'The male victim injected the succinylcholine into his own arm. He had a little less in his body, but just enough to paralyse him.'

'Why do you say he injected himself?'

'Because it was injected downwards. If I was to give you an injection in your arm, I would inject upwards. I see this in a lot of addicts who have overdosed.'

'This succinylcholine, can I get it from a chemist? Can a doctor prescribe it?'

'This is the scary thing. It's hard to get hold of. Typically, you're only going to be given it in a hospital during surgery. Take a look at this,' Brenda Hu passed a blown-up photo of Tal Greenberg's wrist.

'What am I looking for?' Sally asked.

'That's a precision cut,' Brenda said pointing at the wound. 'Right along the ulnar artery, deep with a scalpel. The good news is she died quickly, and she probably didn't feel a thing. With the amount of succinylcholine, she had in her, she would have been in a state of paralysis. I think whoever did this wanted the male to witness the female die. It's probable that the male victim was in a state of paralysis and unable to help the female at the time of her death.'

'What can you tell me about the male victim's eyes?'

'He was awake when it happened and again it was expertly done.' Brenda Hu said.

'Is that admiration I detect in your voice?' Sally asked playfully.

'Not at all. It's just that in all my years as a pathologist I've never seen anything like this. It's my conclusion that you might be after some kind of modern-day Jack the Ripper.'

'Imagine being alive through that,' said Sally, looking at the photos of the eyeless man, who had given her nightmares the night before.

'You're dealing with someone who has vast medical knowledge of medicines and is, or has been, a surgeon,' Brenda Hu said.

Agent Anderson sat down on the chair that was behind her and started to spin around on its wheels while staring up at the ceiling. Her mobile rang and she looked at the number. It was Special Agent Tim Baines in charge of the Miami field office.

'Agent Anderson, where are you now?' Sally thought he sounded unusually uneasy.

'I'm down at toxicology with our victims.'

'Meet me down at Miami International Airport.'

'Why? Are we going somewhere?' She said half-jokingly.

'Leave now and I'll fill you in once you're here.'

As Agent Sally Anderson drove to the airport, she kept thinking to herself, a doctor? A surgeon? That's a person you would trust. The Greenberg's had no family in the States, so a family member was out of the question. And there was no forced entry and no witnesses. How? Sally knew she would need help; she was a long way from understanding this. She thought the killer, probably only one, took gratification in the understanding that they had total control. Sally played it out. She pictured Tal Greenberg welcoming the killer into her home. Hello doctor, please come in, make yourself at home. My husband won't be long. Tal Greenberg wasn't important to you, was she? Adar was the one you wanted to gain satisfaction from, wasn't he? Tal was just a pawn to sacrifice. Sally suspected the killer was a male, in his early thirties to late forties. Sally had done a check on the database for similar murders to the Greenberg's and got nothing. Only the Mexican cartels were doing similar shit and they wouldn't normally stop at the eyes. Then there was Tim Baines, if I'm meeting him, something big is going down. Those eyes though. Christ.

Agent Anderson was directed to a holding room by two policemen. The airport was packed with people coming and going, smiling and crying. Some poor, young, naive girl was bawling her eyes out as she was being padded down by two female officers. In front of the bawling girl was another female officer with a dog who had presumably caught the prize. On the table was an open suitcase. There were all the things you would expect to find in a young girl's luggage plus a big bag of pills. That's someone's daughter going away for a while, Sally thought.

Special Agent Tim Baines was sipping a coffee and pacing around the small holding room when Agent Anderson walked in. Sally was immediately taken aback by his appearance and Tim Baines saw it on her face.

'That bad?'

Sally smiled. 'You look like you could do with some sleep.' And a change of clothes, a shower and a shave, Sally thought. It was quite something to see her boss looking this way. Normally he was very well dressed and not a hair out of place. Now he resembled a criminal who had spent a night in the cell.

He smiled at this remark and for a moment she thought he looked quite handsome.

'Would you like a coffee?'

'I'm good, I've had my coffee fix this morning,' Sally said. 'What's happening?' Sally was eager to know what all this was about.

'Let's take a seat.' They both sat down opposite each other. Tim Baines ran a hand through his normally perfectly combed short brown hair, that now resembled a bird's nest. 'In forty minutes at 11:55 there will be a plane arriving from Tel Aviv with three Mossad agents on board. They are to assist us with this investigation. Your investigation.' He said pointing a finger at Sally.

'Why are three Mossad agents coming here to assist us with this investigation?' Sally asked, slightly confused.

Tim felt her look of concern. 'We ran a background check on Adar and Tal Greenberg. Turns out Adar Greenberg is a "Section 12".'

'I'm not familiar with a "Section 12", sir. What is that?'

'It's confidential. Was confidential,' and then laughed. 'Bloody spooks. The FBI headquarters in Washington have reluctantly given us his folder. Adar Greenberg was Mossad, now retired, even though once you're in, you're never really out.'

'He is now.' Sally added.

Tim smiled again. 'Because of the excellent relations between our two countries, Washington wants us to bring them in on this one. Be that as it may, they have been told that we are in charge and that they are here to assist us with the investigation.'

'Doesn't sound like a problem,' Sally said.

'I've dealt with Mossad before, and they can be sneaky. They keep their cards very close to their chest. I've spoken by phone to a Gavish Molcho, who has sent the agents over. He's given his word that his agents will share everything that they know about Adar Greenberg with us.'

'I thought you would have taken me off something this big?'

'You were top of your class. Plus, you're young and eager to impress. Tell me, how did you feel when you entered the

Greenberg's home and saw what you saw?'

Sally pondered for a moment, then answered. 'I was a little excited, I'm ashamed to say, sir.'

'Don't be. It's perfectly natural.'

'Sir, are we under pressure to get this right?'

'We always are, but when Washington tell you not to fuck this up and you have three Mossad Agents coming over looking for payback, you know your ass is on the line.'

'I think we're after someone who has an excellent knowledge of medicines and a background in surgical procedures,' said Sally.

'A doctor?'

'Yes, a doctor. Someone trustworthy.'

'Male, female?'

'I would say a male, in his early thirties to late forties.'

'Look at me,' Tim Baines said, holding her stare. 'You fucking got this. If you need anything, anything at all, any hour of the day, I'm only a phone call away. I have complete faith in you Agent Anderson.' Sally blushed and felt real pride for the first time since joining the FBI. His words made her feel invincible.

'I'm going outside for a cigarette. When I come back, we'll go meet our friends from Israel.' Sally opened up the file that was on the desk. Adar Greenberg "Section 12" - Intelligence, counter-intelligence, coups, assassinations, it had it all. The guy certainly didn't like sitting around. In January 2010 Adar Greenberg planned and helped carry out the assassination of Mahmoud al-Mabhoud in Dubai. Mahmoud al-Mabhoud who was a senior figure in Hamas, didn't stand a chance. Eleven Israeli Agents in full disguise participated in his assassination and within nineteen hours of landing in Dubai it was all over. They had stopped Mahmoud from meeting a top Iranian backer. It was also retribution for the murder of two Israeli soldiers in 1989 during a Palestinian uprising when Mahmoud was a commander. It was a near perfect operation. Unfortunately for Adar and his team the whole mission was picked up on CCTV. It made international news and was in every paper throughout the world. Israel didn't comment. Adar and the other agents were all held in high regard by Mossad after the mission. As a result of their faces being plastered in all the papers all over the world, the eleven agents all had to take desk jobs after the mission. Sitting in an office was too much for Adar Greenberg, so he retired to Florida, where he was murdered in a very gruesome way.

# 5

Mustafa Khoury walked up to the front door of the Greenberg's abode, past the beautiful hibiscus plants in full bloom and the amaryllis bulbs of bright pink and blood orange. The garden smelt very pleasant to him. He knocked on the door, instead of pressing the doorbell. He was not nervous any more, the butterflies in his stomach had settled. When he killed the Mossad Agent in Melbourne, he had been nervous. He had thrown up twice before and again once more after killing the young man. The second in Lyon was a little easier. He had known the agent would take a short cut through the ally at the back of the strip club, where there were no surveillance cameras. Mustafa had knocked the man unconscious, drugged him then dragged his body behind a dumpster, where he killed him in his gruesome trademark fashion. He hadn't noticed the tramp sleeping opposite until after he had done the deed. He had been clumsy and lucky.

'Doctor Nissan. How lovely to see you. Did you have trouble finding us?' Tal Greenberg asked smiling. It was a warm and genuine smile. Mustafa thought he noticed something else in that smile as well. Was it loneliness? 'Please come in, make yourself at home.'

'Please, call me David.' Mustafa replied in a softly spoken voice and stepped inside, accepting his hosts invitation to enter. He was now the vampire, and he surveyed the killing ground.

Mustafa Khoury a.k.a Dr David Nissan quite liked Tal Greenberg. He was sure that if his wife would have known her when she was alive, that they would have been good friends. They were both gentle souls. Unfortunately for Tal Greenberg, Dr Nissan saw her as a means to an end. He was certain she knew what her husband had done in his previous life. She may not have known all the little details, but a wife knows, and that to Mustafa made her an accessory. Also, if by killing Adar Greenberg, the man who was responsible for killing Mahmoud al-Mabhoud, he had to kill his wife, then so be it. He was Godless now anyway. He had given up the light and was now the angel of death.

'Can I take your coat?' Tal asked frowning. 'You must be baking with that thing on in this weather?'

Dr Nissan let out a small laugh. 'It's a habit of mine never to leave home without it. My arthritis plays havoc on me when it gets cold. I keep forgetting I'm in the Sunshine State.' He placed the small black polyester doctor's case he had been holding in his hand, down by his feet. Tal Greenberg shivered when she saw the case. She suddenly thought of a documentary she had watched about Jack the Ripper and the real possibility that he may have been a doctor. Dr Nissan took off his thick black winter overcoat that he found very uncomfortable to wear in such heat and passed it to his host. 'Thank you.'

Tal took the coat and hung it on one of the hooks on the wall. 'Rest easy, the weather here hardly ever takes a turn for the worse.'

'That is good to know.'

'Have you been on your rounds?' Tal asked.

'Rounds?' Dr Nissan responded not quite understanding the question.

'Yes,' Tal said, pointing at the case down by his feet. 'Have you been seeing patients?'

'Ah-yes.' And he threw back his head and smiled a lovely smile. The act Mustafa put on was that of a man much older than he really was. He hunched a little and walked slowly and pretended to have aggressive arthritis. He spoke softly, but then he had always spoken softly. He came across as fatherly and kind too, but he knew how to be those things anyway, because he used to be those things. He had a pale complexion and looked slightly anaemic. His hair had gone grey when he was in the hospital in Beirut, and he had not done anything about it. When he looked into the mirror he saw it as a reminder, that he had lost everything. He kept a thick moustache, that was not quite grey, but thought that it helped him look older.

'Can I take it for you? And those gloves?' And another shiver went through her.

'It's no problem, I'll keep hold of it for now,' Dr Nissan picked up the case and patted it. 'A good doctor never parts company with his or her case. They never know when they may be called upon to act,' Dr Nissan looked down at his gloved hands that were cradling his case. 'As for these gloves, my arthritis is having a sing today and as ugly as they are, they do help a little.'

'Of course,' Tal said and nodded sympathetically. Instantly feeling sorry for the kindly man before her. 'Please take a seat. I'll make us some coffee.'

He walked across the gleaming white tiled floor that would soon be covered in blood and sat down on the sofa. Across the room a painting depicting a fishing boat in a storm caught his eye. He couldn't say why but for some reason he disliked it immensely. He opened his case, took out a syringe and placed it behind him on the sofa.

'Am I to meet your lovely husband that you have told me so much about?' He asked as Tal entered the living room with a tray of coffee and biscuits and then sat down beside him.

'You will indeed. I told him all about you. He will be home in about half an hour. You're a bit early, I wasn't expecting you until four.'

'I only had two patients to visit, as one cancelled and also I was worried I might not be able to find your lovely home,' he slapped his thighs gently with his hands. 'I'm sorry if I have put you out my dear.'

'No, no, no, not at all. Prompt people are my favourite people.' Tal said waving a dismissive hand in the air.

'I remember now that you said he wouldn't be home until about half three because he plays golf in the afternoons.' Dr Nissan said putting a hand to his head. Tal restrained herself from laughing at this action because for a moment Dr Nissan reminded her of Detective Columbo.

'All that man does is play golf. Lives and breathes it. I do believe he's addicted. Sometimes I think I've lost my husband to golf.'

As Tal Greenberg poured the coffee into the cups, Dr Nissan pointed across the room. 'That's a lovely painting.'

Tal smiled and turned to look at the painting and before she could utter a word, she had been injected in the back of the neck with succinylcholine. Succinylcholine works quickly and Tal Greenberg was in a state of paralysis within a minute. The total look of surprise on her face made Mustafa turn away from her. A minute later she was out cold. Her eyes were still open. Mustafa didn't like that, so he closed them with his fingers. He wondered what went through her mind, before she had lost consciousness. Did she realise she'd been had? They had met in the park the afternoon before. He had known she would be there. Cadoc had been following her for weeks and knew her routine. Every Thursday same time she would take a stroll around the same park and then sit on the same bench and read. She was very predictable and very lonely. It was on the bench that they became acquainted. It was that easy.

Mustafa opened his case and placed a second syringe on the table. He then walked behind Tal Greenberg with a scalpel and put the instrument to her neck and waited for Adar to walk through the door. Mustafa was thinking of his wife Adeline, when he heard the Chevrolet pull in and Adar get out and walk up to the front door. Mustafa straightened Tal Greenberg's head, her eyes were closed, and she had been dribbling; her pulse was very weak. Adar walked in whistling Spanish Harlem. He walked like a man without a care in the world. He had on chequered golf trousers and a yellow polo top. He stopped whistling when he saw a man he had never seen before, standing behind his wife with a scalpel to her neck.

'Tal!' Adar Greenberg screamed.

Mustafa stood calm and composed. He was the conductor of this orchestra. He was the one in complete control. 'Mr Greenberg, I believe? We haven't had the pleasure of a proper introduction have we, but these things happen.' He said with a grin, still holding the scalpel to Tal Greenberg's neck.

'Tal darling, are you all right?' Adar spoke looking at his beloved wife. Not knowing if she was still alive.

'She can't answer you unfortunately. Drugged, but alive.' Mustafa said comically. He was enjoying himself.

'What the fuck is this?' Adar snarled, approaching the man with the scalpel to his wife's neck.

'Don't take one more step or she dies.'

Adar did as the man commanded. 'Is it money you want? Jewellery? Just tell me and you can have it, just don't hurt her. Please I beg you.' Adar Greenberg said, falling to his knees imploring the man before him.

'Please Adar,' Mustafa chuckled mockingly. 'My God man, have some dignity, get on up. On the table is a syringe. I want you to inject yourself in the arm.'

Adar looked at the syringe on the table, then got to his feet. 'You're not here for money, are you?' A little sense of realism came to him now as he looked into the man's eyes.

'Did you think that by living in the land of the plenty. The great US of A, you could out-run all the horrendous crimes you had once done. You couldn't have been that arrogant to think that one day someone like me wouldn't come knocking.'

'She had nothing to do with the things I've done. She knew nothing.' Adar said pointing at his wife, with tears running down his face.

'It's always the innocent who suffer the most,' Mustafa replied.

Adar stared down at the syringe, 'Promise me, you won't harm her?'

'We are running out of time Mr Greenberg.'

'Promise first?' Adar cried.

'You are not in any position to negotiate.'

'Promise?' Adar demanded, gritting his teeth, as tears rolled down his cheeks.

'You have my word. Now inject yourself.'

Adar picked up the syringe with shaking hands. He sat down on the sofa next to his wife and put the needle to his arm. He paused, looking at his wife and then up at the man standing behind her. 'She came home yesterday and told me she had met a nice Lebanese doctor in the park. She told me how she had felt pity on you because you were a widow with no family over here. She invited you to our home because she really does care about people. She's not like us.' Adar said crying.

'I never lied to your lovely wife, well only my name,' Mustafa smiled down at Adar 'I haven't been the one deceiving her.' He said shaking a finger at Adar.

'What are you talking about?'

'Come now, Mr Greenberg, we've been watching,' Adar closed his eyes. 'For a man who leaves home to play golf every day, you play remarkably little golf.'

'You rotten bastard.'

'Or is golf another word for fucking a hot young yoga teacher behind your lonely wife's back?' These words seemed to cut right through Adar Greenberg's soul, and he looked like he had been slapped across the face. 'I am a widow. I have no family any more. My wife and children were killed when an Israeli missile destroyed our home. My children adored me,' Mustafa said with a lump in his throat.

Adar moved his eyes from his wife's face to the syringe and his arm and injected the poison into his own vein. Once the syringe was empty, he looked back at his wife and spoke these last words. 'Darling, I love you.' Adar felt his body stiffen. Five minutes later he was no longer in control of his muscles. He was dazed but awake, aware of some impending doom. His eyes were the only thing he could control.

Mustafa walked around to the front of the sofa and turned Tal Greenberg's wrists around so that they were facing upwards. He stood to the side and with one quick action, cut open her left wrist. Blood flew out in front of her covering the coffee table and floor. Mustafa walked around the pool of blood, knelt down and looked into the eyes of her helpless husband.

'I know, I lied,' Mustafa said. If Adar's eyes could act, they would strangle the monster before him. 'This monster you see before you, is one you helped create. You are just as guilty as I am for your wife's death. If it's any consolation, it was quick and painless for her. I can't say that it will be for you. What I do now to you is pure evil. I only do it because you and your kind our blind. You do not see the harm you have inflicted.' They were looking into each other's eyes now, their faces close, so close they could feel one another's breath. There are no words to describe what Adar Greenberg felt when Mustafa Khoury moved the scalpel towards his left eye. Mustafa pulled Adar's eyelids apart with his left hand and with his right moved the scalpel slowly, inch by inch towards the cornea. There was nothing in the world Adar Greenberg could do. Part of him wanted to die now, Tal was his world. Yes, he regularly cheated on her, but that was only because of his own insecurities. He was terrified now. He willed his body to move one last time. Nothing. He cursed himself for letting his guard slip. The sharp point of the scalpel pierced the eye. The scalpel went through the lens and the iris, then cutting downwards through the retina, Mustafa severed the optic disc and the central retina vein, destroying the optic nerve. Yellow blood poured down Adar's cheeks and Mustafa thought it was as easy as cutting a tomato. He then proceeded to cut around the sclera and after a quick circular motion with the wrist, he was able to remove the mangled eye from its socket. Mustafa then put the eye in an air-tight plastic bag, like the ones his wife used to use to keep food fresh. Adar Greenberg had lost all consciousness when Mustafa finished with his left eye and was near death. Mustafa did exactly the same to the right eye, putting Adar in complete darkness, but this time he went a bit deeper at the end cutting the central retina artery. He watched Adar bleed out for ten minutes, then checked his pulse. Adar Greenberg had joined his wife in the afterlife.

'Throw out the worthless slave into outer darkness; in that place there will be weeping and gnashing of teeth.' Mustafa said, looking down on Adar, quoting Matthew 25:30.

Mustafa Khoury aka Dr David Nissan put his black winter overcoat back on, pulling up the collar to hide his face and walked out the front door of the Greenberg's home, closing the door behind him. It was a beautiful sunny day. He walked past the lovely smelling flowered garden on the left and the shiny red Chevrolet parked on the drive. Dr Nissan turned right at the end of the drive and walked past eight other homes in the suburban neighbourhood. Three children about the same age as his children when he last remembered them, were playing hopscotch. They had not a care in the world and there was no danger of a bomb dropping on them at any time. He walked past a balding man, who was very much overweight, washing the wheels of his car. The balding man glanced up at Dr Nissan and then went back to concentrating on his wheels. Just before he left the quiet suburban street to cut through a playing field and walk through a small nature reserve, where on the other side was a lay-by and a car waiting, Dr Nissan returned a smile to an elderly lady who was pruning her rose bush. Amazingly when asked by the police no one recalled seeing anyone enter or leave the Greenberg's home. No one remembered a pale man carrying a doctor's case, wearing a black winter overcoat on one of the hottest days of the year.

# 6

Friday June 2nd 2017
Miami International Airport 11:50

The plane from Tel Aviv touched down on the tarmac five minutes early. It was a smooth fourteen-hour flight, and in that time Malia Kimani had not slept. She had the dossiers on all three of the dead agents spread around on the two empty seats either side of her. She read each dossier twice and the only link she could find was that they were all Jewish men and were, or had been, Mossad Agents. She was glad the plane had landed and the flight was over. Malia didn't mind flying, but she thought that if she had to put up with Netzer and Ron snoring for another hour, she would open the airplane door and jump out. The landing of the airplane had not even woken the two men up. It was only when the plane stopped and the seat belt sign went off and passengers started taking their hand luggage out from the overhead compartments that Netzer and Ron, who were both seated across from Malia in the middle section woke up.

'We're there already?' Netzer yawned and stretched his arms up in the air.

'Yep.' Malia said, looking towards the front of the plane, waiting for the door to open.

'You look tired, didn't you sleep?' Netzer asked, grinning.

'I am super tired and no, I couldn't sleep. I had work to do.'

'I thought the mission was a dream.' Ron said, standing up laughing, still half asleep.

'Nope. It's not a dream but it's beginning to look a lot like a nightmare,' Malia said, not looking at them.

'What's wrong with you?' Ron asked, not really caring.

'She didn't get any sleep,' Netzer answered

'Well, I had a great sleep. Feel like I'm ready to take on the world,' Ron said.

'You two were chopping down trees in your sleep,' Malia said. She was not impressed with them as agents. If she didn't know them as being agents, she would have guessed they were a pair of stoners, who never paid child support.

'I need a shit,' Netzer added.

Tim Baines and Sally Anderson watched as the passengers from the United Airlines flight walked through the gangway and into the terminal gate. Sally gave Tim Baines a nudge and pointed towards a young, tall, pretty black girl walking in front of two scruffy looking men. Sally thought both men looked like they were heading towards, a midlife crisis. They both had on Hawaiian shirts and jeans and wore flip flops.

'Please tell me that's not them?' Tim Baines whispered.

Sally smiled and replied, 'Maybe they're under deep cover.'

'They look more like drug mules than Mossad.'

'I bet you had some shirts like that sir, back when you were hitting the seventies disco scene.'

'Watch it Anderson, I'm not that old.'

Malia who was walking ahead of her two companions caught Sally Anderson's eye.

'Malia Kimani?' Tim Baines asked, holding out his badge.

'Yes.'

'I'm Special Agent Tim Baines and this is Special Agent Sally Anderson.' Tim Baines said, introducing them both to Malia and then shaking hands.

'I take it they are with you?' Sally asked nodding towards Ron and Netzer.

Malia sighed. 'Yes. Yes, they are,' Malia turned around and saw that Ron and Netzer were now thanking two pretty air stewardesses for a great flight. 'They've just woken up and are a bit slow.'

'I bet.' Tim Baines said.

'Have you any luggage to collect?' Sally asked Malia.

'Only them.' Malia said, gesturing behind her with her thumb.

Sally laughed at this remark. She liked Malia straight away.

'Netzer and Ron. I believe?' Tim Baines asked, holding out his hand to greet the two men.

'I'm Ron Yaffe and this dodgy looking fellow with me is Netzer Akerman. Sorry about our appearance, this was all sort of last minute.'

'Not a problem. This is Special Agent Sally Anderson and I'm Special Agent Tim Baines.'

'Nice to meet you both.' Ron said.

'Hi.' Netzer said and gave a wave.

Sally made a mental note to herself. Ron Yaffe — handsome, dark reddish hair, got a Freddie Mercury thing going on with the well-groomed moustache and top teeth protruding out slightly. Netzer Akerman — curly, dark blonde hair, with deep blue eyes. Looks like someone who might try and score crack at some point.

'We have put you up in the Hilton here at the airport.' Tim Baines said.

'Nice. Mini bar?' Netzer asked jokingly. Netzer liked to give the impression he was a bum, an obnoxious joker who didn't take anything seriously. It was all an act. Okay, he liked a drink, even that was a bit of an act. He could read people better when they underestimated him.

'We've set up a twenty-four-hour communication line in your rooms between you, Tel Aviv and the FBI headquarters here in Florida. We also have a helicopter that can be ready at a moment's notice any time, day or night.' Tim Baines said.

'Fantastic. I understand we don't have any witnesses to the murders,' Ron asked.

'Currently no.'

'CCTV?' Netzer asked.

'We are still going through it. But nothing of yet,' Sally said, looking slightly embarrassed.

'Would you like to freshen up before we start? Maybe catch a few hours' sleep?' Tim Baines asked.

'Me, no, I slept on the plane,' Ron said. 'Actually, I'm right where I want to be. Am I correct in thinking you have a visa department here at the airport?'

'You are correct,' Tim Baines said.

'Brilliant. Could we get a list of everyone who has applied for a visa from within France in the last month and then the same from Australia to France?'

'It might take some time, but yeah, sure.'

'Let's start now then. We should start first with Middle Eastern people,' Ron said.

'I believe this is the work of one man. A man with vast

medical experience,' Sally added.

'Outstanding Agent Anderson,' Ron said impressed. 'That narrows it a little. We should start with every medical professional who has entered the country in the last two weeks.'

'Who is also a Middle Eastern terrorist,' Netzer said, fishing for a laugh, but not getting one.

'Have you access to Adar and Tal's bank accounts? Also, a list of their friends and last known contacts?' Ron asked.

'We already have them, the autopsy report and photos of the crime scene. Would you like to go to the crime scene?' Sally asked.

'Close by?' Netzer asked.

'South Florida. The way I drive we'll be there in an hour.' Sally added.

'Was either of them having an affair?' Netzer asked.

'Adar Greenberg was,' Sally answered.

'I knew it. You can take the man out of Israel, but you can't take Israel out of the man.' Netzer said looking at Ron, who was smiling.

'Who was the woman?' Ron asked.

'A twenty-one-year-old rich chick yoga teacher,' Sally said. 'She was most likely the last person to see Adar alive, we think,' then added. 'Apart from the murderer.'

'How's her alibi?' Ron asked.

'Tight. She was still lying in the motel bed they had just screwed in, and ordering a club sandwich from room service, as Adar Greenberg and his wife were being murdered.'

'Take me to the crime scene. Seems like a sensible place to start,' Netzer said.

'Okay,' Sally said.

'Lead the way,' Netzer said and the two of them left Malia, Ron and Tim.

Tim Baines smiled awkwardly at Ron Yaffe. 'Shall we go to the visa department then?'

'Yes. But first I must have a cigarette and a strong coffee,' Ron said.

Tim Baines smiled again. He was starting to like this guy. 'You took the words right out my mouth.'

'What should I do?' Malia asked, as the two men started to walk off.

Ron walked back to Malia. 'Get some breakfast, some sleep and meet back up with us in a few hours. I need you fresh.'

'You're in the Hilton under the name Lincoln. We regularly use it for our international friends,' Tim Baines said and then the two of them continued on their way.

Suddenly Malia Kimani was alone in the airport, surrounded by thousands of people. She got a taxi to the Hilton, checked in under the name Lincoln. The receptionist made a phone call, and the reservation was confirmed. Malia ordered room service for the first time in her life, ran a bath and then went to sleep in a bed that looked like it could sleep six people.

# 7

Police tape ran around the Greenberg's home and Netzer gave a sly grin, wondering how this would affect house prices in such a pretty neighbourhood. 'It's gonna be like the house from Halloween that's abandoned, and kids dare one another to go inside.' Netzer said.

'Beautiful day in the neighbourhood?' Netzer remarked, getting out the car and waving across at a grim-faced neighbour.

Netzer and Sally walked through the front door of the Greenberg's house, ducking under the police tape. Sally was astonished by what she saw. All the signs of the horror that had happened were gone. The house now looked like a show home.

'The cleaners have been in,' Sally said, looking at the sofa.

Netzer ignored the sofa and walked straight past Sally to the kitchen. Netzer opened a cupboard drawer and took out a plastic container.

'What are you looking for?' Sally asked.

'Bamba,' he replied and then held up an orange-coloured snack bag with Hebrew writing on the front.

'Is there information inside?' Sally asked.

'Something better than that.'

'What?' Sally asked, standing next to Netzer as he opened the packet.

'Soft puffs of beautiful peanut butter. Snacks that the Gods made. Want one?' Netzer offered Sally the bag.

Sally put her hand to her head and felt stupid. 'We are supposed to be looking for something to help us find the murderer,' Sally said, visibly pissed off.

'Well, we're not going to find it here.' Netzer said, stuffing his mouth with Bamba.

'Then why the hell are we here?'

'Bamba. I knew Adar. I knew he would get this shit imported.'

Sally stormed off, biting her lip, not wanting to ruin international relations so early on. Netzer jumped a little when he heard the front door slam shut. A minute later Netzer came out still eating from the giant bag of Bamba. Sally stood on the driveway looking down the street, with her arms crossed across her chest.

'Look, Agent Anderson, the killer never drove in this way,' Netzer said, pointing down the street. Sally glanced at him and saw that he was not acting up now. 'Where does this path lead?' he asked, already walking along it.

'To the children's playing field,' Sally said.

They both stood at the edge of the playing field. A concrete path cut through the middle of the playing field, then climbed slightly then led down towards a nature reserve, where there was a small pond by its entrance.

'No surveillance around here?' Netzer asked.

'None.'

'Then this is the way the killer came and left,' Netzer declared, pointing towards the tree line of the nature reserve.

'We've combed every inch of the playing field and nature reserve. We found nothing.'

'I bet there is a car park or rest area on the other side of this nature reserve,' Netzer said smiling.

'A lay-by. Again, no cameras.'

The two of them walked through the nature reserve to the lay-by.

'This is where the killer entered and left from. This is where the car was parked,' Netzer said, finishing off the last of the Bamba and dropping the packet into an overflowing waste bin.

'It's very possible,' Sally agreed. 'We've considered this already.'

'What is at the entrance to this lay-by, Agent Anderson?' Netzer asked looking down the narrow winding road.

'The freeway. And yes, the freeway has hundreds of cameras. We have gone through them all. Checked every surveillance video that works in every rest stop and motel in both directions for miles. Nothing out of the ordinary. We have nothing because we don't know what or who we are looking for.'

'You have the car the killer was in. You have him, Agent Anderson,' Netzer said lighting a cigarette.

'We have literally thousands of vehicles going across the highway every hour. It runs for five hundred and forty-five miles, through thirteen counties. It's one of the busiest interstates in the United States. We might as well be looking for a needle in a haystack,' Agent Anderson responded looking at Netzer, who was smiling.

'Only we need not worry about all those miles and all those counties. We only need the camera footage of cars going past before the entrance to this lay-by and after. Then we will know which cars stopped off here. We know the day that they died and roughly the time. So, we should be able to find a match, a number plate, a rental company and then hopefully an address and an identity.'

Agent Anderson's eyes lit up. 'That might just do it. Come on, let's go.'

'I'm following you, Agent Lady.'

Just before they got back into the car which was parked outside the Greenberg's home, Netzer ran back inside the house and came out a minute later with another giant bag of Bamba.

'You've got a serious problem,' Sally said looking at Netzer, filling his mouth with the golden snack.

'I know, but there are worse things in this life to be addicted to.'

'You don't think this is the work of one man, do you?' Sally asked.

'It's highly unlikely. I think the killer must be getting some form of help. Someone else is doing the leg work.'

'I believe so too, and that is what frightens me,' Sally said.

'Where to now?' Netzer asked, plugging in his seatbelt.

'To the Florida Department of Transportation to get this fucker,' Sally said, pulling away.

'Now you're speaking my language,' Netzer said and smacked his hands together in delight.

# 8

Friday June 2nd 2017
Miami International Airport 12:35

Standing at 6'2 and weighing an impressive one hundred and eighty-five pounds, Mike McGavin strolled around the department of U.S Immigration and Customs with the air of someone who loved his job. A patriot, who lost a thumb in the First Gulf War, when it was shot off by an enemy sniper whilst he was lighting a cigarette. He was proud to lose his thumb for his country, but angry with his president at the time for not following the job through. A Texan, whose love for his beloved Dallas Cowboys was only equalled by that for his wife and two daughters. He had been the head of U.S Immigration and Customs, for five years at Miami International Airport. To Mike McGavin his guys and girls who worked for the U.S Immigration and Customs were the first line of defence for the country. His country, the home of the brave. His soldiers as he called them, loved him. He ran a tight ship and always taught his interrogators, investigators and security personnel to always make the best decision for the country and be ready to be accountable for their decision. Sentimentality had no place in Mike McGavin's airport.

Mike McGavin was in his office having his daily meeting with Homeland Security when Tim Baines and Ron Yaffe walked in, they had just finished their cigarettes and coffee and were ready to get down to business.

'Gentleman. I'm sorry,' Tim Baines said, opening the door to the office without knocking.

The men all turned around and looked at Tim Baines. 'Buddy, we're having a meeting,' Mike McGavin said leaning back in his chair, upset with the intrusion.

'I'm sorry, but it's very important. I'm with the FBI.'

'If it was that important my people would know about it,' one of the Homeland Security people said, as the other two looked Tim Baines up and down and dismissed him.

'Look, agent,' Mike McGavin said.

'Try special agent, I'll be the one who's in charge of the Miami field office,' Tim Baines said correcting Mike McGavin. The Homeland Security boys gave Tim Baines a second surprised look and Ron nodded his head in admiration of the man he had just had a cigarette with.

'You have our attention,' Mike McGavin said straightening up.

Tim Baines and Ron Yaffe walked in and sat down at two of the leather chairs at the other end of the table.

'If you wouldn't mind, gentlemen,' Tim Baines said looking at the Homeland Security personnel and then at the door.

'If there is a risk to the homeland or the airport, we should know,' one of the Homeland Security guys demanded.

'No risk involving you,' Tim Baines replied. 'Just small fry stuff.'

'What's this about?' Mike McGavin protested.

'Please feel free to phone Washington,' Tim Baines said and walked to the door and opened it. 'Gentlemen, please. Get the fuck out!' he said in his most passive tone, looking down at the Homeland Security boys.

The Homeland Security boys looked at one another in disgust and then at Mike McGavin. Mike McGavin shrugged his shoulders, as if to say it's out of my hands. Ron sat silent, looking at the table. The three stooges got up and left the room, they didn't see the slap across the face, but they sure as hell felt it. Tim Baines closed the door and then sat back down.

'So, what can I do for you?' Mike McGavin said taking off his cowboy's cap and scratching his bald head with his thumbless hand.

'First of all, we need to know how many middle eastern medical professionals have entered the country in the last two weeks. Just men for now and let's start with Miami,' Ron Yaffe said still looking down at the table.

'And who might you be?' Mike McGavin asked agitated with all that had gone on.

'I'm here as a friend,' Ron responded, looking up at the man.

'You're Middle Eastern, aren't you?' Mike McGavin asked. 'I lost a thumb fighting you fuckers.'

'I never knew the United States and Israel had a war. Who won?'

'Mossad,' Mike snapped.

'Time is of the essence,' Ron said calmly.

'How long will it take?' Tim Baines asked.

Mike McGavin picked up the telephone and spoke to his secretary. 'Barbara, get Dug Daniels from the south terminal and Isabelle Martins from the north terminal to meet me in my office ASAP.' He put down the telephone and looked at Tim Baines. 'Tell me, who are we looking for?'

'A murderer,' Tim Baines said.

'A potential terrorist!' Ron Yaffe said looking up at the two men. Tim Baines looked shocked at this statement. 'Come on. Has it not occurred to you too?'

'If you're holding anything back, now is the time to tell us. We were told everything would be laid out on the table,' Tim Baines said angrily.

'And it has. I'm just saying it is very likely our killer is getting help. There could be a terrorist cell working right here in Florida or close by,' Ron said, pointing down at the table.

'Be careful. You say killer, we got a manhunt. You say terrorism and we have a nationwide search involving every department in the country, even the ones you haven't heard of yet, from here to Timbuktu. The possibility of lockdowns, curfews, vigilantes, racism. Airports will shut down, stocks will fall and we could even have a crash.' Tim Baines warned, with sweat running down his face.

'So, this is just a hunch?' Mike McGavin asked, looking up at Ron.

Ron nodded to everyone's relief. 'But it's very unlikely this person flew here expecting to return home. And I would be astonished if he's not getting help.' Mike McGavin and Tim Baines both sunk back into their chairs.

'Who are these folks you've got coming here?' Tim asked Mike.

'My best people. They'll find this guy if he came through here.'

Two minutes later Isabelle Martins and Dug Daniels entered the office, with looks of concern on their faces. They were both thinking the same thing, cuts and layoffs. Why else would they have an unscheduled meeting on a Friday afternoon. Dug Daniels suddenly remembered reading somewhere that most layoffs were announced on a Friday. They were soon both put at ease when Mike McGavin told them that a potential terrorist had entered the country. They were given a list of what to look for. Twenty minutes later Dug Daniels and Isabelle Martins were sitting next to a kid, no older then eighteen, scrolling through a database of millions. Luckily, and unfortunately, after 9/11 the United States government allowed the NSA to connect every airport in the world, whether they knew it or not, through a super-computer. At Miami International the security systems database they could connect to was called Red Storm Revival. Five minutes later in the small, neon-lit room, that hardly anyone knew existed, Dug, Isabelle and the kid had a list of sixty-one names. They took the list back to the office where Tim, Ron and Mike were sitting drinking coffee. The kid who was hired straight out of high school by the NSA went back to playing computer games. The kid only answered to the NSA. At the airport only Dug Daniels and Isabelle Martins could ask him to run a search, but they had to jointly ask him. Mike had to approve the search and the kid had to confirm the search by text message to his NSA boss. Finding anyone through Red Storm Revival was easy. Finding a Middle Eastern, medical professional was even easier. Middle Eastern men, or people who looked Middle Eastern were categorised as potential risks. If a person of interest has a cell phone, it can be listened to. If that person is on social media, the kid can access it and all their contacts and so on. If you use your credit card anywhere in the world the kid can see where and what you purchased.

Dug Daniels, Isabelle Martins, Mike McGavin and Tim

Baines read out the sixty-one names, where they flew in from, their country of origin, where and when they applied for their visa and if they arrived alone. Ron Yaffe drew up a scoring system on a white board. If a person ticked all four boxes his name was circled as a possibility, the rest were temporarily dismissed. In the four boxes were. 1) Male, Arrives Alone. 2) Country Of Origin - All Middle East. 3) Flew In From Europe (Preferably France). 4) Applied For VISA In Last Three Weeks. At the end they were left with just two names. The first name was a Dr David Nissan, born in Lebanon, arrived alone on a J-1 Visa, and flew in from Belgium two weeks ago. The second name was a Dr Mohammad Saleh, born in Jordan, arrived alone on a J-1 Visa, and flew in from Germany ten days ago.

Dr Mohammad Saleh was sixty-two years of age, and this was his ninth visit to the United States in the last six years. Dr David Nissan was much younger, thirty-six years of age and this was his first visit.

'This is our man,' Ron said slapping his hand on Dr David Nissan's name on the whiteboard.

'How do you know?' Tim Baines asked.

'Right age, and he flew in from Belgium,' Ron said staring at the name and smiling. Inside he was saying, 'I got you fucker.'

'Belgium?' Tim Baines said confused.

'We have it practically blacklisted in Israel,' Ron said still staring at the name.

'Find out all we can on this Dr Nissan. See if he has been to Australia as well.' Tim Baines told Dug and Isabelle.

'He would have changed passports in Europe,' Ron said knowingly.

'Check anyway,' Mike McGavin said.

'And get a photo of this man!' Tim shouted before Dug and Isabelle left the room in a hurry.

At that same moment Tim Baines's mobile phone rang. He had the Star Wars ringtone and Mike McGavin lost the little bit of respect he had for the man. It was Agent Anderson on the other end telling Tim they were on the way to the Florida Department of Transportation or FDOT for short. Ron saw relief upon Tim Baines's face, as he closed his eyes and smiled, like a man who has held the urge to urinate for some time.

'Good girl. Call me when you get the plate,' Tim said gleefully, before putting down the phone.

'What we got?' Ron asked, sensing good news on the horizon.

'Your man and my new top agent think they can get the plate. They are on their way to the Florida Department of Transportation now. I'm betting the name registered to that car is our Dr Nissan.'

Half an hour later Dug Daniels and Isabelle Martins walked back into Mike McGavin's office that was now a makeshift control centre. Tim Baines was pacing the room, badly wanting a cigarette. Ron Yaffe was pouring coffee from a jug that Barbara had just brought in. Mike had told Barbara to order five pizzas, fearing that this could turn into an all-nighter.

'Five pizzas?' Ron remarked, amazed and counting the people in the room. 'Are we expecting an army?'

'I like pizza,' Mike replied proudly. Only in America, Ron thought.

'This is Dr David Nissan,' Dug said, holding up a blown-up sized passport photo of Mustafa Khoury. Ron snatched the photo and looked at the man, thinking he might recognise him.

'Seen him before?' Tim asked.

'Never,' Ron replied. It was a determined face he was staring at, but the eyes, the eyes were vulnerable.

'We don't have a lot on him,' Isabelle said, looking at a single sheet of paper with Dr Nissan's information on. 'Born April 20, 1981, in Lebanon, studied to become a Cardiologist at the American University of Beirut and Graduated 2007. No wife, no children. Nothing on parents or siblings. Lives alone in an apartment in Lebanon. Works at the Saint George Hospital University Medical Centre. No phone number and he is not on social media. Also, we can't find any photos of him at the university. His passport is clean, issued in Lebanon. No criminal record, and this is the first time he has entered the United States. He flew in from Belgium and that looks like the first country outside Lebanon he has ever been to. No address in Belgium either.' Isabelle said passing the sheet to Ron.

'It's like the guy's a fucking ghost,' Tim Baines said.

'He was issued with a valid passport, granted by the Lebanese government. It was clean and he was cleared,' Isabelle said.

'Bank account?' Ron asked.

'Yes, he must have used a credit card here?' Tim jumped in.

'He has a US currency card, which was preloaded in Belgium. There is $4,825 on it,' Isabelle said.

'Put an alert on it now.' Tim Baines said, slamming his fist down on the table. 'If he uses it, we'll nab him.'

'I will, but we've already checked. He hasn't touched it yet.'

'Where's he staying? He must have checked in to somewhere?' Tim Baines asked, raising his voice.

'He was registered to stay at a motel in Wildwood, but he never checked in.'

'And I suppose he hasn't rented a car either?' Tim asked, already knowing the answer.

'I'm afraid we have nothing. He's here, he hasn't left the country.'

'Let's put a block on his passport as well,' Mike McGavin said.

'Already done it,' Dug Daniels said.

'Was he picked up at the airport?' Tim asked.

'He purchased a bus ticket with cash to Fort Lauderdale, but we don't know if he got off there as the cameras on the bus were out,' Isabelle said.

'Question the bus driver, he might remember something.'

'We are tracking him down now, but my guess is he won't remember.'

'That means he's getting help,' Ron said, looking at Tim Baines glumly.

'Let's hope Sally and your man can get a plate,' Tim Baines said, pinning their hopes on them.

'Let's not count on this man making too many mistakes,' Ron said, looking at Dr Nissan's photo.

The room fell silent and when Barbara walked in with the pizzas, she got the same feeling she got the year before at her mother's funeral.

# 9

Friday June 2nd 2017
The Florida Department of Transportation, Fort Lauderdale
17:17

Agent Anderson and Netzer walked into the Florida Department of Transportation about the same time Mike McGavin was tucking into his sixth slice of pepperoni pizza. Agent Anderson showed her FBI badge to the Security guard and a young girl with an award-winning smile walked over from the reception desk. Netzer kept his hands in his pockets and looked like a lost child.

'How can we be of assistance, Agent Anderson?' said the young receptionist, glancing at Agent Anderson's badge.

'We need to find a vehicle that may have been used in a crime,' Agent Anderson said.

'Please take a seat and I'll call someone to come down.'

'Thank you.' Sally sat down and watched the girl make the phone call.

Netzer walked over, picking his nose. 'Any luck?'

Sally saw that his little finger was moving around in his nose, and she gave him a look of disgust. 'Are you digging for treasure?'

Netzer smiled. 'No, I have a scab. It's really itchy and my fingers are too big.' He looked at her hands, 'You look like you have thin fingers, can you help a spook out?'

Sally raised her eyebrows. 'Gross.'

Across from them an elevator door opened and a black guy in a wheelchair came out. He had Rastafarian type hair, with thick dreadlocks and wore a bandanna. He glanced up at the receptionist and she nodded towards Agent Anderson and Netzer.

'You need to find a car?' He spoke with a cool cat voice and Sally thought he sounded a lot like a crush she once had at school.

'We do.' Sally confirmed.

'I'm your man.' He said pointing his thumb at his chest and looking at Netzer.

'I'm Netzer,' Netzer said holding out his hand.

'Israeli?'

'You got it,' Netzer said.

'Netzer, I'm Ben.' Ben then looked at Sally. 'And you're FBI.'

'Agent Anderson, but you can call me Sally.'

'I'm guessing this is big. We don't normally get the FBI and Mossad knocking on our door.' Netzer winked at Ben and Sally smiled.

'Shall we go find this vehicle,' Netzer said.

They took the elevator up one floor and came out into a control room. Maps and monitors of Florida were on every wall. Telephones rang constantly, red lights flashed on the big screens to indicate where accidents had been reported. Staff directed emergency services and it seemed that there were at least a hundred different conversations going on at once. You couldn't pin-point one conversation, they layered on top of each other. Runners ran between technicians and offices where management meetings were being held. There was no catastrophe in Florida, this was just another run of a mill day for the Florida Department of Transportation.

'Look at it. Organised chaos.' Ben said.

'How do you stand the noise?' Sally asked.

'This is peaceful compared to Korangal Valley,' Ben said reflectively, for a moment going back in time, when he served with the Second Battalion, 12 Infantry Regiment.

'Afghanistan, is that where you got injured?' Sally asked.

Ben laughed, spinning around to look at her. 'Dumb luck. Two months after coming home and surviving that hell hole, I get hit by a drunk driver.'

'That's about as fucked up as it can get,' Netzer said.

'Tell me about it. One minute I'm crossing the road with a taco, the next I'm in this chair.'

'I wouldn't have pegged you for the military,' Netzer said.

'I know, right. The weed helps, I get it for the pain, and it helps with the flashbacks.'

Ben's monitor was decorated with dancing Buddhas on springs and a flask of coffee, that probably had more whiskey in than coffee, Netzer thought.

'I like your Buddhas,' Sally laughed, pushing down on one and watching it spring up.

'They're good company. Down to brass tacks. Do we have a make or plate to play with?' Ben asked.

'We have nothing,' Sally said. 'We only have the date and a rough time we think the crime occurred.' Ben gave them a bemused look. 'But we think we know where the car was parked when the crime was being committed. We believe the car came in and went out from the West Dixie highway. It's the only entrance and exit. Even though there is no camera at the entrance.'

Ben cut her off. 'You want the camera before and after the entrance.'

'Exactly,' Sally said.

'Easy,' Ben said.

'Easy, really?' Sally returned, surprised.

'What date and time do we have to play with?'

'Friday, May 26th, between midday and 5pm,' Sally said.

'Where on the West Dixie Highway?'

'A turning into Greynolds Park between 179th Street and 173rd street.'

'I went there last year to a reggae concert,' Ben said typing the address into the computer. 'We have one camera after 173rd street and one before 179th Street. Now we put in the data. We want every vehicle that past between those two cameras between midday and 5pm. We want the speed every vehicle travelled at. Then we can see all the vehicles that stopped between those two cameras and hopefully find your vehicle.'

'How long will it take?' Sally asked.

'I'd say no longer than ten minutes and we'll have a list for you.' Ben patted his monitor, like it was a pet.

'Is there somewhere I can smoke?' Netzer asked.

'Go out the same way you came in and walk around the back of the building, there's a smoking area.'

Eight minutes later the monitor beeped, and list of vehicles showed up on the screen.

'We have a list of 13,630 cars,' Ben announced. 'Now we tell it to take away all the cars that took under ten minutes to make the journey between the two cameras.'

Thirty seconds later the monitor beeped again.

'How many are we left with?' Sally asked eagerly. Everyone's heart was beating fast now. They could smell the prey.

'Only ten cars took over ten minutes,' Ben said.

'Can you print out all the information you can on those cars?'

'It's already coming out,' Ben said pointing at the printer. Sally gave Ben a high-five.

Sally phoned Tim Baines to tell him the news. The pizza was all gone now. Ron was laying down on the sofa and staring up at the ceiling.

'We got ten names,' Sally said trying to keep her composure, underneath she was excited.

'Are any of them a Dr David Nissan?' Tim Baines asked.

'No,' Sally said.

Netzer studied the list, only one name stuck out. Everyone else on the list had your typical American name, but not this one. Mr Cadoc Elneny.

'I'm sending you a photo of Dr David Nissan, we think he's our man. Can you get facial recognition?' Tim Baines asked.

'Can we get facial recognition?' Sally asked Ben.

'Shouldn't be a problem, where should I start?' Ben asked.

'With this one,' Netzer said pointing at the name of Mr Cadoc Elneny.

Ben entered the registration for Mr Elneny's silver 2007 Honda Civic.

The photo of Dr David Nissan came though the other end and Netzer picked it up, looked at it for a moment and then placed it on the desk.

'The speed cameras in Florida are a thing to marvel. They

can produce crisp images of the vehicle, driver and front seat passenger. In Florida you don't need to have broken the speed limit for your vehicle to be captured on camera. These cameras are live and record everything.' Ben announced.

'Big brother is watching us,' Netzer remarked, putting his hand on Ben's shoulder and looking at the screen, waiting to see the face of Dr David Nissan.

A photo appeared, clear as day of the driver, presumably Mr Cadoc Elneny. There was a man sitting next to him in the front passenger seat. It was Dr David Nissan.

'Got him,' Netzer smiled and nodded at Sally who was still holding the phone.

'What address do we have for Elneny?' Sally asked.

'32077 North East, 9th Avenue, Pompano Beach, Florida,' Ben shouted.

'Fuck, that's close,' Sally gasped.

'What's that address?' Tim Baines asked.

'It's super close. Pompano Beach, sir, 32077, 9th Avenue.'

'That's only twenty-five minutes away,' Tim Baines said.

'We're closer, sir, we can—'

'That's a no,' Tim Baines said, cutting Sally off. 'Give me a second.' Tim Baines studied a map that Ron Yaffe had just ripped down from the wall in Mike McGavin's office. 'Meet us in twenty minutes on the corner of North East 24th Street and North East 12th Avenue. That's a couple of blocks down from Elneny's.'

'Yes sir.'

'Good work, Agent Anderson,' Tim Baines said.

'Thank you, sir.'

As soon as Agent Anderson put down the phone, Netzer looked her squarely in the eyes. 'I would appreciate a firearm.'

'That's not going to happen without Tim's approval.'

'You're telling me I can't have a gun in Yankee land, I thought they grow on trees here,' Netzer said sarcastically.

'Very funny,' Agent Anderson returned.

'But everyone is going to have one,' Netzer said imitating a sulking child.

'Anyway, we want to take them in alive.' Agent Anderson reminded Netzer. She studied him for a moment.

'Of course, but you don't go to bed with a whore without wrapping up.'

As they drove to meet the others, she was suddenly concerned about Netzer's true intentions.

# 10

Friday June 2nd, 2017
Pompano Beach, Florida, corner of 24th Street and 12th
Avenue 18:20

Agent Anderson and Netzer parked up next to a beaten-up old
camper van that had a peace sign painted on the back doors.
Sally watched as three children raced up the street on bicycles,
it made her happy to see the children having fun. Her palms
were sweating, and she rubbed them on her trousers and Netzer
noticed.

'Don't underestimate these men. If they notice anything
out of the norm.'

'I know,' she said cutting him off.

'This your first time?' Netzer asked smiling. He had
yellowish teeth and his skin was oily and she thought of him
as someone who only showered on special occasions.

'I've been with tactical before,' she replied sounding
annoyed, more annoyed than she intended.

'As an observer?'

'Yes,' she said gritting her teeth.

'You shot at a human before?'

I'm coming pretty close to shooting you, she thought.
Netzer read the anger in her face and felt her look. Netzer
turned and looked up at the sun that would not be setting for

another hour or so. He started to whistle a familiar tune, Sally recognised it, but could not put her finger on the song.

'What is that you are whistling?' she asked trying to break the tension between them.

Just before he could answer Tim Baines and Ron pulled up next to them.

'Who we got coming, sir?' Agent Anderson asked a tired looking Tim Baines.

'SWAT are about five minutes away.'

'Have we got anyone watching the house?' Netzer asked.

'Two agents posing as Jehovah witnesses are in a house across from Elneny's now. The Honda is on the drive and the curtains are pulled. According to the neighbours, Cadoc and his mother have lived there for about four years. She is very elderly, and he is very pleasant. Cadoc volunteers down the homeless shelter regularly. Just recently another man has been seen staying there. They hardly leave the house,' Tim Baines said.

All four got out the cars when SWAT arrived in an unmarked white van. Tim Baines climbed into the back to brief them and Netzer and Ron smoked a cigarette together.

'Where's Malia?' Netzer asked Ron.

'Still in bed, we don't need her. Hopefully, by the time she wakes up, this will be wrapped up.'

Tim Baines jumped out the van holding a phone to his ear. 'We're all ready to go, just waiting on your boys, sheriff.'

'Who we waiting on now?' Ron asked Tim Baines when he got off the phone.

'We need local law enforcement to tag along, so everyone can say this went down legally.'

'Too many fucking people,' Ron said, with his hands on

his hips.

'We do things the right way in this country,' Tim Baines said pointing at the floor with his finger.

'We're already parked out here in broad daylight, with our dicks in the wind, while the whole fucking neighbourhood is probably taking photos and putting them on Facebook.' Both men were clearly agitated, and the heat was not helping.

A minute later two Broward County Sheriff cars pulled up and Tim Baines walked over towards them.

'Hey boys, we want a Cadoc Elneny and a man going by the name Dr David Nissan, there may be three people in the house. We have to assume they have weapons. Just stay two hundred yards behind and bring some popcorn.'

'Sure thing,' one of the two Sheriffs said laughing.

'Fuck me, they must think they're going to a shoot up on their daddy's ranch,' Ron said, unimpressed by the amount of different law enforcement agencies that had gathered.

Tim Baines walked back over towards Ron Yaffe, who was looking in the back of the van, at the ten men who were heavily armed.

'Two five men teams will hit the house in five minutes, after they have opened the front door. We will breach from the back and the east side of the home.' Tim Baines banged on the front window of the van, 'All right, go boys.'

'Believe me, if these guys are even half-decently trained, then they have envisioned this scenario and are ready for it. If you want your men to walk away from this alive, don't for one minute go in all guns blazing,' Ron pleaded.

'What would you do then, wait until they leave the house?'

'Yes,' Ron returned quickly.

'Time is against us. If there is a cell operating in this country, we need to know now. End of.' Tim ended the conversation and phoned the agents posing as Jehovah witnesses in the house across from Elneny's. 'It's a go, in two minute walk over to Elneny's and SWAT will back you up.' He put down the phone and took a deep breath. 'Right ramblers, let's get rambling.'

'Do we get guns?' Netzer asked.

'You won't need one,' Tim Baines said, wiping his forehead with a tissue.

Ron and Tim got in one car and Netzer and Agent Anderson got in another. They drove in single file towards the house with the Broward County Sheriffs following behind.

Ron felt helpless, and the skyline was turning golden red. Special Agent Tim Baines had all his cards on the table now. Sally had reservations about the operation, but she was enjoying the thrill. Netzer looked void of all emotion, to Sally he profiled the perfect sociopath.

A female agent, with ten years' experience on the force and her male colleague with eight years', approached Elneny's home. The lawn was cut and looked lush green. The house itself looked well maintained with double glazing windows which looked newish, and it wasn't totally unusual for the curtains to be pulled all day in Florida in June. It was very hot, and the evenings had been getting stupidly humid recently. They knocked on the door and saw the curtains in the living room move slightly. No one answered and after a minute they rang the bell and took a step back on the porch, holding their leaflets. Their 9mm handguns were in a holster in the back of their trousers, safety off, ready to use, like in their training. To the left of the agents who were dressed in full Jehovah witness attire, were the first element of the SWAT team, the second ready to breach from the back of the house.

Then the agents heard the key to the door turn and bolt move up and to the side. The agents smiled, as an elderly lady wearing a dressing gown and slippers opened the door. She appeared to be on the better side of seventy and did not smile. Diabetes had claimed the vision in her right eye two years earlier and her eye was completely bloodshot and lost forever. Doctors put this down to her high sugar diet. It was true, since arriving in America with her then, ten-year-old son Cadoc, in 1980, she had become a lover of all things sweet.

'What do you want?' she asked softly, trying not to show her blackened teeth.

'We would like to share God's word with you. The spiritual command given to Jesus and his followers,' Agent Oliver Hanson said, whilst Agent Karen O'Brady, who was unaware she was seven weeks pregnant held up the Holy Bible, King James Version.

'I'm okay, thank you.'

'Do you believe in God?' Agent O'Brady asked, glancing behind her to see if there was anyone else in the house. The question seemed to Mrs Elneny to be very personal, and she didn't like the tone of the bible bashers voice, it was very flat and to the point and more of a demand to know. Manar, meaning guiding light was born in Egypt in a small Bedouin village called Sallum, near the Mediterranean Sea and next to the border with Libya. Her marriage was arranged, and she was married at fourteen years of age to a man four years her senior. She didn't think much of Jafar when she first laid eyes on him. He had a cruel face; a scar ran across his right cheek from an unfortunate accident that had happened when he was ten years of age. A goat had kicked him, and he had fallen backwards down a small ravine and cut his cheek on a jagged rock. He was conscious of his scar and for this reason he rarely smiled. Also, Manar was a little taller than Jafar and she hated that, and the other girls in the village joked about it. All her worries were soon put at ease. Jafar the goat herder let her keep her Ird, which means honour, for three months after the marriage. Ird is something a woman is born with, and she loses it after sexual transgressions has taken place, the longer she can keep it, the more respect she gains. The girls in the village who laughed at her for marrying a smaller, quiet and unattractive man all lost their honour on their wedding night. She went from disliking Jafar, to respecting him and then loving him all in about the space of a year. He was gentle and loved to tell jokes. Manar had two miscarriages before Cadoc was born in 1970. On July 21$^{st}$, 1977, Libyan forces invaded the border village of Sallum and on the the 22nd of July 1977. Jafar was struck in the back of the head by a stray bullet. He was not recorded as one of the one hundred casualties of the three-day war. Three weeks after mourning the loss of her husband, Manar the widow took her 7-year-old son Cadoc and left her home in the Bedouin village, the place she was born and had lived her whole life. They sneaked out in the middle of the night under the cover of darkness, without telling a soul. She paid a smuggler to take her across the Mediterranean Sea in a skiff to Italy. Two days and two nights later they arrived in Athens, Greece. Three of the ten migrants who paid the smuggler to take them across the Mediterranean died of hypothermia on the skiff and were buried at sea. Manar and her young son claimed asylum as refugees in Athens, thinking at first it was Italy. She told the authorities in Athens she had fled her old life to save her son, because she was scared for his life. This was the truth. She got a job as a cleaner in Athens at a nice hotel and by chance she met an American man, a diplomat, he took pity on her and arranged for her and her son to go to America. It's the land of milk and honey, she told Cadoc. He was a young boy, he had lost his father whom he loved, had been taken away from his family and spent nearly three days in a skiff that nearly capsized twice and now he was told he was going to the United States of America. In America Manar raised Cadoc as a proud Sunni Muslim. She loved Islam, but as the years past in America, she and Cadoc lost touch with Islam. Manar never remarried, never even looked at another man, only the guy from Magnum P.I, Tom Selleck, yeah, she liked him.

'I do,' she answered truthfully.

'Good,' Agent Oliver Hanson said, putting his foot in the door so that she could not close it. Manar Elneny gasped as she saw the first Swat Agent holding a Heckler and Koch MP5 sub machine gun in full body armour approach the door and then go inside. Agent Hanson put his hand across the elderly woman's mouth so she could not scream and held her up against the door.

The curtains in the upstairs window moved and Ron noticed that the last two SWAT Agents approaching from the side of the house were in sight of the window.

'Something's not right, your men have been seen,' Ron said opening the door to the car that was parked up under a tree about fifty yards away, facing the house.

'Get back in the fucking car,' Tim Baines sneered, trying to grab at him from the driver's seat.

'Get them out of there,' Ron said, turning back to look at

Tim Baines, with a total look of terror on his face.

Cadoc Elneny sat on the floor of his room, the room he had lived in since the age of sixteen, when he and his mother had moved from New York. He held the detonator in his shaking right hand, thumb on trigger, ready to lightly press down. He knew this day might eventually come. His mother who was at the front door with the agents knew not of the man her son had become. She had no idea she had chewed down her last twinkie. Mrs Elneny thought her son could do no wrong, he had a good job as a computer programmer and regularly worked from home. He volunteered with the homeless, helped coach a little league team, even though he didn't really like baseball. In reality, Cadoc had been fired from his job two months prior. In fact, it was at a works Christmas party a year before, when he overheard Lucy Taylor, a systems analyst, whom he had had a crush on for over three years, tell two male colleagues that if the Arabs didn't have Israel to fight, they would be fighting each other. Lucy had just slammed down two tequila shots with the men and was on her sixth glass of red wine. Whether Lucy Taylor believed what she had said or not seems in-coincidental now. It was the catalyst for change in Cadoc, a man who already felt like an outcast in his adopted home country. He had been bullied his whole life for having a different skin tone. He came to the country as a young boy with dreams and love in his heart and year by year, and one derogatory comment after another slowly destroyed his love. Cadoc knew it wasn't going to get any better for him, when two planes flew into the world trade centre. Despite his open condemnation of this terrible act, the name calling only got worse, he felt the glares on the bus and in the supermarket. People treated him like a terrorist before he ever became one. It was at this Christmas party, waiting in line to collect his jacket from the cloak room, with his ticket number in hand, that he first thought about revenge. He thought no more of Lucy Taylor, who drunkenly staggered into a taxi with both her male colleagues from the Christmas party, one of whom filmed the threesome on his iPhone. Cadoc still helped her at work when she asked for help, laughed at her crap jokes that were funny once, when he was in love with her. He was reliable, great at his job, a good rag head terrorist she thought. He was a model employee up until he was fired for nothing more than poor time keeping. It was hard, helping plan the murder of so many and at the same time write a program for people who hated you. It wasn't hard finding fellow radicals online; he was clever with computers and stayed safe. Cadoc became friends with a person who called himself Samuel. They started off talking about Islam, America and life in general. Samuel was the friend Cadoc always wanted, he listened to Cadoc's life story and then exploited it. Cadoc was easy to indoctrinate, he was a recruiter's dream. Samuel, the ISIS recruiter had sunk his hook in, he told Cadoc how to act, what books to read, told him that he could have his jihad. The two men never met, but the network is wide and Samuel made all the necessary checks on Cadoc. When Samuel was absolutely sure of his man, he told him a man would be coming to Florida and Cadoc would help him and house him. In return the man would help him make a bomb. The man coming was Dr Nissan.

'Allahu Akbar, Allahu Akbar, Allahu Akbar.' Cadoc shouted from his room and then pressed lightly down on the trigger. The blast was huge, car windows half a mile away shattered, Ron Yaffe who was arguing with Tim Baines by the car flew backwards five yards. The two five-men SWAT teams didn't stand a chance, Agents Hanson, O'Brady, her unborn baby and Manar Elneny were also killed. The Elneny home and two of their next-door neighbour's homes were completely flattened. Luckily, both neighbour's homes were unoccupied at the time of the explosion. Cadoc's jihad was complete, he had used enough Triacetone Triperoxide, or TATP to level a street. Mustafa Khoury who had left the night before, had helped Cadoc put the mother of Satan bomb together. The highly sensitive crystalline powder that had blown up so many clumsy terrorists over the years had been put together perfectly here.

# 11

Wildflowers of dark blue, violet and purple danced in the warm afternoon spring wind. The old general was laid out on a trunk of an uprooted cedar tree that had fallen the previous winter.

'You smell that?' General Fouad Aoun whispered softly into the wind.

'What is that?' Mustafa Khoury asked, sniffing the air, hands on hips, head up with one foot on the trunk of the cedar. The young, widowed doctor was fixed now. His legs had mended well, all the nurses and all the doctors had put him back together again.

'Lebanon. It's Lebanon.' The old general sat himself upright on the trunk of the cedar, nearly rolling off backwards in the process. Mustafa smiled and the old general laughed.

'You didn't need to come,' Mustafa told his old friend.

'I thought I still might have one last chance of talking you out of this,' The general said, looking out across the valley towards the city of Zahlé and behind that Mount Hermon to the east and Mount Lebanon to the west with the Beqaa plateau between them.

'I have to do this.' Mustafa said, turning away from his

friend.

'You're a doctor, not a killer. The world has enough murderers in it. Please let's go home.' Fouad walked over and put a hand on Mustafa's shoulder. 'This won't bring them back; it will just take you further away from them.'

Mustafa reached backwards and put his hand on the General's. 'I must do this, my friend, I must.' Mustafa was close to tears and his voice was breaking.

Both men stood silent for a moment, thinking, in front of them bright pink beds of silene colorata flowers had formed in the fields. Their deep thoughts were broken off from the laughter of two children approaching down from a rocky pass, where an old settlement wall once stood, but now only a few stones remained. The children went in between the rocks and stones and started to pick some of the bright flowers. One of them caught Mustafa's eye and waved at him with a flower in hand and then ran off again.

'Serapias vomeracea,' Fouad remarked.

'What's that?' Mustafa asked, slightly confused.

'It's an orchid. They were picking orchids, the children. It was named after Serapis, the god of fertility and the afterlife.'

'How do you know all this?' Mustafa asked smiling, genuinely impressed at Fouad's knowledge of orchids.

'My grandmother would take me flower picking when I was little. She showed me the flowers that had healing properties, the flowers that were poisonous and the flowers you could eat.'

Mustafa smiled again and looked at his wristwatch that his wife had brought him a year before she and their children were killed. She had brought him the wristwatch, not as a birthday gift, or anniversary present. No, it was because he was

106

a horrible timekeeper. On the back of the watch was inscribed "Hurry up XX". 'It's time.' Mustafa said, starting to walk slowly towards Fouad's car, a badly beaten-up box with four wheels and a dodgy handbrake, because a general's pay in the Lebanese army wasn't the greatest. Fouad said nothing, he just nodded in defeat and then looked out across the valley.

The General drove on slowly, while Mustafa looked out the window, knowing that there was no turning back now. The General had insisted on driving Mustafa to the Hezbollah training camp in the Beqaa Valley. He had taken Mustafa, the young man he loved like a son, the son he never had, into his home after he left the hospital. He watched on helplessly, as the love that once showed in Mustafa's heart dissolved. He only lived for revenge now. He had asked the General to use his influence and ask Colonel Walid if he could join his elite Hezbollah unit. Mustafa had heard that Colonel Walid was a fearsome man, who trained his men to be fearless and take no prisoners. Colonel Walid had even survived two Israeli assassination attempts, the last attempt taking his left eye and nearly his life. It was not without good reason he had tortured and killed a young captured IDF soldier in front of onlookers in 2006. Colonel Walid's hatred for Israel was the reason Mustafa wanted to join his unit, also known as "Walid's death squad". The car pulled to a stop, where a boy no older than ten years of age was sitting, waiting on a rock and smoking a cigarette. This was the goodbye, the boy would take Mustafa the rest of the way on foot to the training camp.

'Look after yourself,' Fouad said, and the two men embraced for the last time on the dusty road.

Mustafa picked up his rucksack and walked towards the boy who was relighting his cigarette. The boy walked ahead of

Mustafa, with his hands in his pockets. The old general watched as they crossed a wheat field, where a thin man with a stick was herding two thin goats. The old general got back into his car and saw the boy lead Mustafa up a slope between two tall cedar trees and then out of sight. The general reversed back up the dusty road in the Beqaa Valley. On the drive home he stopped to pick some wildflowers that he would later lay on his wife's grave. Two weeks later General Fouad Aoun died of a heart attack in his sleep.

Colonel Foziah Walid was sitting on a stool in a circle with five other men peeling potatoes into a large pot when one of them caught sight of the boy and Mustafa walking towards them through the forest. Walid glanced up once at the man walking with a boy, and then went back to concentrating on his potatoes. When Mustafa and the boy arrived at the camp, the boy who now held a stick in his hand pointed with it towards where the men were seated peeling potatoes. The boy then ran off down the hill towards where a group of boys were playing football. Mustafa stood still, sweating from the walk that had taken almost an hour. His leg was pounding with pain, but he hid the pain well. He was just about to go over to the men peeling potatoes when Walid stood up and gestured, with the knife and a potato in his hand, for Mustafa to come over. Mustafa approached the short man, who squinted even in the shade of the tall trees.

'I'm reporting for training,' Mustafa said, uneasy and feeling nervous and not really knowing what to say. The men who were seated around the potato pot, burst in to a fit of laughter. Walid did not smile; it was an action he had not yet mastered in his thirty-nine years on planet earth.

'You can start with pealing some potatoes,' Walid said,

passing Mustafa the potato and knife. Walid was unimpressed with the man he saw before him. He saw a tall, gawky man who was sweating and out of breath after a brisk walk through the forest. He had taken him on as a favour to General Aoun, a man he had only ever met once, years ago, but nevertheless respected. Mustafa took the potato and knife, dropped his rucksack and sat down with the other men and began to peel. Mustafa did not know if it was Walid who had just given him the potato and knife. He did not know what Walid looked like. Mustafa looked up at the stocky man, who was now standing on his own and smoking a cigarette. He didn't look much like a colonel. He wore a loose green wool jumper, army trousers and brown sandals. His once pale skin was now heavily sun bleached and it made him look a lot older than he actually was. Mustafa thought this man was too short to be Colonel Walid, even though he had no idea what the man himself looked like. All the stories Mustafa had heard had put an image of a giant of a man into Mustafa's mind. Okay he was of a stocky build and looked villainous, with his thick chevron moustache and stubbly beard and grey hair combed back, but this man was not him, maybe a second in command, but he was not Walid. Also, Walid was meant to be missing an eye, this guy had both his eyes. This guy resembled an angrier version of Joseph Stalin and that was a hard thing to do.

'That will do,' said one of the men who was peeling potatoes.

'We are done, colonel,' another man said, looking at the angrier version of Joseph Stalin.

Colonel Walid, the man Mustafa had mistaken for a regular soldier walked over, stared into the pot and nodded approvingly. 'Good, good, take it to the cook.' Walid then turned his stare to Mustafa, who quickly stood up. It was then that Mustafa noticed Walid's glass eye. 'Walk with me,' commanded Walid.

The two men walked down the hill towards where the boys were playing football. The children were using their shirts for goalposts and the ground was uneven in places. 'I understand you are a doctor; we need good doctors here,' Walid said, not taking his eye off the football match.

'I am,' he said, then paused. 'But.'

The Colonel turned to Mustafa. 'But? Please do go on.'

'I didn't come here to be a doctor. I came here because I want revenge. I must avenge my family,' Mustafa said spitting his words. Walid saw the anger in the man's eyes and knew he meant it.

'The Americans killed your family, didn't they?' Walid spoke softly, wanting the man to break. Walid enjoyed watching men breakdown, so he could build them up again. Mould them.

'The Israeli's.'

'Yes, but with American money.' Walid said, smiling for the first time and it was an awful smile, filled with blackened teeth and a lifetime of hate. Mustafa started to sob, with his head down; Walid's smile grew to something grotesque and some of the boys playing football stopped to stare. Walid saw before him that this man would be easy to shape. Shape into a weapon. He didn't need breaking; he was already broken.

'The Israeli's, the Americans, I want to get them all,' Mustafa declared, opening himself up.

'You will, you will,' Walid turned Mustafa away from the football match, put an arm around his shoulders and walked him back up the hill. 'You must keep this hatred inside and use it to avenge your family.'

The camp was well hidden from the air. Nature was their defence from the sky. Tall trees, high hills and caves gave them the perfect cover. Even though they took orders from the Lebanon government, they trained more in guerrilla warfare. The unit was fairly small and comprised of thirty-five men including Mustafa and five women. Two wooden barracks for the men and one for the women. The kitchen and mess hall were in one cave and a tactical station was in another. A tent was used as a makeshift hospital for the wounded and was currently empty, it had very little supplies of medicines and essential medical equipment. Walid pushed the women in the unit just as hard as the men. He took extra satisfaction, when fighting ISIS, with the women on his side. Whenever they captured Islamic State soldiers, Walid would get the women to execute them. Knowing that being killed by a woman would rob them of their paradise. Soldier's widows and their children were also allowed to stay at the camp, and live in tents and small huts, and work the land. They also helped with the cooking, laundry, and trained as nurses and teachers for the children. It was a small community. Walid's unit was battle hardened, they had been fighting ISIS with the Syrian army and with the help of the Americans for the last three years. When Mustafa turned up, they were just getting ready to go east towards the Qalamoun mountains and link up with the Lebanon Army under the control of Commander Ali Khalil Alian. Mustafa only had three days of tough training before heading off with the unit to the Qalamoun mountains. Colonel Walid would have normally preferred to give a new recruit more training than just three days. But in a way his hands were tied, he didn't have a doctor in the unit and the only two other men with medical experience were not trusted by the rest of the men in the unit, because they had let so many die. Also, Walid knew that the best training a raw recruit could get was often war itself, that's where you found out the men who had character and men who had none.

# 12

Monday May 4th 2015
Qalamoun Mountains, Lebanon 09:00

High up in the cloudless spring sky, that looked down on the trenches on the Lebanon side of the Qalamoun mountains, which had been dug the previous winter, thousands of white storks were migrating north from Africa. The Lebanon army was ready for a defensive and every soldier was expecting an ISIS/Al-Nusra Front offensive any day. Mustafa sensed it too, it was in the air, like that sweet smell just before a summer storm. If Colonel Walid had his way, there would be no defensive. It was his view that the defensive was totally unnecessary and showed weakness, when he told the top brass exactly how he felt, they decided to leave him out in the cold, with regards to future military planning. On the morning of the 4th May Colonel Walid was smoking a cigarette laced with hashish, watching his men and women check and recheck their M16 rifles. Most of them had been to the Qalamoun mountains before with Colonel Walid and knew what to expect. Whilst soldiers in other units were spread out, some eating, some sleeping, some reading Walid always had his unit ready, ready for anything, at the drop of a hat. Everyone in the unit knew he smoked hash, they could smell it on him, but no one begrudged him. He told himself he was not an addict, but the truth is, he was. Deep down he knew it too, and this he also blamed on the Israeli's. It was after their last attempt on his life, that took his eye. Walid was told that the bullet was resting on the optic nerve and its removal could cause further bleeding and even death. The pain was very real and brought on excruciating headaches; when normal pain killers wouldn't work, a doctor suggested hashish.

The picturesque morning was interrupted by the sound of self-propelled howitzer firing from the Syrian army, this was as the Al-Nusra Front and ISIS were over-running several positions near the Assal al-Ward boarder. Colonel Walid's unit were ordered to make their way to the village of Tfail and secure it. Tfail is the highest village in Lebanon, with an elevation of 1660 meters.

Grey and black smoke had now penetrated the clear blue skies that stretched along the Lebanon-Syria boarder. Howitzer fire sounded closer and more desperate and gun fire could be heard in all directions. When Mustafa got to Tfail, Colonel Foziah Walid ordered half his unit to enter the village from the west, whilst he led the other half, that included Mustafa, around to the east. A point man was sent ahead through a narrow pass that led around and down to a clearing, where there was a road that was easily accessible for a tank to pass along. The aim of the game was for the point man to be seen and start firing at the enemy and draw them up the pass towards the unit who would be waiting above on the ledges. It was a gamble splitting up his unit, but colonel Walid had always been lucky in war. As Mustafa sat next to him on the ledge overlooking the pass, he saw the anticipation and excitement of the fight on the colonel's face, for him this was living. Mustafa suspected that if peace was called tomorrow, and the war would end, Walid would simply die.

'Where is he?' Walid was looking down the pass that was laden with natural obstacles of rocks, boulders and small trees, not impossible for a tank to move up, but very difficult and narrow to accommodate a unit with it. A moment later M16 fire was heard, followed by rapid AK-47 fire. A minute later a blast roared through the pass, echoing at the same time, smoke flumes appeared at the mouth of the pass, then more AK-47 fire.

'It's a tank,' one worried looking solider said, squatting next to Mustafa, both hands shaking. Mustafa saw that the soldier was very young.

'It's me, don't shoot.' A voice cried out and a figure appeared through the smoke, it was the point man limping, gunless, holding his left leg at the thigh.

'They've taken the bait,' one soldier shouted out across from the opposite ledge.

'Be quiet,' Walid snapped.

'I'll go and get him,' Mustafa said looking down on the point man, as he staggered up the pass and collapsed behind a thick shrub.

'No stay, he will be fine,' then after a moment's pause, 'If he is lucky.' Walid said this without concern, giving Mustafa a quick wry smile and Mustafa felt this was Walid attempting humour. Walid looked down along the ledge at the brave men and women behind him. 'No one fire until they are directly below us.'

Two Al-Nusra Front fighters came through the smoke wearing black bandanas and holding AK-47's. One of the men walked up the pass a little further, he was the bait for the enemy. The Al-Nusra Front fighter then stopped and stood about three feet away from the injured point man who was hiding behind the shrub. The other Al-Nusra Front fighter then went back through the smoke, seconds later the ledge started to shake, as a tank turret poked through the smoke. Voices came through the smoke and then the tank started to move slowly up the pass. Al-Nusra Front fighters followed either side of the tank and behind it.

'Not yet,' Walid said softly.

Mustafa looked across the pass towards the other ledge where two soldiers were standing, holding RPG-7's, ready to move forward and fire. A Toyota pickup followed behind the tank with a mounted 50 calibre machine gun on the back. A black Al-Nusra Front flag, with white Arabic writing, was attached to the front of the Toyota and it waved in the breeze. Five more fighters followed behind the dusty red Toyota.

'They're too close to each other,' one soldier announced, sounding excited.

Colonel Walid waved across to the other side and the two soldiers with the RPG-7's stepped forward to the edge of the ledge and fired down on the tank. At the same time Colonel Walid cried out, 'Now, give them hell.'

A blinding yellow flash and a roar of explosion was followed by terrible screams from the Al-Nusra Front fighters, the screams rose up as if they were coming up through the pits of hell. M16 fire rained down from all angles, smoked covered the pass and then two more RPG-7's hit the Toyota.

'It's a turkey shoot,' the soldier next to Mustafa cried out, and he did not look worried any more. A dreadful satisfaction had replaced his worries.

Soldiers were looking down, shooting at anything that moved in the smoke.

'Die, you sons of whores,' one soldier screamed out, firing his M16.

'No paradise for you. This is a woman who kills you,' one female soldier shouted, firing down. Laughter from the ledges met the screams from fighters below, dying in the dirt.

'Cease firing, cease firing,' Colonel Walid called out. 'Mustafa, go check on Muhib.'

'Yes, sir.' Mustafa turned and ran down the pass, without a moment's hesitation. Muhib was the name of the brave point man, who had acted as the bait. Mustafa found Muhib, pale and passed out, behind the shrubs. He held clenched in his right hand a knife, ready to fight to the end. His left hand was soaked in blood, still holding on to his bloody thigh, a pool of blood had formed around his legs and the brave man appeared to have wet himself. Mustafa knelt down and checked his vitals; he found a faint pulse. The other soldiers in the unit were coming down the pass now. The pass that was clear and alive only a few minutes before, was now blanketed in thick diesel smoke, hiding the cries of the wounded. One soldier ran past Mustafa and disappeared into the smoke. Mustafa watched as another soldier came down and walked past him. Mustafa called for the soldier to help him with Muhib, but the soldier ignored him. The smoke cleared a little and he saw the soldier standing over a heavily wounded Al-Nusra Front fighter, whose limbs were cramping up. He was looking up towards the sky and crying for his mother. 'Mother, mother,' blood was oozing out the corners of his mouth as he cried out. The soldier thrust the end of his M16 rifle into the wounded Al-Nusra Front fighter's mouth and stirred it around forcibly, as if it was a spoon in a cup of coffee. Mustafa cringed as steel smashed against fragile teeth, breaking them.

'Arghh,' the fighter screamed out terrified, paralysed, blood foaming from the mouth, eyes bulging out cartoon like. He was hellishly aware of what was happening to him.

'Time to die.' Bang.

Mustafa lifted Muhib's wounded leg on to a rock, so it was elevated, then cut along his trouser leg with scissors that he produced from his small medical pack. He found the entry wound just above the knee, put his forefinger deep into the wound and found that the bullet had fractured the femur, but thankfully not severed the femoral artery, which it was now resting on.

'Muhib, Muhib,' one of the female soldiers cried out, running over. 'Will he live?' she asked despairingly, holding his face. 'Wake up, I command you, wake up,' she sobbed. They were lovers, they tried to keep it a secret, but eventually like all secrets everyone found out. Colonel Walid knew about them too but decided to let it be.

Mustafa told the girl, and she really was just a girl probably no older than twenty, to put pressure on the wound, while he tied a tourniquet above the hole. The thigh had swelled fast, too fast for Mustafa's liking, also it had turned blue, and that was never a good sign. He knew from his time in ER, that a wound this bad was life threatening, and that was in a hospital, they were in the highest village in Lebanon and in the middle of a war zone.

'Why don't you take the bullet out?' she begged, stroking Muhib's face. Mustafa saw she had the greenest eyes of any woman he had ever seen.

'I can't, that bullet might be the only thing keeping him from dying.' Mustafa didn't know if the look she gave him was anger or shock, maybe both.

'Please keep him alive.'

Colonel Walid came over and looked down on the three of them. 'Is he dead?' He asked the question in the same manner a child asks its mother what's for dinner. The girl looked straight ahead dumbfounded.

'No. But he will die soon if we don't get him to a hospital.'

Walid nodded, weighing it up in his mind. 'Okay, I'll call in the cavalry.' And then casually walked away.

Muhib started to come around, shaking his head from side to side, moaning. He looked like a vampire had sucked the life out of his body. By some miracle he was still alive.

'Muhib, Muhib.' The girl grabbed his face, showering him with kisses.

Mustafa squirted a mild solution into the wound to clean it, then dressed it with a bandage.

'My sweet, it's so painful, I'm so, so cold,' Muhib murmured, looking into the girl's deep green eyes.

'You fight it, you'll be in the hospital soon my love.'

'I love you,' Muhib whispered.

'And I you.'

Mustafa produced a morphine tartrate from his medical kit. Muhib and his lover watched on as Mustafa injected the solution into his thigh. 'This will help with the pain.'

'Morphine?' the girl asked. Mustafa nodded, then stood up, rubbed his knees and looked down the pass at the carnage. The screams from the wounded Al-Nusra Front fighters had stopped now. The soldiers were piling up the dead in what looked like a small mound, they had stripped them bare and left them for the flies. It was a massacre. A total of forty-five Al-Nusra Front fighters were killed in the ambush. More than half of them were murdered after the initial ambush, whilst injured and dying.

Mustafa found Colonel Walid at the mouth of the pass, sitting on the floor on his own, with his back turned away from what had just occurred. He was smoking one of his hash cigarettes and staring out at the openness, like a surfer who sits on the beach and watches the waves in the evening. He had not a care in the world.

'How long until the helicopter arrives?' Mustafa asked, kneeling down opposite the Colonel.

'They couldn't give an exact time,' Colonel Walid said, blowing a cloud of smoke into the air. 'It's been a busy morning.'

'He'll die if it doesn't come soon,' Mustafa stressed.

'That's war.'

'Don't you care?' Mustafa snapped.

Calmly Walid spoke. 'Fifty-nine.'

'Fifty-nine, what?'

'If Muhib dies, he will be the fifty ninth soul to die under my command,' and then raising his voice a little louder, with more emotion in it. 'And I see them all in my dreams at night. Every last one of them.'

Mustafa said nothing.

They walked back up the pass together and stopped where the bodies of the dead had been piled up on top of each other. Two of the dead Al-Nusra Front fighters had been decapitated. The heads had been put on wooden stakes that had been hammered into the ground. 'They call me a butcher, but if I don't train my soldiers to be ruthless in battle, it might be their heads on those stakes. If I had more soldiers like these, our troubles here would be over very quickly.'

No helicopter came and Muhib died that evening in the

arms of his lover, in a tent in the village of Tfail. The next morning Muhib was buried, and the unit moved out. Over the next couple of days Hezbollah and the Syrian Army seized control of a number of important hilltops overlooking Assal Al-Ward, killing many rebels.

On May 13th the strategic hilltop of Tallat Mussa was captured. Colonel Walid's unit led the assault, under the cover of darkness, climbing the slopes in sub-zero conditions and a hailstorm, that seemed to grow in ferocity with every advance. Rebel snipers picked off soldiers who struggled to find adequate cover in the darkness. Mortar fire rained down on them, but still they advanced, led by Colonel Walid from the front. Walid was a firm believer in leading from the front. A soldier next to Mustafa was shot in the belly, and he died a most painful death. Near the top they linked up with the Syrian Army and proceeded to clean up the remaining pockets of rebels. Four soldiers in the unit were killed taking Tallat Mussa.

By the end of June, Hezbollah and the Syrian Army had near total control of the Qalamoun mountains. The media soaked it up and it was just what the army needed after so many defeats. ISIS had been defeated in battle and lost some ground, and just at the right time, when the Lebanese and Syrian governments were coming under increasing pressure to produce a victory.

# 13

Two red dusty pickup trucks slowly bounce along the uneven terrain between the crop fields carrying bundles of cannabis. At the end of the field the pickups pass a Hezbollah soldier sitting under a tree in a deck chair. The soldier is wearing sunglasses, with a scarf around his face to protect him from the crop. He has an assault rifle resting on his lap and he nods at the drivers as they drive up the cemented incline, that leads to a garage. They stop at the garage, and four women in headscarves come out from inside the garage. The drivers who are wearing scarfs, baseball caps, jeans and sunglasses help the women carry the bundles of cannabis, into the garage. The bundles, wrapped in white tarp are stacked between two concrete pillars in the shade. Once the pickups have been emptied, the drivers leave to collect more bundles. At the back of the garage is the cannabis factory. Two of the women pass the cannabis through a mechanical separator that works non-stop and sounds like a steam train approaching. A thick green haze clouds the air, as the sticky green, spiky leafed plant breaks up and falls to the floor. A girl no older than thirteen continually shovels the remains into a massive pile, ready for another girl to collect in a bucket. The girl with the bucket is named Ranim, she is fourteen years old and totally alone in the world. Unlike the other Syrian women, she works with, Ranim will not be going back to neighbouring Syria after the harvest. All the women Ranim works with hate the prospect of heading home, back to Raqqa, the de facto capital of ISIL, but they have families there. They know all too well what will happen to them if Islamic State finds out they had been working with cannabis. Ranim knows too, her cousin had both her thumbs cut off by Islamic State. Soon after that, she killed herself, jumping in front of a truck. One morning Ranim awoke to find that her mother had passed in the night, presumably from heart disease. She had complained of chest pains in the night and died before first light. As Ranim looked at the lifeless body of her mother, whom she loved, a fantastic weight released itself from her soul. No longer did she have a reason to stay in Raqqa and live, in fear, and with no other relatives alive, Ranim decided to leave for Lebanon. Leaving the brutality and starting a new life.

Ranim carries the broken-down cannabis over to the other side of the factory, passing through a roll of plastic curtain strips that hang down from the ceiling and smell of cannabis. Ranim leaves the bucket with two old women who are sitting on stools and shifting the remains through a rectangular mesh sieve screen. Ranim takes their empty bucket and starts again. The old women rub the cannabis gently through the sieve with their hands, to extract the powdery kief, which contains the trichomes (THC) from the other contaminates. The powdery kief is then collected and taken to another part of the factory, where another woman presses the kief between two hot plates at a temperature of about three hundred degrees fahrenheit. This pressing process transforms the kief into a solid dark slab of hash about the size of a brick. The hash is then left to be cooled, then wrapped and stored in a dark room. Later the hashish will be smuggled all around the Middle East and Europe, helping to fund Hezbollah and at the same time getting university kids in London studying Middle Eastern Conflict Resolution in Divided Societies stoned.

Just north of the factory overlooking the seventy hectares of cannabis, Samir Ephrem sits with his back against the white stone wall of his drug lord son's villa. The old man is a traditionalist, he moves the prayer beads slowly through his hand with worry. He worries what God will make of it all. The old man remembers the wheat fields that once grew and how beautiful it was to watch the crop swirl in the wind. He remembers carrying his son high upon his shoulders so he could look far out over the hectares that once flourished and they did once flourish. There were some good years and some bad, but in the end the bad years were too many. Wheat prices fell year on year with competition and the government struggled to find payment for the harvests. It was his son George who saw the future, a solution to their problems. The old man didn't want it, the illegal crop. Drugs was dirty business, unfortunately the way the economy was and with his age, he had little choice. George may have been a poor farmer, but he was an excellent businessman. With cannabis being cheaper to cultivate and easier to look after than wheat, their first harvest proved to be very profitable. A year later in 2012 government special forces burnt and destroyed nearly all the cannabis crops in the Beqaa Valley. After that the farmers started to arm themselves. When Hezbollah offered their protection for a percentage, and with government forces now preoccupied with fighting ISIS, farmers like George welcomed them with open arms. The returns were enormous, even with giving Hezbollah a cut of the money, George was making close to two million dollars a harvest.

The old man turned his head and watched in disappointment as the vehicle raced up the dirt track that led to the villa. He saw the rays of sunlight hit the shiny monster, as it past the ancient olive trees that had stood for hundreds of years, and that lined the dirt track on either side. The vehicle halted to a dramatic stop, throwing dust into the air and scaring off the birds. George stepped out of his brand-new silver bulletproof Chevy Tahoe with two other men. The old man thought his son looked like a gangster. He was dressed from head to toe in black, all Armani, all made to measure. Even his hair was black, combed back with too much gel. His hair was not naturally black, he dyed it black. His trophy wife who was probably on another one of her shopping trips to Paris, or Milan had told him that black hair was a sign of a powerful man. The old man stood up using his cane that his father once used and past down to him on his deathbed. He was hoping one day he would pass it to George, but he knew now looking at his son there was slim chance of that. The old man stood in his country clothing, a red and white keffiyeh on his head, held in place by a black aqel rope made from goat's hairs. A faded blue shirt unbuttoned at the top showed his tanned chest, and baggy beige trousers and sandals that looked like they were from the time of Christ.

'I would like to introduce to you my papa, does he, or does he not look like Yasser Arafat?' George asked, walking in front of his two guests. He smiled at his father, who didn't return the smile. Yet still there was a striking resemblance to the former PLO leader.

'You smell funny,' Samir Ephrem told his son as they embraced.

'It's aftershave, don't you like it papa?' The old man waved away the question with his hand.

'I would like to introduce you to the famous Colonel Foziah Walid and his right-hand man Mustafa.'

The old man nodded at the men. 'Welcome.'

'They would like to meet Samuel.'

Ignoring this, the old man who was studying his son, who he had not seen for over a week, said. 'You look different, uglier somehow.'

George started to feel embarrassed and began to sweat. 'You're just getting older, papa.' George answered laughing nervously. In fact, George was different, his wife, who was half silicone herself now, had talked George into getting a facelift making his cheekbones look more prominent.

'I'm going for a walk.' The old man said, leaving the three men.

George, Walid and Mustafa sat down at a table under the shade of a tree, with a bottle of arak, some fresh warm hummus and some pita bread.

'Pay little attention to my papa,' George said, breaking pita bread up in his hands, whilst watching the old man walk slowly over towards the cannabis factory. 'He still thinks we should be growing wheat and begging for money, living every day in fear,' George threw his hands in the air. 'Well not me.' He declared in a sudden burst of emotion, poking his forefinger to his chest.

'They project all their fears and desires on to us.' Walid said, pouring the arak into three colourful mosaic goblets.

'So, Samuel?' Mustafa jumped in, wanting to know more

about the man they had heard so much about from George. Over the past few years George and Walid had become quite close. Not only did Walid's special forces unit protect George's cannabis crops from being destroyed by government forces, but they also helped smuggle the hash out the country. Three weeks back, George drove into Walid's camp, having done more cocaine than a runway model and was tanked up with alcohol, smelling like a brewery. This wasn't his first drunken visit to the camp and as usual he was talking about anything and everything. Walid found George to be a very entertaining drunk and liked listened to his extravagant stories until he passed out, never really taking anything he said, as truth. Only this time he mentioned a young man named Samuel.

'Samuel was a recruiter for ISIS but became disillusioned with their ideology and barbaric nature. He escaped from them, crossing the border under the cover of darkness. One of the girls' — he paused for a second thinking about the young girl and smiled — 'Ranim, a real beauty, found him hiding in a cotton patch behind her tent, near death, with hyperthermia and starving. Ranim came to me and I got a doctor for him, because I'm a good person,' he said, looking around for approval.

'Yes, you are,' Walid said, lying.

'Good man,' Mustafa said nodding, feeding George's ego.

'Ranim nursed him back to health. When Samuel recovered, he confided in me at first sight, breaking down and confessing to me everything, as if I was a priest,' George recounted smugly, leaning back in his chair.

'You're a good man,' Walid said.

'I felt pity on the young man, he had the weight of a thousand corpses resting on his soul. Another man, my neighbour, anyone, would have turned him in, or killed him, but not me, not George, I gave him a new life working for me.'

It turned out to be a clever and very lucrative move. Samuel was a genius and in return for his new life Samuel set up a computerised irrigation system, that was easy to manage and cost efficient. He also set up a network for accounts and bookkeeping, where it was easy to record financial transactions and analyse the cost of operations, taking them from the Stone Age to the present.

'I can't wait to meet him,' Mustafa said.

'I'll take you to him.'

Since their return from the Qalamoun mountains in June, Walid and Mustafa had been secretly planning an attack on Israel and America. So secret Hezbollah didn't even know of it, and they certainly wouldn't have approved of it. Walid and Mustafa had the financial resources through the smuggling of drugs and weapons. They had the backing of one, or two, government politicians who were sympathetic to their cause, so passports and visas would be easy to obtain. Walid also put Mustafa through extensive mental and physical training, where he was denied sleep and food for days at a time. He was given names and dates to remember then interrogated and tortured. He had lessons in the history of America and weapons training, where he was taught that any household object could be made into a weapon. It was real tradecraft stuff, escape and evasion skills, how to pick locks, jack a car, surveillance techniques, disguises, make up lessons and most importantly how to make bombs, the big kind. They also had targets, a list of several Israeli operatives from all over the globe. It cost a huge sum of money getting the targets. Mustafa's final destination would be America, but he would need somebody to help him once he got there, ideally an American, who was born in the country, or who had lived there for the majority of his life. Someone respected in the community, so that Mustafa's arrival would not draw on too much attention. The problem was they had no one. So, when they heard of Samuel the former recruiter for Islamic State, they had to meet him.

It was a two-mile drive away from the farm and on the main road that led all the way to Beirut, the Mediterranean and beyond. A line of off-white tents stretched along the roadside, as far as the eye could see. The misplaced, forgotten and lost. Samuel and Ranim were among them, the lost. Syrian refugees escaping the war, the war they never asked for. When George pulled up in his bulletproof spaceship he couldn't have looked more out of place. A patterned rug was hung on a line between two trees and an old woman was ferociously beating the dirt from it with a thick piece of wood. An old man was sat on an upside-down bucket, looking into oblivion, whilst holding a cannabis bud to his nose. Innocent children played tag, shoeless and half naked, laughing without a care in the world, too young to notice their plight. Another woman with her shirt sleeves pulled up to the elbows swept the dust from the entrance of her tent.

Samuel was watching television with two of his neighbour's children, when George called him from outside the tent. His baseball cap and scarf were hung over the chair outside and a pair of old Adidas trainers, that were worn to the soles and that hurt his feet when he stepped on uneven ground, were outside the entrance to his tent. Samuel jumped up and walked over to the door, whilst the children carried on watching cartoons with fascination.

'Mr George,' Samuel said, popping his head around the

corner. Samuel's smile soon left his face when he saw the two men with George. For a moment he thought George had sold him down the river.

'Don't worry, they are friends. May we come in?'

Samuel nodded, knowing he really didn't have much of a choice. 'Certainly, Mr George.'

'You're not too tired, are you?' George asked and then turning to Walid and Mustafa. 'Samuel gets up very early and assigns the jobs and checks the irrigation system.'

Samuel managed half a smile. 'No. I don't sleep much these days.' This was the truth. The nightmares came like clockwork, nightly and debilitating. Regularly waking up soaking with sweat, even on a cold night. He remembers the towns they took. Still sees the faces of the homosexuals with their hands and feet bound together. The look in their eyes just before being flung off the tallest building in town. He hears the tank creeping along slowly. Sees vividly the prisoner, a young man full of despair, lying down before the tank and waiting for it to crush his head. The cries are what wake him up. Samuel always wakes with the screams from the new-born baby. The baby is naked. His parents have just been dowsed in gasoline and set on fire. Samuel looks into the screaming eyes and knows he is godless.

'Would you like some tea?' Samuel asked his guests, inviting them to sit down on three cushions on the floor.

'Yes please.' Mustafa answered, George and Walid nodded to indicate they did not want any.

Samuel poured a cup of tea and handed it to Mustafa. 'What can I do for you gentlemen?'

Walid walked over towards the television, smiled at the children and then turned the volume down.

'These men would like to ask for your help,' George said.

'I'll try,' Samuel said nervously, uncertain of the men and uneasy about their arrival.

Walid was sat like a child with his legs crossed, looking up at Samuel who was standing. 'We understand you are a very talented individual.'

'Am I?' Samuel blushed, thinking for a minute that this might be about his irrigation system that he had set up.

'You are,' Mustafa said, taking a sip of tea from his cup.

'We need you to help us recruit an American. Like you once did for ISIS,' Walid said passively.

Samuel gasped in shock. The colour left his face and he looked like he might be sick. Walid stood up and patted the children on the head, turned the television off and gave them a coin each. The children smiled when they saw the shiny coin and then ran out of the tent. Samuel started to pace around the room, then his legs started to shake. He fell to his knees crying and grabbing at his genitals. Mustafa walked over, knelt down and put an arm around his shoulders. George left the tent, feeling uncomfortable. He was surprised by Samuel's reaction. He lit a cigarette, wishing he had never brought the men to Samuel's door.

Back in the tent, Samuel was sobbing. 'I don't do this any more. Please. I am a good person.'

'We know. But if you help us this one time, I personally promise you that you will never be made to answer for the horrific crimes that you had a hand in.' Walid spoke calmly, with Mustafa holding the young man up.

Mustafa turned to see a beautiful girl standing by the entrance. It was Ranim. Just for a moment he thought it was his eldest daughter all grown up.

'Ranim,' Samuel pleaded holding out his hands to her, hoping she could save him. Since having nursed him back to health, Ranim and Samuel had found comfort in each other's loneliness. Even though her tent was just down the road, she more or less lived in Samuel's. She loved him and he her.

'Are you a friend of Samuel?' Walid asked the girl standing before him. She had heard enough of the conversation to realise what was happening. She had walked past George outside, standing shell shocked by his car and regretting his drunken mouth.

She looked down at Samuel without expression. Now was not the time to show emotion. 'And what can you do for us?' she asked, looking into Walid's cold eye.

Walid gave a sly smile. A deal with the devil was on the cards. 'What do you desire?'

Samuel looked confused, looking at both parties.

'Lebanese passports.'

Walid considered it in his mind, looking at Mustafa who was wiping the tears and snot away from Samuel's face with a tissue and then back to the girl. Walid liked her, she was to the point and strong. 'Maybe, maybe.'

'He will do what you ask of him and in return, we get passports and $10,000 and then we never want to see you again.' Ranim held all the aces, and she certainly wasn't going to fold with this hand. They needed Samuel's help, his knowledge of manipulation, and she was in command of Samuel. Ranim didn't care of the consequences of their actions. She didn't care about the United States of America. Why should she, she thought, they never helped her when ISIS invaded her homeland. She was in total control now. This was their chance for a new life. A fresh start.

'Deal,' Walid agreed. $10,000 was nothing to him and he had the connections to get the passports. It was a small price to pay, and in return they would get their cell in American.

Samuel reluctantly did what they asked of him. He was the middle-man between them and Cadoc Elneny, who would eventually blow himself up in his home taking with him his mother, twelve FBI agents and an unborn baby, with a bomb that Mustafa Khoury had helped him make. But Cadoc wasn't the only person Samuel recruited. A wealthy American couple also fell into his web. For this Walid paid Ranim and Samuel double what they had asked. The young couple were overjoyed when they received their new passports. Their new lives. They left the Beqaa Valley on a bus bound for Beirut, hand in hand, with wonder for what the future might hold. The young woman formerly known as Ranim cried when she saw the Mediterranean Sea for the first time. Walid had considered disposing of them. He didn't want any loose ends, but Mustafa made him promise to leave the young couple alone.

# 14

Friday June 2nd 2017

Broward Health North Medical Centre, Pompano Beach, Florida 22:00

Malia Kimani's eyes opened. Startled, temporarily forgetting where she lay. The phone next to the bed was ringing. Not her bed, not her phone.

What? Where? Then at once it all came back. Hilton, I'm in the Hilton.

She picked up the phone. 'Okay, I'll be right down.'

It was dark outside. How long have I been out, she wondered?

A young man was waiting for her in the lobby. 'I'm Agent Scott, I'm to take you to the Broward Health North Medical Centre.'

'Is there a problem?' Malia asked.

The young FBI Agent hesitated for a moment. 'There's been an incident.'

'An incident?'

'Yes.'

'What's the incident?'

'Agent Anderson will brief you at the hospital, that's really all I can say right now.'

Agent Scott tried several times to make conversation with

Malia on the drive to the hospital, but Malia was not interested in small talk. She just looked out at the night, with the window down, letting the breeze hit her hair.

When they arrived at the hospital Malia thanked Agent Scott and got out. She walked along the line of drop off points amidst an array of ambulances, taxis and police cars. At the entrance a grief-stricken, black women, was being held by her two sons, who were also crying. A man clearly in distress was on the phone telling someone on the other end that it was happening and that they should get here now. A bewildered female paramedic in bloody overalls strolled across to the circular intersection and sat under a palm tree and lit a cigarette.

Malia walked in from the humid night into a claustrophobic bustling nightmare. The queue at the reception desk was long. Hundreds of conversations were taking place. It was a cauldron of noise, and it was packed. Relatives paced up and down, people were sleeping on the floor. A maintenance man in blue overalls was on a ladder, trying to figure out why the air conditioning was out. His young apprentice stood at the foot of the ladder looking uninterested and sweating, everyone was sweating. Fans were scattered all about the place, but they did little to help. A large black woman got up from her chair with great effort and walked over and stood next to one of the fans, blocking its air flow and an argument broke out. Everyone was agitated. When Malia finally got to the reception desk, she was met with a tired looking girl who seemed more concerned with keeping herself cool, with her mini handheld fan, than looking up on the system to see where Malia had to go.

'I was told Agent Sally Anderson of the FBI would be

meeting me here, but I can't see her.'

'That is most unfortunate,' the receptionist said, giving Malia a smug grin.

'If you could just point me in the right direction?' Malia asked politely.

'Are you, yourself with the FBI?' The receptionists asked, still holding that smug, shit eating grin and suddenly Malia realised that this blonde looking Barbie doll with the fake tits was being deliberately awkward.

'No, I'm working with them,' Malia said biting her lip. 'I thought you might be able to help me out?'

'I didn't think you were with the FBI.' The receptionist said and turned to her colleague, a long faced pasty girl who had on more eye makeup than a prostitute with a heavy-handed, short-tempered pimp and they both raised their eyebrows.

'I never said I was.'

'Have you any identification with you?' She had closed her eyes now and was leaning back into her chair, with one hand on the desk and the other moving the mini handheld fan across her face.

Malia felt and overwhelming urge to jump over the desk and jam the fan in the Barbie dolls mouth and down her racist throat. 'I have not,' Malia said, sounding fed up.

'Well.'

'Well, what?' Malia interrupted.

Barbie doll opened her eyes and slammed the mini handheld fan back down on the desk. 'I will not be spoken to in such a tone by a...'

'By a nigger?'

Barbie doll blushed with embarrassment. 'I suggest you

lower your tone. With, without prop—, proper identification.' She was flustered now. She had just been called out.

Malia leant in on the desk and Barbie doll drew her head back in fright. 'Just tell me where to go bitch?'

Barbie doll gasped in horror.

'We. Can. Not. Help. You. Without. Proper. Identification.' Her long faced pasty colleague jumped in, coming to her rescue, punctuating each word and looking Malia up and down resentfully. 'Now take a seat or leave, there are people here who need real help.'

Barbie doll had regained some composure now. She smiled at her colleague then brought the fan back to her face again. 'You go girl.'

'I'm about one more bitchy ass comment away from jumping over there and fucking you two up.'

'Security!' The long-faced pasty one screamed.

'You can't talk to us like that,' Barbie doll cried.

'Security!'

'Better call a medic as well, cause when I'm finished with you, you'll need one.'

'Malia?' A voice from behind.

Malia turned to see Agent Anderson standing behind her smiling, with her hands on her hips. 'You having fun?'

'Security!'

'It's okay, this ones with me.' Sally said, producing her FBI badge.

'You know this crazy woman?' long faced pasty asked.

'I sure do.'

They walked along overcrowded corridors, a maze of patients, young and old laying on trolleys, waiting for available beds. Doctors debated over charts and X-rays, whilst nurses in sneakers were running the nightly gauntlet between departments. An elderly woman was staring up at the flickering fluorescent lights on the ceiling. Tears were rolling down her aged cheeks and urine was running down one of the legs of her trolley and a small puddle was forming on the floor. They passed a room where a priest was reading the last rites to a bald man who was surrounded by loved ones. In another room a girl of about Malia's age was receiving a round of applause from family members and hospital workers as she hobbled around on crutches. They saw an old man wearing only disposable underpants and one slipper in a wheelchair being chased by two nurses, who were screaming for him to stop.

Sally and Malia got into an elevator with a worried looking obese woman who was holding a drip trolley that was attached to her arm and a nurse who was leaning against the wall with her eyes closing.

'You look like you could do with a coffee,' Sally said, smiling at the nurse.

'With some whiskey in it for a kick,' the nurse added, opening her eyes. She had a southern accent and was very pretty.

The elevator opened and the nurse and the obese woman with the drip trolley got out.

'Good luck,' Sally said.

The nurse turned and looked at her watch. 'Only five more hours.'

The elevator closed. 'Are Ron and Netzer all right?'

'Ron took a knock, but other than that he's fine.'

'What the hell happened out there today?'

'We identified the target, as a one Dr David Nissan, a

Lebanese national. We traced him to the home of a Mr Cadoc Elneny and his mother, both American citizens,' Sally paused and ran her hand across her tired face. 'We sent in two Agents posing as Jehovah Witnesses, with two five-man SWAT teams backing them up, then out of the blue the house blew up killing everyone.'

'When will we know if our man was inside?'

The elevator opened and they got out. 'We have forensics combing the crime scene as we speak, but to be brutally honest it's a bloody cluster fuck.'

'We need to know soon, if he's still alive, it's only a matter of time until he strikes again.'

'My colleague's body parts are scattered all over Pompano and are being marked with little blue flags. We don't know which torso belongs to which head. We're talking a whole block,' Sally snapped back angrily.

Malia lowered her head for a second and then raised it again. 'I'm sorry, I truly am, I'm only blunt and to the point because time is of the essence. If he wasn't in the house, he's planning his next attack. The explosion may have brought him some time, but he won't hang around long. We have to assume he is alive. We have to assume the worst,' Malia put a hand gently on Sally's arm. 'I know I can be a bit of a bitch sometimes.'

Sally laughed and smiled. 'It's me as well, I'm tired as hell.'

Malia thought the day was starting to show on Agent Anderson's face. Malia, on the other hand, was fresh faced and well rested. She felt like a lioness ready to chase down her prey.

Ron Yaffe was sitting up in bed with his left arm in a sling and a bandage wrapped around his head. Netzer was sitting on a chair with his feet up on Ron's bed, eating the meal a nurse had just brought Ron. Both Sally and Malia gave a grimace as they watched Netzer eat.

'We forgot all about you,' Ron said, looking up at Malia from his hospital bed.

'And look how you're paying for it now,' Malia returned.

'And just how exactly would you have stopped a mad man from blowing himself up?' Netzer asked, lifting his head up from the tray of meatloaf and spitting his words and food across at Malia.

'You eat like a starved pig,' Malia remarked, looking down pitifully at him.

'You know what, I'm almost finished, you can run and get me some more of this lovely meatloaf if you like, you people are good at that. Running.' Netzer said.

'You piece of shit,' Malia said, moving forward and front kicked him in the side off the chair. Netzer gave a moan as he fell to the floor with the meatloaf tray landing upside down on his lap. Sally Anderson pulled her back and Netzer stood up quickly, still chewing and smirking.

'Right, that's it, break it up,' Ron shouted from his hospital bed. 'For fuck's sake, break it up.'

At that moment Tim Baines walked in. 'What's going on here? Are you fighting? This is a hospital; you can't fight in here.' Sally turned to her boss, still holding Malia. She thought that he looked like he had aged another ten years since the morning at the airport.

'Everyone take it easy, it's been a long day,' Ron said trying to calm the situation. 'Malia, Netzer didn't mean that, did you?' Ron looked at his old friend. 'Did you Netzer?'

'No,' Netzer said, turning towards the window and wiping the meatloaf from his jeans. And he didn't mean it, he just hated to lose and today they lost, in fact they got their ass kicked.

'Why did you go in all gun-ho?' Malia asked, speaking to Ron calmly.

'He didn't want to. It was my call. This one is solely on me,' Tim Baines said, holding his jacket down in between his hands.

'Not true, sir.' Sally said.

Tim Baines nodded his head. 'Like it or not, my decision cost the lives of twelve good people.'

'Nonsense,' Netzer said, waving a hand.

'That's right,' Ron said. 'We have to forget about the past now. It won't do for us to dwell, nothing is gonna bring the dead back. We need to work together in harmony and if we do that, we will get results. Tim, what are forensics saying?'

'Forensics,' Tim sighed. 'Forensics are still picking up the pieces. We should know more tomorrow.'

'Good,' Ron said.

'We've brought some time from the press; I'm guessing twenty-four to forty-eight hours. Washington, are holding off the other agencies for now. We've put out that there was a gas leak and that seems to be sticking for now, but once the press helicopters eventually release images of the blast, which as sure as you're born, they will do, Homeland Security and everyone else will be all over this. An expert in a bow tie will be on television telling the nation, heck the world, that these images don't look like no gas leak.'

'This needs to be kept small. We don't need other parties interfering with this. Our man must think he has time. The second his face appears on a television screen, he'll act, he's proven that much.' Ron said.

'Let's hope he's dead.' Sally said.

'Let's,' Tim said.

'Has it occurred to anyone that our man knew we would trace him to Cadoc's home? I believe he must have another base, another cell somewhere.'

'We are checking to see if Cadoc rented or brought any vehicles in the last month. We have people going through his accounts, telephone records, everything,' Sally said.

'Hopefully Cadoc's hard drive from his computer withstood the blast. I've made it a priority to find. We have the very best people who can go through it,' Tim Baines said.

'Brilliant. I'm betting that if there is another cell operating, that the group who put our man in contact with Cadoc Elneny, have also put him in contact with the place he is at now,' Ron said. He had suffered a concussion but was still the sharpest person in the room. He swung his legs out of the bed and took the sling apart on his left arm, his elbow was still swollen from being dislocated. He tried stretching his arm out and began moving his fingers, he had temporarily lost the feeling in his hand, but it was coming back now. As he stood up and began to take the bandage off his head, laughter erupted in the room.

'What?' Ron asked, standing in his Homer Simpson underpants.

'Nothing,' Malia said trying to regain her composure.

'Don't they sell adult underpants in Israel?' Sally asked laughing hard and setting Malia off again, even Tim Baines who looked like he had been dragged through hell was laughing.

142

'Very funny,' Ron said putting his jeans on. 'Where is my shirt?'

'They destroyed it when you came in, crimes against fashion,' Sally said, setting Malia off laughing again.

'Seriously though, where is it?'

'It was ripped to pieces; we'll have to get you a new one downstairs in the shop,' Sally said.

# 15

Saturday June 3rd 2017
The Home of Carol and Franklin Wheeler, St Pete Beach, St. Petersburg, Florida 06:57

Mustafa Khoury and his two children knelt excitedly, as they watched the foamy bubbling dying waves roll in and approach the moat that surrounded their sandcastle on the beach. The waves began to trickle in, and the little ones giggled, jumping up and down in delight, as the circular moat filled. Their little hands soft and gentle resting on his shoulders, like little harmless weights that he had helped bring into the world. Mustafa turned to see Adeline, standing and smiling, her hair lifting angelically in the breeze. Was there ever a more beautiful woman he wondered. Adeline raised the camera to take a photo. Suddenly there was a darkening. Excited fascination disappeared from the faces of his daughters and what replaced them was a lost blankness. The sun was dissolving, apocalyptic clouds appeared on the horizon, unworldly like. Mustafa Khoury was slammed forward with ferocious force, a jolting push in the back, he felt the little hands disappearing from his shoulders. He landed on top of the sandcastle destroying it, the water in the moat was dark now, and was thick with blood. Everything began spinning, his world going black. He turned back and his family were gone.

Mustafa opened his eyes and was back in the nightmare he had been in since his family were snatched away from him. He was lying on a bed in the garage basement of Carol and Franklin Wheeler's home. What awoke him from his dream state was the Wheeler's slamming the front door to their waterfront property. The eccentric millionaire couple had just come back from their daily early morning run.

Mustafa had not ventured upstairs in the daylight since the night Carol and Franklin had picked him up, under the cover of darkness, a block from where the now recently deceased Cadoc Elneny had lived with his mother. There were no reports of a terrorist incident, instead local television news stations were saying a gas leak had caused a major residential explosion, with multiple casualties.

Mustafa showered and shaved in the garage bathroom, that was bigger than most people's living room. He walked to the wardrobe and took out a pair of jeans and a red Nike t-shirt, luckily, he was the same build as Franklin Wheeler. Carol was frying eggs naked when Mustafa walked in the kitchen, she was not embarrassed when she saw Mustafa.

'I'm sorry' Mustafa said, turning quickly.

'Don't be, this is how God created me, clothes are an invention of the devil's making,' Carol said, facing him full frontal, with a spatula in hand.

Mustafa turned to look at her. A woman nearly approaching fifty, with the body of a woman half that age. The best breasts money could afford, Dr Horowitz had done a fantastic job, and a six pack and muscles that would give Madonna a run for her money. She also had unshaven genitalia, that looked too big for her frame. She was a natural blonde but dyed her hair red, and her green eyes were very seductive, and Mustafa couldn't help but find that he was attracted to her. In the late eighties Carol Saint-James, as she was known, before she took her husband's name, was a nude model and even posed for Penthouse magazine and eventually, like most models, made some soft-core pornographic movies. A producer on one such movie invited her to a pool party in the Hollywood Hills where she met a dashing young man named Franklin Wheeler, who had seen the future of porn in video and not cinema. He invested heavily in the pornographic video industry in the late seventies, helping revolutionise the way people jerked-off forever, and by the late eighties was living the dream. For Carol and Franklin, it was love at first sight and by 1991 they were married. Children soon followed, two of them, a boy and girl, Billy and Sandy. The years went by, and life was good for the Wheelers, video changed to DVD and Franklin didn't miss the gravy train. In April 2010 tragedy struck, seventeen-year-old Billy and fifteen-year-old Sandy were killed when they were hit by a speeding motorist whilst out cycling on the Pacific Coast Highway between Santa Monica and Malibu. The car driver, a one Juan Carlo, had recently split up with his boyfriend and was on his way to confront him after taking a dangerous cocktail of alcohol and drugs. The combination of rum, cocaine and MDMA, proved to be cataclysmic for the siblings. Juan Carlo passed out at the wheel, approaching from behind Sandy and Billy, first making contact with the back of Sandy's bike at a speed of approximately seventy-five miles per hour, knocking Sandy up and over the front of her racing bike and into oncoming traffic and over two lanes where she was hit by the 534 Metro bus. Billy was next, he turned his head just in time to see his sister fly through the air and splatter against the bus. It was actually the back wheel of his sisters Bianchi racing bike, that brought him down, smashing against the back of his bike helmet, but even his bike helmet couldn't save him from the front wheel of Juan Carlo's Subaru Baja, which crushed Billy's head like a watermelon in a hydraulic press. As for Juan Carlo, his Subaru skidded to safety, with him sleeping like a baby, head resting on an airbag. He only knew of the accident when he woke up in the hospital, suffering with a horrendous hangover and mild case of whiplash. Shortly after the deaths of her children Carol Wheeler had a breakdown and missed most of the trial of Juan Carlo. Franklin Wheeler, or the porn King of LA, as Juan Carlo's defence team labelled him went to the trial every day. He watched in anguish, as Juan Carlo's legal team made Juan Carlo look like the victim. They told a story of a poor Cuban boy, who came to the country with his aunt, after the death of his parents, and how they lived in a one-bedroom flat above a Chinese restaurant in Miami, with rats and cockroaches running around. The defence team, made up of three black lawyers, played on the heart strings of the mostly black jury. One elderly black female juror even started to cry when they were told that at the age of fifteen, Juan Carlo was beaten up and hospitalised with a broken jaw and several broken ribs for being a homosexual. The jury were told that after the attack Juan Carlo had dropped out of school, left his aunt, who was now a heroin addict and prostitute and got a bus to Los Angeles, where he planned on becoming an actor. In Los Angeles, Juan Carlo's dreams of becoming an actor faded like so many peoples do, casting after casting, rejection after rejection. Soon he was just another nobody in the city of angels, walking the boulevard of broken dreams. He picked up odd jobs here and there, working as a receptionist, a gardener, at a car wash, even washing Kevin Spacey's car once, but it was in a nightclub working on the floor, collecting glasses, that his life changed forever. It was January 2009 when Juan Carlo met the man of his dreams, DJ Eric Dalton, handsome, rich, gay and proud. A month later Juan Carlo was living in Eric Dalton's condominium and working as his personal assistant, a job he knew absolutely nothing about. They travelled America and the world together, DJ Flavour Man, as Eric's fans knew him was in high demand. With the lifestyle came parties and drugs and by January 2010 the relationship had become strained, Juan Carlo found out that Eric was seeing other men and was planning to leave him. In court Eric Dalton testified that Juan Carlo could become erratic and even sometimes violent towards him. In March 2010 he left Juan Carlo, telling him he had to be out of the condominium by the end of April. On the morning of Sunday 25 April 2010, Juan Carlo in a fit of desperation and after contemplating taking his own life, started drinking heavily and taking whatever drugs he could find in the condo. He then jumped in his blue Subaru Baja that was brought for him as a birthday present three months earlier and decided to drive to where he believed Eric Dalton was staying, with the idea of winning him back, but on the way passed out at the wheel, subsequently killing the Wheeler children. As California law doesn't notice diminished responsibility, the defence team pleaded mental infirmity, stating his mental state at the time was unbalanced, and that he should not be held responsible for his actions, asking the jury to consider manslaughter instead of murder and recommending to the Judge a light sentence. The jury bought it and the judge sentenced Juan Carlo to just four years in prison, 730 days for each Wheeler kid, saying that Juan Carlo seemed genuinely remorseful for his actions and that one hazy error in judgment, shouldn't warrant a life behind bars.

Franklin Wheeler sat alone as the sentence was read out, never taking his eyes of Juan Carlo and his black defence team, who celebrated like they had just won the Super Bowl. On another day, a different jury, made up of rich well to do white people, and a judge who was not married to a former Miss Havana, might well have put Juan Carlo behind bars for life, but this was not one of those days.

Carol Wheeler was sleeping in her dead son's bed, arms clung around one of Billy's old teddy bears, when Franklin wandered in through the front door of their soulless home. He had been parked up in the driveway for a good half hour before he finally got out of the car. It was around midnight when Carol Wheeler left Billy's room, she was still holding the teddy, as she staggered hazily downstairs, finding Franklin lying in the foetal position on the rug by the fireplace. Next to his scrunched-up body was a .38 Special double action Revolver, that he had loaded and not yet used. It had been pressed against his temple, put in his mouth, held under his chin, even aimed at his heart, but he just didn't know if it would work, also he didn't want to leave Carol with more grief, he especially didn't want to fuck it up and become a vegetable. Carol knelt down beside him, picked up the firearm and rested it down on the mantle above the fireplace where the children use to have their stockings hanging at Christmas.

Los Angeles was dead for the remaining Wheeler's. Franklin cashed in his chips with the porn business, and the couple moved to Florida, making the opposite journey Juan Carlo had made several years earlier.

Thanksgiving 2013 was the day a bolt of lightning struck

down upon Carol and Franklin. The couple were sat naked in their living room, zombified, watching television on a comedown from a cocaine fuelled Thanksgiving gingerbread party, that was held at a neighbour's house where guests had to come dressed as Pilgrims and Puritans. On the television came a charismatic young man preaching the word of God, he caught their eye and awoke something inside them. Televangelist Pastor Jesse Jacobs spoke to them through the screen, standing on a stage in front of his flock, holding a microphone in both hands, with a picture of Christ dying on the cross behind him. Carol began to weep almost immediately, probably with the help from the emotion of the drug binge, but to her, Pastor Jesse Jacobs was her son reborn. The resemblance was uncanny, same height, eye colour, glittering white teeth, combed over blonde hair, strong well-educated jawline, even the mannerisms; the same way Billy would shake his head in delight, the athletic erect walk. History always talks of chance meetings and coincidences for Carol, and for Frank Wheeler, who would follow his wife anywhere, it was destiny. To them, stumbling upon the Assemblies of Christ's show was predetermined. Wearing a dazzling cream suit, Pastor Jesse Jacobs spoke of the demon running the country, a reference to Barack Obama, and how the tornadoes in north Texas, earlier that year, that left six people dead and cost the economy $272 million dollars in damage, was God's way of letting us know he is unhappy. Pastor Jesse Jacobs told them the country should expect more killings of the innocent, like at Sandy Hook elementary school and the cinema in Aurora Colorado, until we deal with the serious moral problems. By moral problems, he meant homosexuality and he equated homosexuals with serial killers, saying the sin of homosexuality confuses young men and turns them into killers. His hatred for Obama was at the heart of everything he said.

'How can you, how can you Mr Obama?' Pastor Jacobs shouted, slapping his free hand against the side of his leg, and then pointing his microphone at the television cameras again. 'How dare you.'

'How dare you?' someone in his congregation shouted out, off screen. His flock were in full motion now. 'How can you support marriage equality?' Pastor Jacobs said shaking his head, looking down at the floor and then pausing for a second. 'God made Adam.' He said with a sly grin.

'Yes, he did, praise the lord,' a woman from the congregation screamed.

'And he made Eve,' Pastor Jacobs said smiling softly, with his arms folded. 'Let me tell you something, we didn't get here today because he made Adam and Steve.' The mob off screen started clapping and cheering and you could almost imagine them swinging from the ceiling like monkeys and picking their own backsides. He had worked them up to the point where they would go and hunt him down a gay kid if he asked it or string up a nigger for him in the name of God. It's fair to say he had the Hitler thing going on.

'Tammy darling, kids, would you come down here please?' he said, turning around, holding out a hand towards where his wife and two children were stood either side of her. Tammy was the picture perfect wife, a bit plump in her red jumpsuit, with an easy-going smile, dated tinted glasses, big rosy cheeks, big breasts, that Pastor Jesse Jacobs would regularly do coke off, something that would only come to light in 2018, when Tammy did a tell all with a magazine, after divorcing Jacobs, because he had been arrested on several counts of child molestation dating back years, which only came to light when Jacobs youngest child found a video that Jacobs had made of him and another man raping a young boy.

'Adam and Steve can't reproduce Mr Obama, but my Tammy can,' Pastor Jacobs said, and kissed his wife on the cheek, bent down and put his arms around his children, pulling them in tight.

He also spoke of how important it is that God gave good Americans the right to protect themselves from evil doers, and that if guns were taken away from good people, we would be defenceless, and our children would be at the mercy of more agents of evil like James E Holmes and Adam Lanza.

'Do you want your children to die?' he asked the audience and then rubbed his children's shoulders.

'No, please God no,' a woman in the flock cried out, as if it was actually going to happen then and there.

'If you love God, send in whatever you can afford, and you will be repaid by the great one in heaven.' The fraudster in the cream suit lied, with the phone number displayed across the screen.

The Wheeler's were sold from that point on. Not only did they regularly tune in and send money, but they also joined a local gun club and became active republicans. They bought all Pastor Jesse Jacobs books, one titled "You, Me and Jesus too" spoke about how white Americans will be a minority in thirty years and how gays, blacks and Jews will be running the world soon. In Carol Wheeler's fragile mind, which was already broken, she saw hidden messages in the text. Pastor Jesse Jacobs was telling her to kill blacks and homosexuals. The match was already there, Pastor Jacobs was the flame that lit it, after all it was a queer that killed her children and a black defence team that got the queer off on a four-year sentence, of which he would only serve three.

Franklin and Carol both found a mutual love for guns, with Carol turning out to be natural. She was even asked to join the local NRA women's club. They cleaned up their act and stopped the drugs and slowed down with the alcohol, but not the swinging. Now they wanted to avenge their children, and with Franklin's knowledge of the dark web, they started talking to a nice young man named Samuel, who wanted to help them.

'Sit, sit,' Carol said, holding the frying pan and directing Mustafa with her eyes, to sit in one of the French chairs.

Mustafa sat down on one of the pastel chairs around the white rustic wooden kitchen table and Carol served the eggs for all three of them on decorative plates, that looked expensive.

'Franklin, breakfast,' Carol called out, and then after a few seconds with no reply. 'Let's start without him,' Carol said smiling, sitting directly opposite Mustafa, with her perfect tits on display, showing them off proudly, like a soldier who has just come back from war with the Purple Heart.

Mustafa was famished, which was a good thing and he managed to keep his eyes down on his plate. Half-way through eating his eggs and toast, his head came up and he made eye contact with Carol's Purple Hearts. Franklin had come down and he gave Mustafa a friendly pat on the back.

'It's good to see you have an appetite, we will all need our strength in the coming days to fulfil the lords work,' Franklin announced, walking around to the front of the table. Mustafa was relieved to see Franklin fully clothed, wearing a t-shirt and shorts. 'That was some bomb you made son,' Franklin said, pouring himself a coffee.

'Can you make another one like that one, but bigger, for us?' Carol asked, reaching over and grabbing Mustafa's hand. Mustafa blushed, not knowing quite where to look or what to say. In normal circumstances he would have got the hell out of that house, these people were clearly insane, but these were not normal circumstances. He needed them and he had nowhere else to go.

'Mother,' Franklin said, putting his coffee cup down. 'I do believe we are making our guest feel uncomfortable.'

Carol frowned and looked down at her breasts, then back up at Mustafa. 'I will go and put a top on.' Carol got up from the table.

'No, no, not at all, I'm just worried about the authorities,' Mustafa lied.

Carol smiled and sat back down. 'See,' she said, looking up at Franklin.

'You have nothing to worry about, the news is saying it was a gas leak,' Franklin said.

Mustafa knew better. 'It's a cover. We should still proceed with caution. Do not change your routine, if you normally go shopping on a Friday, go on a Friday.'

'We have it delivered,' Carol said jumping in.

'Ok, but you get the picture. Change nothing, keep up appearances.'

'Understood captain,' Carol said and gave a salute.

'Show him your new toy,' Franklin told his wife. Carol jumped up from her chair and clapped her hands together like a child and ran out the kitchen, with all the grace of a crack addict running away from the law.

'New toy?' Mustafa asked. For a second, he pictured a dildo and was relieved when Carol came back with a shotgun.

'Same one the legendary James Holmes used to kill those sitting ducks in the cinema,' Carol said proudly, posing with her 12-gauge. 'It's a Remington 870, the gun I've always wanted, and now I have it.' This was followed by a fist pump.

'Does she, or does she not look like one mean sexy bitch?' Franklin asked Mustafa, then slapped his wife's pasty firm ass.

'Woo,' Carol jumped in joy.

Mustafa nodded, he was thinking that he did not want to die with these people. He wouldn't mind killing them, but not dying with them.

'Today, we show you the target,' Franklin announced, putting his arm around Carol.

'America will be a better place, after our sacrifice,' Carol declared.

Franklin walked over to the radio and switched it on, instantly turning the volume up, and hopping from side to side, as Men Without Hats blasted out The Safety Dance. Carol joined her man and the two of them danced like two blind lunatics.

Mustafa sat awkwardly, watching the monstrosity unfold in front of him, feeling violated somewhere deep down, like a child stumbling upon his parents having sex, suddenly knowing too much too soon, and for a second, just for a second, he wished he had let Walid kill Ranim and Samuel.

# 16

Saturday June 3rd 2017
Young Palms Fundamental Elementary School, St. Petersburg,
Florida 13:36

They parked up outside the St. Petersburg Mercy Gospel Church, a small white bricked building with a high blue wooden roof, that pointed towards the heavens. The unlikely trio got out of the newly restored sandy coloured 1979 Buick century turbo coupe, Carol opening the door, and pushing forward the front seat for Mustafa to get out.

'Is this the target?' Mustafa asked, bending down to tie his shoelaces.

'It's a secondary target,' Carol said, arms folded, wearing a white wife beater, breasts pushed up, and leaning against the Buick, engine cracking, calming down in the summer heat.

There was singing coming from inside the church and on the lawn was a billboard, with a blown-up picture of a young black woman, who was smiling. The billboard read 'Saturday June 3rd, 2017, celebrating the life of Selina Lee Jackson, 33 years of age. Officiating Dr D Danny Hall and eulogist Reverend Michael P Perkins.'

Carol studied the picture, then turning around to her husband and Mustafa, with a grin, 'This bitch was thirty-three, just thirty-three fucking years old.'

'Must have been drugs,' Franklin said, putting his sunglasses on, trying his best to look cool.

'Or a drive by, these fuckers love shooting each other up.' Then she fell into a fit of hysteria. A fit of hysterics only suited to those who have been touched by psychosis. Mustafa looked wearily at the woman. At them both for that matter.

They walked on past the church and turned right down 25th street. One hundred yards down they came upon the main target. Mustafa stared at Young Palms Fundamental Elementary School, and for the first time in a long time, he doubted the monster he had become. The choir was in full force now, singing Goin' Home. Mustafa thought he would certainly be going to hell, after this.

Mustafa was standing by a small white picket gate that led to the main building. It had purposely been made small for the little children. Mustafa could see into one of the classroom windows, children's drawings were sprawled all about the walls. A short distance to the left of the main building was a playground. Franklin and Carol Wheeler stood either side of him. Two demons.

'I know what you're thinking, it's been done before,' Carol Wheeler said, hiding something back with a sly smile. She walked in front of him, and Mustafa followed her with his eyes. 'But this Wednesday at noon, a very special visitor is coming here.'

'Who?' Mustafa asked.

'The mayor,' Franklin said.

'Mayor Jake Kellerman,' Carol said. 'A very special friend of former President Nigger man himself.'

'And he only ever travels with his aid and a driver,' Franklin said, giving Mustafa a playful nudge with his elbow.

'Why's the mayor going to be coming to this school?' Mustafa asked.

'Something to do with the principle's unique methods of teaching,' Franklin said.

'Apparently since she took over a couple of years back, test results have gone through the roof,' Carol said.

'A real crusader for children's nurturing. What's her name again, hun?' Franklin asked his wife.

'Principal Gilda Coleman,' Carol said, then a moment later she added. 'She's probably a dike, with a name like Gilda.'

'And the Mayor will definitely be here this Wednesday?' Mustafa asked.

'Most definitely. I even phoned the school to confirm, after I read about it online. Wednesday will be the last day before they break up for summer,' Carol said.

'He'll be here,' Franklin confirmed.

'Okay then,' Mustafa said, looking at the school. 'This will be where we'll make our stand.'

The monster was coming around again now. A smile began to grow on Mustafa's face and somewhere far away he could hear his old friend, Walid, laughing with delight.

The mourners were leaving the church, and the choir was singing Be Not Afraid, as the deadly trio got back into the Buick and drove off.

All the murder planning had made Franklin Wheeler hungry, and he insisted they find somewhere to eat. They pulled into a Big Daddy Burger and BBQ, one of those old-fashioned drive thru places that are scattered all over America. For Franklin it was the nostalgia of it all, he loved the greasy food, the people watching, passing through from place to place

— truckers, bikers, the wanderers and the lost. They got a booth by the window; the walls were decorated in old Hollywood. A signed black and white picture of Clark Gable looked down on them above the window. A young waitress, no older then eighteen came to take their order. She wore a scandalous pink uniform that stopped way above the knees, just about hiding her innocence, or lack of it. Her name badge read Lucy and she kept a pen behind her ear, where her blonde hair was tied back. Her order pad stuck out her little white front pocket that she also used for tips. Her white slip-ons, were like the menus — covered in grease. Franklin and Carol each ordered a Big Daddy chilli burger, while Mustafa just went for a small chocolate ice cream cup. When it arrived, Mustafa thought there had been a mistake.

'Sorry Lucy,' Mustafa said, looking at the mountain of chocolate in front of him. 'I only wanted a small one.' A rupture of laughter arose from the girl, the Wheelers and the table across from them, where a family was celebrating a birthday.

'This is America!' Franklin said, 'We don't do small.'

'I'm glad I didn't order a large.' Mustafa smiled, holding his spoon and looking at how, exactly, he was going to negotiate the chocolate mountain that was already beginning to drip on the table.

'I have faith in you,' Lucy said, giving him a wink.

Mustafa watched in amazement as Franklin and Carol ate their Big Daddy chilli burgers. Grease oozed from the meat and half-way through the eating of the thing, and it was a thing, the plate was floating in a lake of grease.

'No wonder we're all dying of heart attacks,' Carol said, after finishing her burger.

'No need for us to worry about that any more,' Franklin stated, looking out the open window, breathing in the sea air that was just out of sight.

'Don't be so melodramatic,' Carol snapped.

Had doubt entered Franklin's mind? Was he having second thoughts? Mustafa thought it might be possible. Sure, Franklin talked a good game, but actually killing someone was different. Mustafa knew that himself. He felt good about Carol, she was the right kind of crazy for this murdering business. Mustafa also knew that between now and Wednesday there was little time and lots of planning. Franklin tipped Lucy generously and a week later the pretty girl-next-door waitress would tell a reporter that the trio were very friendly and seemed just like any other regular folk.

# 17

Saturday June 3<sup>rd</sup>, 2017
Pompano Beach, Florida, corner of 24th Street and 12th
Avenue 14:55

A marquee stood on the road, outside the rubbled remains of
the former Cadoc Elneny's home, that was now an active crime
scene. The whole street had been evacuated now and FBI
agents were combing the area for evidence and picking up the
remains of their dead colleagues. Body parts were found
scattered around the neighbourhood and carefully collected. It
was hot, Florida summers are always hot. Heat and raw meat
don't do well in the open air, and where there's rotting meat
there's flies. They were a good indicator of just where to look
for their fallen friends. Thousands of the little buggers
swarmed together on piles of stinking human flesh, that could
mostly only be described as looking like blended pasta. At just
about the same time the Wheelers were finishing their big
Daddy chilli burgers, Cadoc Elneny's computer was found
under an upturned bathtub, and by some miracle was in pretty
good shape. A team of IT technicians quickly went about
rebooting the computer inside the marquee, that was now also
a computer forensics lab.

Tim Baines was on a flight to Washington, to put out some
flames with the disgruntled head honchos and he had left

Agent Anderson in charge.

'How long until we can get this baby up and running?' Sally asked the three men, who were hooking up wires and connecting devices into other pieces of expensive looking electronic equipment.

'With any luck we should have this "baby", as you call it up and running in no time,' one man said, never taking his eyes away from his work.

'Like, no time when exactly?'

The same man, who was now lying on his back on the plastic blue tarp underneath the table where the computer stood, ignored her for a few seconds while he fiddled with a connection, then answered her. 'Like now,' and just like that it was on. 'Now we have to find the dirt on this guy and I'm guessing it's well hidden, but we're sly,' he said smiling.

Another IT technician who was typing on a keyboard at a ferocious speed, glance up at Agent Anderson. 'We got something.'

'What we got?' Agent Anderson asked, leaning in.

'JPEGs.'

'What's a JPEG?' Netzer asked.

'Images,' Malia said, stunned at Netzer's lack of basic computer knowledge. 'Christ, it's frightening that you have so much responsibility.'

'Steganography?' Netzer asked, kneeling down beside the IT technician.

'I think so,' the IT technician said, bringing up a picture of a boat on the FBI computer that was connected to Elneny's computer.

'Crafty little bastard hid the data he didn't want anyone to find in an image of a boat,' Netzer said looking up at Malia, who was now looking back at him slightly puzzled.

'You nailed it,' the IT technician said.

'It's going to take a while. Why don't you guys piss off and leave us to concentrate. We will let you know when we have something,' the IT technicians who appeared to be in charge said. He was a very serious, handsome looking guy, who looked like he may have played some football in college and dated the prom queen. The other two technicians looked like textbook nerds, with their short, neat hairstyles, both with quiffs, one wearing a pair of horn-rimmed glasses. A good Saturday night for them was Warcraft and a pizza.

'How long until you have something?' Sally asked.

'Not long, stay close.'

'What should we do?' Malia asked.

'We should help,' Ron said, looking across to the other side of the marquee, where body parts were being brought in.

Sally, Netzer, Malia and Ron went about the rubble, laying little blue flags down as markers, when they came across something that maybe once belonged to a person. Sally was walking about five feet behind Netzer, who was whistling that familiar tune once more.

'What is that tune? It's so familiar to me.'

'It's Span—'

'Over here,' Malia called out, waving for their attention.

When Sally, Ron and Netzer got over to her, Malia was sitting on a grass verge that was now a grey colour from the dust. She was looking a bit fresh under the collar too, staring at the little blue flag she had just laid down on a broken kitchen table that Cadoc and his mother once sat at, where Manar did her puzzles.

'Under there,' she pointed at the table.

Ron carefully lifted up the table wearing latex gloves. He quickly turned his head and gasped when he saw the mess underneath, not from the sight so much as the stench. Sally fell backwards a step and Netzer put out an arm to catch her, but she regained her footing.

'That's just fucked,' Netzer remarked, holding his hands against his mouth from the smell.

Looking at the decapitated fly ridden head of Manar Cadoc, Netzer suddenly remembered the tragic story of Roei Hosh. Roei Hosh was an old man who had lived in kibbutz Lahav when Netzer was growing up, their homes directly opposite one another and only separated by their front lawns and a road that hardly anybody travelled up and down on. All the kids on the kibbutz thought Roei mad, and in truth he probably was. The adults on the kibbutz excepted him, but were also embarrassed of him, maybe some of it was shame on their part. He lived with his mother and worked in the horse stables on the kibbutz, feeding, haying and grooming and all the other tasks that came with the job. He was regularly seen walking the kibbutz and talking to himself, wearing the same blue shirt and shorts every day, like some cartoon character. He ate with his elderly mother every lunchtime in the dining hall, where the children would watch, point and laugh at him, as kids do. Netzer never did though, he felt sorry for his neighbour and always gave him a wave when he saw him. Netzer would wake at night sometimes, hearing the screams from his neighbours' home, nightmares straight from some dark place in time. When the young chubby Netzer would ask his father about Roei, his father would just tell him that Roei was a good man, who had suffered a great deal. Netzer knew of suffering and nightmares, often crying out for his dead mother, only to be comforted by his father, who had basically died the day she did. It was his uncle who finally told a thirteen-year-old Netzer about Roei. Uncle Meni Akerman sat in the porch, that the two of them had just painted, and lit a big fat joint.

'What's the story with Roei?'

'Roei Hosh, your neighbour?'

'Yeah.'

'Where do I start?'

'Like, why does he wear the same clothes every day?'

'That, Mr Picasso,' Meni said jokingly, studying the porch they had just painted, 'you can blame on the Yom Kippur war of 1973.'

Netzer leaned forward and his eyes lit up, eagerly wanting to know the story. 'Go on uncle, do tell?'

Meni laughed that stoner laugh and passed the joint to his nephew. 'You kids always want to know of the macabre.'

'Off course, it's fascinating,' Netzer said, taking a toke, then coughing a cloud of smoke out into the warm afternoon air, that now smelled of wet paint and weed.

'Pass it back now, don't Bogart me.'

Netzer passed the joint back, still coughing. 'It's strong.'

'You know Roei and your father were friends?'

'No. No, I didn't.' Netzer said surprised.

'Truth be, if Roei hadn't come back from that war fucked up, he would have probably married your mother.'

'What?'

'True story. They were a couple in 1973. So, this, what I am about to tell you, stays between me and you, all right Picasso.'

'Okay.' Netzer said, red eyed and dazed from this

165

revelation and the dope.

'His platoon or unit or whatever the fuck he was in got ambushed near the Golan Heights.' Meni said, he himself had never actually served in the army on account of his eyesight that made it hard for him to concentrate on things for very long. Meni claimed the pot helped his sight, but this was probably crap, Netzer thought. 'They were retreating with no cover, over an open field of land, running like wildebeests from the lions, only these lions, used mortars. His whole platoon got killed that day, all his friends, apart from Roei. One of his friends on the retreat ran past him and when Roei turned to look at his friend, he was headless, still running.'

'Like a chicken,' Netzer said, shocked.

'Yep. Anyway, when he awoke in the army hospital a few days later with only a few minor wounds, the nurses had dressed him in a blue shirt and shorts.'

'Who told you all this?'

'Your mother. She tried to help him after he came home, but he never came back from that place. He wears those same clothes to remind him of his friends. I think the nightmares you hear from his room at night, are of that day and place he never left.'

The young Netzer took another drag and then was suddenly back in the present.

'You're gonna want to come and have a look at this,' the handsome IT technician called out from the entrance of the marquee.

'It appears Cadoc Elneny had been speaking to a person named Samuel on the internet.'

'Do we have a second name? An address?'

'No second name. And I would guess from the grammar,

that Mr Samuel is of middle eastern descent, probably Syrian or Turkish,' the IT technician they called Pete said.

'Why do you say this?' Sally asked.

'A common mistake we see all the time from recruiters from this region,' Pete said, pointing at the screen. 'Look here, where Samuel tells Cadoc — he coming.'

'They talk about Islam, about Cadoc's troubles with women, isolation and racism. This is textbook ISIS recruiting,' Pete said, pushing his horn-rimmed glasses back up his nose. 'All done from Lebanon or Syria, it's difficult to narrow it down at the moment.'

Ron tapped Malia on the shoulder. 'Get on to Gavish. Ask him if there are any known ISIS recruiters going by the name Samuel.'

'We're doing that now,' Pete said, eating a cheese stick.

'What's troubling you?' Sally asked Ron, who was looking concerned.

'This isn't ISIS,' Ron said.

'This is interesting,' the other nerdy looking IT technician they called Chris whispered in a low tone.

'What?' Sally asked.

'Five days ago, our Mr Cadoc joined a dating agency. Now why would you join a dating site, if you're planning on blowing yourself up?'

'One last fling?' Pete suggested.

'You would get a hooker, or an escort for that. No, this is something else,' Chris whispered, with his face close enough to the screen to kiss it.

'Can you find out who he's been talking to?' Sally asked.

'This guy's been using a dating site to talk to someone here in Florida,' Chris said, turning and smiling.

Malia came back into the marquee, holding her cell. 'Gavish is looking into it.'

'Is it possible to see if Samuel has talked to anyone else here in America?' Ron asked, kneeling next to Chris.

'It will be extremely difficult. Finding this was easy, because the security firewall on this end was easy to break.'

Malia's cell rang and she walked back out of the marquee.

'What's the dating site called?' Netzer asked.

'FlirtatiousBeginnings.com' Chris replied.

'Never heard of it.'

Malia came back into the marquee. 'He's ISIS, but went quiet, a few years back. Never recruited Americans before either. Last reports say he was in Syria.'

'That was quick,' Sally said, almost amazed.

'Those Mossad gang have got more fingers in pies than anyone else,' the handsome IT technician said, who was named Devin.

'I love a pie,' Netzer said, then winking and blowing a kiss in Devin's direction.

'What if Samuel is not working for ISIS now? What if he hopped across to Lebanon and got picked up by Hezbollah, or some fraction of Hezbollah?'

'That's a lot of what ifs,' Sally said, raising her eyebrows.

'I'm positive our Dr Nissan is Hezbollah and Samuel has helped him get here,' Ron said, rubbing his left elbow with his right hand. Ron turned to Malia. 'Send Tel Aviv Dr Nissan's picture and ask Gavish to run it through our connections in Lebanon. I'm betting you we get something back.'

'Like I said, fingers in pies,' Devin spoke, with a vicious smile. He had nothing but contempt for Mossad. A few years back Devin was stationed in El Salvador with the DEA, when a two-year operation was ruined. Devin and his team were days away from capturing Medardo Lopez — drug lord supreme and help stop the supply of cocaine crossing the border and eventually ending up in Miami. Temporarily anyway. But Medardo Lopez also had his fingers in a lot of pies, shipping guns to Africa, that eventually wound up in the hands of Hamas. This, in the eyes of Israel, was a no no, and Medardo Lopez had to go. He was assassinated in a whore house and up in smoke went a two-year operation the DEA had been putting together. Medardo was the man, who if captured, would inform and would open up the whole El Salvador/Miami network.

'St. Petersburg,' Chris shouted, beckoning everyone with a wave of his hand.

'I hate St Petersburg,' Netzer remarked, reminiscing.

'St Petersburg, Florida, not the Russian one,' Chris said, looking up at him.

'Oh, you guys also have one,' Netzer said, trying to seem interested.

'What you got?' Sally asked.

'Someone was chatting to Cadoc on FlirtatiousBeginnings.com. It's an internet cafe called Geeks and Treats, near St. Pete's beach.'

'Address?' Sally asked.

'1335, 5th Street.'

'Chris, you come with me and Netzer,' Sally said, pointing at the IT technician. 'Jesus, I hope they have operational surveillance cameras,' Sally said, looking up and pleading to the heavens.

'If not we're sure to run in to some geeks with treats,' Netzer said, looking around for laughter, that didn't arrive.

'You guys stay here and see what else you can dig up,' Sally said, walking backwards out of the marquee, pointing at Ron and Malia.

Chris the IT technician jumped up from the desk he was seated at, with the look of a man who has just been released from a long sentence in prison. Malia, on the other hand, looked like someone had just spit in her face. She fell into one of the chairs and slumped down like a kid who realises it's not pizza night and mum's cooking liver that's as tough as an old boot, with onions.

'Shotgun,' Chris called out, almost running for the car.

'They don't let you out much do they,' Netzer said.

'No sir, they do not,' Chris said, checking his firearm.

'Are you fucking serious?' Netzer said, looking at Sally from the backseat. His facial expression was somewhere between disgust and disbelief.

'What?' Sally asked, looking back at Netzer in the backseat, his face now buried in his hands.

'This guy,' Netzer said, looking up and pointing at Chris. 'Even he has a gun.'

Sally smiled. 'Yep hun, now put your seat belt on please.'

As they drove off Ron stepped out of the marquee and lit a cigarette. He was hoping his old friend Gavish would come up with the goods on Dr Nissan, or whatever his name was.

# 18

Sunday June 4th 2017
Nicosia, Cyprus 02:06

Gavish was in the Nicosia international airport in Cyprus, less than three hours after Malia had sent him the photo of Dr David Nissan, and in four hours he would be back in Tel Aviv.

Gavish took a taxi from the airport to the Hilton hotel. He paid the driver in cash, then spoke quickly to the doorman, who gave a nod of approval to the concierge. Gavish then walked into the marbled floor lobby and sat in one of the big red chairs that could probably fit two people and picked up a copy of National Geographic Magazine. He had been reading the magazine less than five minutes when an old man with a walking stick waddled up to him and sat down in the seat next to him.

'My doctor tells me I need another hip replacement,' the old man said, sitting up straight, still holding on to his stick.

'Do you have a name for the face?' Gavish said, eyes never leaving the magazine, he had never actually been reading.

'Are you a believer in retribution?' the old man asked, leaning forward on his walking stick, not wanting to fall too far back in to the seat. At his age resting for too long had its disadvantages. He hated how his body was falling apart now.

Everyday something new would trouble him. Some mornings after waking from a good sleep the cracking of his joints would sound like some nightmarish orchestra playing only for him.

'Someone once told me, whatever side you're on, you're right,' Gavish responded, placing the magazine back on the glass table in front of him.

The old man looked down for a second nodding. 'For this one you must take some responsibility.'

'Really,' Gavish replied, looking amused.

'This is a monster that you created.'

'How is that?'

'His family were killed by one of your bombs. You took away everything he had and everything he's ever going to have.'

'Name?' Gavish asked sharply.

'Mustafa Khoury. Dr Mustafa Khoury.'

'Hezbollah?'

'No. He's one of Walid's men. Do you know Colonel Foziah Walid?' The old man didn't wait for a response. 'You should, you've tried to kill him enough times.'

'Are you telling me some off-shoot of Hezbollah, some gangster army, are running a mission right under the noses of the government?'

'That's the way business gets done all over the world. You know that better than anyone. Does your government know we're having this conversation? I suspect not. You've helped us in the past and now we're returning the favour. My informant in Beirut wants you to know, whatever is going down, it's nothing to do with the Lebanese government.'

'Where's Walid now? They can stop this,' Gavish spoke, sounding a little desperate.

'How long have we known each other?' the old man asked his young friend.

'Over twenty years, when you were with SLA.'

'You were just a young kid. An idealist, a person who really wanted to make a difference. I remember that you were shedding tears the day we had to flee. What was the date?' the old man asked, already knowing the answer.

'We handed over control to Hezbollah on the 22nd May 2000 and two days later we left,' he paused for a moment looking sadly at the old man, the old man who since that day, was a refugee. 'We were one of the last to leave. I will never forget watching them drag Haddad's statue through the streets of Marjayoun, laughing at us and firing their guns in the air.'

'We all lost something that day. Many of my friends who stayed were tried for treason and executed,' the old man said. Tears were rolling down his wrinkled face now.

Gavish put his hand on the old man's arm. 'I know.'

The South Lebanese Army, or SLA was a sad chapter in the history of Lebanon. A romantic failure. A mainly Christian fighting organisation, supported by Israel to overthrow the government and Hezbollah.

The old man stood up. Gavish was waved away when he tried to help him. 'I have to keep on reminding myself I am one of the lucky ones. Cyprus is a nice country. Whenever my body aches, or I have to get up three, or four times in the night to take a piss — you will have that to look forward to, don't worry about that,' he looked Gavish in the eyes. 'I think of the people who stayed, the people we failed, the ones whose children and wives were gang raped and slaughtered by the vengeful mob.'

'We can't change the past, but we can still change the

future,' Gavish said, bluntly.

The old man, who was slowly making his way back towards the other side of the lobby, where there was a set of elevators, turned to his old friend. 'I'm sorry I couldn't be more helpful, but it was nice to see you again.'

# 19

Outside Geeks and Treats a teenager was lying against a wooden bench under the shade of a giant Captain America patio umbrella. Captain America was looking angry and thirsty for some vengeance. Someone had drawn a penis in black marker pen next to the mouth of the past out teenager. He had dyed orange and purple spiked hair, but that was self-inflicted. The Nirvana t-shirt he wore was about ten sizes too small for him and his big round belly rose like a mountain, making his t-shirt look more like a tank top. In his left hand was an energy drink still half full. On another bench a few feet away, sat a group of Asian kids all on their laptops. They were together, but also completely alone. They were playing against each other and very engrossed in what they were doing. Netzer studied the youths and thought that World War three could be taking place around them and still they wouldn't look up from their cyber world.

'Virgins of the world unite,' Netzer said looking around. 'You should fit right in,' Netzer said, slapping Chris on the back.

'The future leaders of the world,' Chris declared. 'In the years to come, they'll be millionaires and you will still be dressing like you've had a breakdown.'

'Women dig me,' Netzer said, looking down at his attire.

Agent Sally Anderson and Chris the IT technician shared a smile, trying not to laugh.

Sally showed her FBI badge to a young girl, no older than twelve, who was sitting behind the reception desk and playing on her cell phone. 'Can I speak to the owner please darling?'

The young girl smiled. 'Uncle, FBI lady wants to talk to you,' the young girl bellowed from the top of her lungs.

Behind the girl, a whole room of zombies looked up from their screens, with their headsets on. One nervous looking stick thin man took his headset off and stood up slowly, composed himself, took a deep breath and walked over towards the reception. He gave the impression of a scout master with his tight brown short shorts and a white polo top tucked into them, fastened uncomfortably together by a belt. Sally gave a little shudder looking at the man's white socks that stopped just below the knees and sandals, that wouldn't have looked out of place centuries ago knocking around Nazareth. The man who was now approaching them apprehensively, reminded Sally of one of her first arrests when she was with the Miami Dade police department. A man dressed not to dissimilar to this one, skinny frame and skinny arms like this one, same seventies porn star moustache like this one, same pale complexion and same nervous air about him. A dog handler who would befriend young children, mainly boys on their own, using man's best friend to lure them in and make them feel comfortable. After he had won their trust, he would then offer to give them a lift home. He raped and killed two young boys before Sally captured him. Both children were found in wooded areas, two months apart, both had traces of dog hair on their skin and clothes and both children came from families that had no dogs. She went house to house questioning people who might have seen anyone unusual in the area with dogs. One day, call it dumb luck, a van cut in front of her. In the back window of the van a couple of dogs were jumping up and down. Sally pulled the van over and talked to the nervous driver, who had never been in trouble with the law before. She asked to see the dogs in the back and unsuspectingly, she took samples of their hair. Back in the lab they matched them with the dog hairs found on the dead boys. A day later the dog handler was arrested, whilst he was having breakfast with his wife and two young children in the kitchen.

'Are you the owner, sir?' Sally asked.

'If it's about Gregg, I told him to go home hours ago. I can't help it that he's always passing out.'

'Are you going to arrest my uncle Roy?' The young girl asked smiling.

'No darling,' Sally said, smiling down at the young girl.

'Ah ah.' Uncle Roy laughed nervously, rubbing the top of his young niece's blonde head.

'Sir, I don't care about some passed out gamer. I have more pressing issues. Am I to believe you have working surveillance cameras in operation here?' Sally said pointing at the camera monitors spread across the cafe.

'Yes ma'am, that's correct. The very finest. We had a few break-ins a couple of months back, so I decided to get the very best in the business. What's this about?'

'We're not at liberty to say at this moment in time,' Sally said.

Chris pulled out a piece of paper. 'Can we see the surveillance footage from Monday May 29th, between 2pm and 4pm?'

'Shouldn't be a problem, just follow me to the office.'

They walked through the room of gamers, who were chasing each other in some altered virtual reality, trying to kill each other, dying, then doing it all over again. It was a tense theatre of human emotion.

'What kind of fucking cover is that? I've been carrying you fuckers all day,' one kid screamed out, slamming his fists on the desk.

'Hey, go easy on the desk, dude, I'm sick of telling you,' Uncle Roy told the angry kid.

'Go blow me, Roy,' the kid snarled back and the room broke into a raw of laughter.

Roy tried to look angry by standing with his hands on his hips. The kid gave Roy the bird and went back to gaming.

'A rowdy bunch,' Netzer said.

'They don't respect me like they should,' Roy said, opening the door to the office.

Roy got the surveillance for Monday May 29th up on the laptop.

'We can take it from here, sir,' Sally said, almost pushing Roy out of the room. 'If we need your help, we will give you a shout.'

Roy looked a bit dejected at this and put his hands into his pockets. Netzer smiled at Roy and then shut the door to his office on him and pulled the blinds.

'That guy gives me the creeps,' Netzer said, turning to look at Sally and Chris.

'He looks very pasty,' Chris remarked.

'Looks like he just woke up from ground zero, that's what he looks like,' Netzer said.

They watched in high-definition colour as kids, mainly, came and went. They saw Roy trip over a chair, stand up and kick the chair and hobble off. At 14:26 in the afternoon a good-looking woman in high heels walked into Geeks and Treats. She talked to the young girl briefly, who was manning the reception and then took a computer in the far-right hand corner, away from the gamers. At 15:37 she got up from the computer, walked to the reception and paid in cash, again briefly talking to the young girl and then exiting Geeks and Treats.

'That's got to be our woman,' Netzer said, 'Nice legs. I would guess she's in her early forties.'

Sally opened the door and walked out the office and up to Roy, who was sat at a computer, gaming. 'I would like to talk to your niece for a second. Would you bring her into the office?'

'What's this all about?' Roy said, turning to look at her, sounding a little annoyed. 'I'm the one who owns this establishment. You should be talking to me.' Roy was putting his foot down; he didn't like the idea of being left in the dark. Damn it if he was going to let the FBI talk to his niece and not him. No, Roy thought, I'm not being ignored. Roy stood up tall, chin up and folding his skinny arms. 'So, you going to tell me what this is all about?'

Sally looked up to the ceiling in disbelief, then leaned in close and whispered in his ear. 'Are you aware of the Florida child labour laws for minors under the age of fourteen?'

Roy gulped and his arms dropped to his side like a rag-dolls and his stomach tightened up and a bad smell filled the air.

'I think Roy shat his pants,' one kid declared.

'We have all the evidence of… what's your niece's name?'

'Ju, Ju, Juno,' Roy stuttered, sweat pouring down his face.

'Lovely name. We have her on camera handling money.'

'Oh God, oh God,' Roy whimpered. His pasty complexion had now turned an advanced looking pale. Sally thought he was going to puke right then and there.

'Now, Roy darling. Go get Juno and bring her back to the office. If you don't Roy, I'll make sure that you pay the maximum fine of $11,000.'

'Ri, ri, right away. I'll go, go, go get her.' His whole body was shaking as he staggered over to his niece. He looked like a man who had just finished a marathon, like a disoriented junkie.

Juno came into the office, hands on hips. 'Lady, you got my Uncle Roy rattled.'

Sally bent down so she was eye level with the little girl. 'Sorry, honey, sometimes you just got to give them a scare.'

'I get ya, but Roy's just about ready to cry. Don't judge him too hard, he's a good one, since mum had a breakdown on account of dad running off with his secretary, or whore as she calls her.'

'You shouldn't use words like that,' Sally said, breaking a smile, with Netzer and Chris grinning.

'I live in the real world. My Uncle Roy,' Juno sighed, looking through the blinds towards where her uncle was sitting and looking sorry for himself, 'he has his faults, but if it wasn't for him, I really don't know how I would have managed these last months.'

'Smart kid,' Netzer said.

'Roy is in absolutely no trouble at all,' Sally said.

'Promise?'

'Promise,' Sally said, holding out her little finger to the girl and they pinky promised.

'So, what can I help you with?' Juno asked.

'Do you remember this woman?' Sally asked, showing Juno the footage of the mystery woman.

'Don't get many like her in here,' Juno said.

'You remember her then?' Sally asked.

'Most definitely. Not our usual clientele.'

'What was different about her?' Sally asked.

'She didn't stink like all the boys. Smelt really fresh.'

'Perfume?'

'Uh huh. I think she was rich.'

'How come?'

'Jimmy Choo's.'

'Who?' Netzer asked.

'It's a shoe,' Sally and Chris responded together.

'And a real person,' Juno said. 'She was wearing a pair. I know all about fashion from my mother's magazines. Her dress looked great as well.'

'You talked to her, do you remember what about?' Sally asked.

'Was she American or foreign?' Netzer asked.

'As American as apple pie.' Then turning back to look at Agent Anderson, 'She was nice, she said I reminded her of her daughter.'

'She tell you her name?' Chris asked.

'Nope.'

'What about signing in or ID?' Chris asked.

'Nope, she paid in cash and tipped me. No one ever tips me. I hope she hasn't done anything bad. I liked her very much.'

'Thanks darling. If you remember anything else, however small, please give me a call,' Sally said, passing over her phone number to the girl.

'Sure thing.'

Netzer opened the door to the office and Juno walked out. Just before the door could close, Juno turned back, unintentionally imitating Lieutenant Columbo, without the cigar. 'There is just one more thing.'

'Go on,' Sally said, poking her head out the door.

'It's probably not important, but I thought it was funny, because she didn't look like the type.'

'Okay,' Sally said.

'She had on the same gold ring as Freya's dad,' she paused. 'Freya's my best friend,' Juno explained. 'A National Rifle Association members ring. My mother says Freya's dad is an idiot.' Juno turned around and walked back to the reception.

Sally felt the hair on the back of her neck stand up, as if a cold chill had entered the room.

'That cuts it,' Netzer said, as if to confirm their suspicions.

'Let's go,' Sally said.

Outside across the road, opposite Geeks and Treats was a car dealership, with surveillance cameras pointing high in every direction. Sally looked at Chris. 'I want you to trace her movements when she left here. Can you do it starting with those cameras up there and others if you need to? She might have parked up around here, or got a taxi, bus, whatever.'

'I'm going to need a small team and some warrants.' Chris replied.

'I'll get you the warrants. And you can have as many people as you want,' Sally said. 'We need to find this woman. We need to find her fast.'

# 20

Sunday June 4th 2017
The Home of Carol and Franklin Wheeler, ST Pete Beach, ST.
Petersburg, Florida 07:00

Twice in the night he had woken, the usual nightmares of loss, breaching his dreams. The damp bed sheets clung to him and when he pulled them away a cool air swept over his sweaty body. His heart pounded in his chest, and he wondered if he had not run a marathon whilst sleeping.

Mustafa picked up the hair clippers and proceeded to shave his hair. He stood staring at himself in the mirror for a long time, admiring what he had done. He ran a hand over his newly bald head, and it felt good. It suddenly occurred to him that he would never see another Sunday ever again. The door slammed upstairs. They were back from their daily morning run. Music blasted out from the radio; Diana Ross was singing about her old piano. Mustafa had decided it was time to test the Wheelers. Talking about and planning to commit mass murder was one thing, doing it was an entirely different entity. Mustafa walked upstairs past Carol Wheeler, unnoticed in the kitchen frying eggs, wearing only a yellow and blue apron. In the drawing room, Mustafa found Franklin Wheeler. He was sat motionless like a doll and holding an empty whiskey glass. A lifeless stare into the abyss. On his lap was some kind of diary. What he needs is a boost, Mustafa thought.

'You need to go on a shopping trip.' Franklin turned his head and looked up at Mustafa, who was holding a piece of paper in his hands.

'Wow, is that you?' Franklin gasped, coming back to life, slightly horrified at the new hair style, or lack of it, that Mustafa now had.

'You think it suits me?' Mustafa asked, running a hand over his bald head.

'It's… it's definitely different,' Franklin said, trying to sound positive, but his face had miserably failed to hide its dislike for what was in front of it.

Mustafa passed Franklin the piece of paper. 'Everything on that list is vital. I need it for the bomb. I suggest not buying them in the same store. Most are everyday items, but you can't buy them all together. Store people are trained now on what to look for.'

'I know.'

'And pay with cash if you can.'

'Of course,' Franklin said, studying the list. 'I'll be careful.'

'It's important,' Mustafa said, meeting his eye, then looking down at the empty whiskey glass.

'It's okay, it just takes the edge off,' Franklin said, holding the glass up. 'I'll go after breakfast.' And he put the list in his breast pocket.

After breakfast Franklin went bomb shopping. Mustafa and Carol, who was now dressed in grey sweatpants and a blue t-shirt, cleared a table in one of the upstairs bedrooms. A blown-up map of the killing zone was placed on the table, showing the church, Young Palms Fundamental Elementary school and the surrounding residential homes and roads.

'What's the plan, captain?' Carol asked excitedly, both hands leaning on the table, eyes wandering over the map, like some demonic flying dragon ready to breath down hell fire on a helpless population.

'We park up at 11:50, outside the Mercy Gospel Church. We wait for Mayor Jake Kellerman to enter the school, presumably through the front entrance. Once he's inside, you'll cut around the back of the school building — making your way down to the playground. Franklin and I will both enter through the front, splitting off once inside — going classroom to classroom.' .

'Lamb to lamb,' Carol jumped in. She was stroking her 12-gauge now and a shudder ran up Mustafa's back.

'How's Franklin with all this?' Mustafa asked.

Carol Wheeler rested her 12-gauge against one of the table legs and walked over to the window and looked out. 'It's a first for him, for both of us,' she said, gently, speaking with candour. 'You don't have to worry about my husband.' She turned to look at Mustafa. 'I'll keep him in check,' and for the first time, she sounded like a normal person. A regular Joe, who doesn't wake up on any given Sunday and plan to kill children. Mustafa saw the honesty in her face and thought how refreshing it was to see. 'Now. What's the plan?' she asked, walking her eyes back over to the map.

'Once inside Franklin will make his way to the main hall, located at the north end of the building,' Mustafa ran a finger from the entrance to the main hall. Carol imagined Franklin walking along the hallway, going from class to class until he hit the main hall, like some gallant knight. 'I'll take the bomb down to the basement, where the boiler room is located.'

'How long will we have before...'

'We will synchronise our watches for 12:15, so we will have plenty of time to get in position. We don't want to hang around long. Police response time should be less than ten minutes from the first shots being fired, less if there just happens to be a random cop car in the area. If I have to detonate the bomb before 12:15, so be it, but ideally, we want as few people escaping as possible. We want total annihilation.'

'What about the Mayor?' Carol asked.

'Try and kill him before we enter. He must die. You'll have roughly three minutes on us.'

'I'll save a shell for myself, if I'm still alive at the end,' Carol said.

'You won't need to. With the size of the bomb,' Mustafa laughed. 'It will probably take the church out as well,' he said, pointing to the St. Petersburg Mercy Gospel Church on the map.

'Boom,' Carol said, pulling her hands apart.

'We've agreed to make a tape so they know why we've done what we've done,' Carol said, and then hesitating for a second. 'Would you like...'

'Would I like to make a tape? No. It will probably anger them even more, if they don't know my motives.'

'Do you know about our children?' Carol asked, smiling at him, tears starting to fill in her eyes.

'Yes. Yes. I Do. Samuel told me.' Mustafa walked around the table of death and gave Carol Wheeler a hug and then he kissed her on the forehead. He had not kissed another woman since he last kissed his wife. She felt smaller than she looked in his arms. He thought if he squeezed too hard, she would break like some fragile porcelain.

'Pastor Jesse Jacobs says God tests us every day. We are made to feel pain, and God will give us the grace to bear pain.' Snot and tears were running down Carol Wheeler's face now as she spoke, still hugging tightly to Mustafa, face squashed against his chest. 'In Corinthians, Paul said. "And he said to me, my grace is sufficient for you, for power is perfected in weakness." God let his own son die on the cross for our sins. And he tested Abraham with Issac, so he could know how that felt.' She let go of Mustafa, pushing away from him slightly, looking into his eyes. 'Pastor Jesse Jacobs says pride is the worst sin of all. For that, I am guilty. I was so, so, so proud of my babies. I loved my little girl and m, m, my boy was so, so perfect.' She screamed from deep down in her stomach and fell to the floor sobbing, spitting snot. Her pain was immeasurable.

Mustafa knelt down beside her, stroking her hair. 'I followed God all my life. For me, God was the sunrise and sunset. Now I want God to see what he has created. He let the Israelis kill my family. He let the Americans finance and protect them. If killing children is okay,' he clenched a fist and raised it, looking up, as if to speak to God, his nemesis — 'then just wait until Wednesday.'

# 21

ST Pete Beach, ST. Petersburg, Florida 12:10

All told, Franklin Wheeler visited five stores and a Thai massage parlour in the St. Petersburg area that morning after breakfast. Whilst lying face down on the floor in Nin's Lotus House massage parlour, having Nin herself press her knees and forearms into the pressure points on his back and bending him into slightly uncomfortable yoga positions, he began to wonder what would come next — if anything. Is there a heaven? Is there a hell? If there was, he would certainly be going to hell. Killing children would be a one-way ticket straight to the cold depths of hell. Shit! Satan himself would probably pick him up. He would probably find himself rooming with Ted Bundy and Josef Mengele. Old Ted with his arm in a cast, asking girls by the lake for a little help, and Josef experimenting on a pair of twins. It's not too late, a voice spoke from deep inside him. A goodness buried somewhere. But it is. I'm in too deep. I have a terrorist in my basement and my Carol's better side of her nature has deserted her.

'You so tense' Nin said, pressing down on his back with her little palms. 'Relaaaax, relaaaax.'

And then there was the bomb list. The guy gave it to me, like it was a list for a fucking cake mixture, an everyday thing. Franklin took a deep breath in and then out heavily.

'Good, gooooddd,' Nin said, speaking softly, bending his legs up to his back now. I have enough pool sanitiser, in the boot of my car to start my own pool cleaning business. An ample amount of paint remover, nail polish remover and bleaching agent. Fuck. What would the cops say if they pulled me over? What would I say? Yes officer, I have a pool the size of Lake Michigan and about two hundred hookers working for me, who like their nails looking spot on. I'm doing some decorating, taking the paint of the wall of my palace. No. Sorry officer, I have a crazy terrorist in my basement and we're making a big fuck off bomb to kill elementary children, oh and the mayor, whom everybody seems to love. No worries, sir, you have a good day now and watch out when you're handling that ammonium nitrate — you could lose a hand with that stuff. Will do officer.

The ammonium nitrate was already taken care of. Fertilizer bought two months before off some dead-beat farmer, who needed the money in Georgia. The nitromethane was a bit more difficult to get hold of. Having to subscribe to Model Cars magazine monthly and then joining a club, had been a pain at first. But after a while, he quite liked taking the model racing cars out around the tracks with the other enthusiasts. It was all done for the fuel. Joining the model car club was a way of not drawing suspicion. It had worked and he had also quite enjoyed it.

Franklin sat in his Buick smoking a cigarette and listening to Joe Cocker tell him that he was so beautiful. He was a secret smoker. Carol knew nothing about it and at this point in time, probably wouldn't care. Cancer wasn't a worry now, nor was AIDS and every other incurable disease out there. Franklin looked lovingly at the cancer stick. The freedom one feels, when one has nothing to worry about, nothing to lose any more is unfathomable for the everyday man. The everyday man, the nine-to-fiver with the pretty wife, two kiddos, a loyal dog and mortgage. He now felt like God. Was he going to go through with it? I am he thought.

A mile from home Franklin stopped at a pedestrian crosswalk. An old woman, dressed in winter clothing, like she was anticipating snow on a hot day was walking a Labrador retriever, or more like old faithful was walking her, pulling her along. Two skateboarders raced across, both wearing baseball caps and backpacks. A weekend working desk jockey with a briefcase marched across with a sad dull robotic look on his fat face. The look of like at any minute on the long commute home from work, he may just decide to walk out in front of a bus, and those reports that needed — that had to be — on his boss's desk by tomorrow morning ASAP, wouldn't be getting there. Then, just as Phil Collins was asking for one more night, a gang of young Cubans wearing bandanas and jeans that needed pulling up, crossed, strutting along, bouncing from side to side. The gang glanced in at Franklin Wheeler with disdain. A cold sweat came on suddenly from nowhere. It wasn't him, but one of the gang brought everything crashing down, back home. His eyes, the way he grinned at him, the grin said fuck you man and your dead children. He was the spitting image of Juan Carlo. He was the reason for everything he had in his car boot and of the man living in his home. He wanted to put his foot down and mow the gang down. He watched the gang pass, walking along the opposite sidewalk and then a horn from behind and another and another. He drove on.

He pulled into the driveway of his home, the Wheeler's bomb factory. In the boot the pool sanitisers, the bleaching agents, the nail and paint removers he had purchased with cash. On the back seat the lab equipment he had purchased from Richardson's Chemists, with American Express. He had run out of cash by the time he got to Richardson's Chemists, and was too tired to look for an ATM. The young dyke at Richardson's, with her face full of metal piercings, had given him a peculiar look when he approached the counter with the trolley full of lab equipment. She even called her supervisor, Al over, giving Franklin a fuck-you smile, as she did. A tall man in his late fifties, easily surpassing six foot five and balding, with dark untrusting eyes looked up from the back room where he was putting prescriptions together. Alfredo, or Al as everyone called him, made his slow walk over to counter. Franklin thought the man looked like the trusted servant in a vampire film. The man who will do anything for his monster master, and who has fantastic strength.

'You making meth?' The young dyke asked, half joking, half not.

Franklin let out an absurd laugh. 'My daughter is a budding scientist and I promised her I'd get her some equipment to play around with. Supervised, I promise,' Franklin said, starting to feel the heat around his collar.

Al studied the trolley from behind the counter, then the man. 'Sorry sir. It's just procedure to do checks when buying lab equipment, that could be used in the manufacturing of drugs, or even bombs.'

Franklin chuckled and put a hand on his stomach, trying his best to look amused. 'That's funny.' To his relief, the young dyke also began to giggle at the idea of this well to do man making drugs and bombs.

Alfredo gave a slight grin. 'But you don't look like a man who needs money that bad or is that unhappy with his life.'

Boy are you in for a big surprise, Franklin thought,

laughing hard with them now.

'You say your daughter has an interest in chemistry?'

'You know kids, once they like something, they have to have all the equipment. I just hope we don't blow the house up.'

Al was nodding happily, 'How very refreshing. Kids these days just want to stay in and play video games. My hat off to you sir. Your daughter sounds like a great kid.'

'She is,' Franklin said. She was, he thought.

'Make sure she's careful.'

'I'll be watching her the whole time,' Franklin said.

'Wait a second,' Al said, he bent down under the counter and came up a few seconds later and produced a magazine. 'Science life,' he said, and handed Franklin the magazine. 'For your daughter. On the house.'

'Really? That's too good of you,' Franklin said, looking at the magazine. On the front cover was a mad chemist with white hair wearing white overalls making colourful, smoky concussions, next to him a table full of lab equipment.

'It's nothing. In that magazine you will find a few simple harmless experiments to try out.'

'Thank you, she will love this.'

'Have fun and be careful,' Alfredo said smiling, then turned and walked slowly back to the back room. The young dyke thought she had never seen her boss look happier in the two years she had worked at Richardson's. Two months later Alfredo Richardson closed the store and moved to Costa Rica with his wife.

'Cash or card?' the young dyke asked.

# 22

Sunday June 4th 2017

The Home of Carol and Franklin Wheeler, St. Pete Beach, St. Petersburg, Florida 15:00

By three in the afternoon Mustafa, Franklin and Carol had set up a makeshift laboratory in the garage. They had dusted off an old air hockey table that had only ever been used once, and that was on the same day it had been delivered. That was over two years ago now, and although Carol and Franklin had thoroughly enjoyed themselves, they soon forgot all about the game. It had a purpose now. On its blue top stood glassware, mixers, filters, distillers, funnels, open containers, stirring rods, a thermometer, a mask, nitrile gloves, two tripods, a set of scales and a stopwatch. At the foot of Mustafa's bed lay a brand-new bathtub and rigged up to the taps were two thin silicone tube pipes which had pressure release valves connected to them. The pipes ran from two separate buckets set high up on a little wooden coffee table. One of the buckets was an old champagne bucket that was once used in happier times. Behind the tub stood six bags of fertiliser and they were piled up on top of each other in two stacks. Behind the fertiliser, against the far wall, was a line of eleven bottles of bleach. A foot away from the bathtub stood a small, dented refrigerator. Packed inside the refrigerator were a few small bottles of diluted water and more importantly pool sanitiser, which contained the hydrogen peroxide. On the floor next to the refrigerator lay two plastic storage boxes. One held twelve 1 litre tins of paint remover, the other held thirteen 500ml bottles of nail polish remover — the key ingredient used for the acetone peroxide. Mix the acetone and hydrogen peroxide together correctly and with a bit of luck, you just might live to tell the tale and create TATP.

It's not that he didn't want the help, Mustafa would have loved a spare pair of hands, or two. Someone careful, someone focused, someone like Cadoc Elneny. Mustafa had liked Cadoc. He found in Cadoc a keen student, intelligent and a steady pair of hands. Mustafa didn't see the focus in either of the Wheelers, or much in the way of intelligence. There was no doubting Carol's enthusiasm, but she was too scatty. She couldn't be trusted in this volatile environment and then there was Franklin. He still didn't completely trust the man. He had to be tested before Wednesday, Mustafa thought to himself. No way can we allow him to have a burst of morality on the day and drive into oncoming traffic, killing them all. Even worse phone the FBI and have them storm the house the night before. Mustafa couldn't have that. Spending the rest of his life in some miserable, white wall padded cell, wearing an orange jump suit and being taken for walks wearing a dog collar. He hated the thought of being waterboarded. He had seen Walid use it. Waterboarding was Walid's favourite torture technique, he even used it on young men, still children really. No, Mustafa thought. He had seen too much. Too much already. He would sleep down in the garage basement until Wednesday. And if the police, or FBI happened to storm the house, maybe he would have enough time to detonate, or at least shoot himself in the head. Yes, from now on he would sleep with the Ruger under his pillow.

'Why don't you two go out for the evening? Spend some quality time together.' Mustafa said, looking first at Franklin and then Carol, making a genuine effort to sound caring. He was using the same gentle tone of voice he had used when he was a doctor, when giving bad news. That life seemed a million years ago now. He was a life saver then. Now he was a life taker.

Carol and Franklin looked at each other from opposite sides of the hockey table. They looked like two nervous teenagers at a school dance, like strangers on a train, catching one another's eye for the first time. Carol's initial disappointment at knowing Mustafa did not want to include her in the bomb making disappeared suddenly, when she caught her husband's eye. Franklin looked overly relieved at the chance to go out for the evening. Even more, she saw the softness in his eyes. His eyes, her son's eyes. She did love him.

'Well, if you are sure you won't need our help.' Carol said, frowning a little.

'The less cooks in this kitchen the better,' Mustafa declared, slapping a playful hand on top of one of the stacks of fertiliser. 'This stuff isn't kind to anyone. It can kill indiscriminately, regardless of how cautious you are.' he continued, grinning and showing off all his un-American yellowish teeth.

Franklin thought he had never seen a man try so hard to grin at that moment. You, my man, grin with the same grace of a toddler taking its first steps. Franklin had to bite his bottom lip to stop from laughing. 'I think we should go dancing, my dear,' Franklin said, holding his arms out to his wife.

Carol fluttered her eyelids playfully at her husband and waltzed over to him. She linked her arm in his and the two of them went skipping towards the stairs, as if it was the yellow brick road.

Mustafa sat upright on his bed, hands resting on his lap, somewhat relieved. Meditating. A man trying to find the calm before the storm. He looked around at the laboratory, then down at his hands. He knew they were good hands. They were surgeon's hands, and they once belonged to one of the best surgeons in Lebanon. I need you now. We shall do our best work, our masterpiece. He heard the shower running above him, distant laughter and singing. The radio was blasting out 80's hits, one after another. An hour later they were gone and there was silence. Mustafa Khoury stood up and set about beginning his masterpiece.

# 23

Sunday June 4th, 2017
My Little Friend Shooting Range, St. Petersburg, Florida
16:00

A rejuvenated Agent Anderson and an itching for action Malia Kimani riding shotgun drove slowly along the winding road that led to My Little Friend Shooting Range. Sally had fallen asleep around one in the morning, on a hard mattress in a cheap motel and when she awoke it was already midday. Sally cursed herself in disgust and disbelief that she had slept so long. The sleep marathon was overdue, much needed and slightly irresponsible. She had spent the previous night getting warrants and dealing with endless paperwork to get Chris and his small team set up. By the time she was done, Chris and his team had the authority to go anywhere in the St. Petersburg area and look back through any surveillance system they wished.

Sally and Malia had left Ron and Netzer with Chris's team, who were to contact her with any important developments. She had checked in with them about an hour before setting off for My Little Friend Shooting Range and the news then wasn't good. Chris had said that they had tracked the woman for about half a mile before and after she had left Geeks And Treats, then lost her after going into a flea market where there were no cameras.

The road seemed to go on forever, flanked by a high concrete white wall, and every fifty meters there were signs reading "SPEED LIMIT 5" followed by a "TRUMP PENCE" sign. Sally shuddered every time she saw "MAKE AMERICA GREAT AGAIN! 2016" under "TRUMP PENCE". You've won, can't you take down the fucking signs now, Sally screamed in her head. Sally loathed Trump. She voted for Hillary and was angry at her for not running a better campaign.

They parked up outside an old white building, that looked like it could do with a lick of paint. Old glory waved high above them. They got out and sat on the hood for a second and watched as the flag waved in the gentle breeze.

'If you want to sing The Star-Spangled Banner, don't let me stop you!' Malia said, looking at a row of never-ending trailers parked up behind them, then back up at the flag.

'My mother keeps telling me I sing like I'm deaf.'

Gun fire echoed, crackling in from the practice range. From one of the trailers came two small identical grey-haired women wearing matching tracksuits and white trainers, walking incredibly fast and carrying their gun bags. They both turned their heads to look at Malia as they approached the building, staring for longer than what would be called comfortable. They stopped at the flagpole, looked up, each put a hand to their chest and said a prayer. They walked up the steps to the old white crumbling building and before entering turned back once more to look at the ugly beast sitting on the hood of the car.

'Ain't they never seen a black woman before?' Malia asked smirking.

'We're in the belly of the beast now. This is Trump

country and don't you forget it, now get your cotton-picking ass off the hood of that automobile,' Sally said, trying her best to impersonate a southern plantation owner.

'Yes misses, I'll do what you says, just don't put me in the hot box again, I'll be good this time,' Malia said, playing along.

'You better, you black devil.'

They laughed all the way to the steps. 'You go in first, they'll probably shoot me if I go in first. Those evil twins are probably taking up position as we speak,' Malia said, eyes watering from the laughter.

The twins weren't waiting for them when they entered. Instead, a big friendly faced man, wearing a black baseball cap greeted them at the front desk. He leaned on the countertop, resting his hands. For a second Malia was hypnotised by the hands. She had never seen hands that size before, they looked like bunches of bananas. He caught her gaze and broke it, she looked up and smiled.

'You ladies here for a gun fitting with Fanny?'

'Not us,' Sally said, looking around the room, then smiling at the man.

'Then what's your pleasure, on this fine lazy Sunday afternoon?' the man asked.

Sally produced her FBI identification, while Malia looked at the photographs scattered around the walls of the room. The room was not what Malia had expected. To her surprise there were no guns anywhere. Four children were sat cross legged watching The Simpsons on a television in the far corner with the volume turned down low. A pretty teenage girl with auburn hair was sat back comfortably on a rocker, knitting something blue with a yarn ball on her lap. In the middle of the room two old men sat eating soup, whilst playing checkers. It was more a parlour — a social club, and not at all what she had expected — a room full of Americans and guns.

'Are you the manager?' Sally asked putting away her identification.

'I co-own this establishment, yes. Had it five years now,' he said proudly. 'Always happy to help law enforcement. What can I help you with?'

Sally produced two photographs taken from the security cameras at Geeks and Treats. 'Can you tell me, sir—'

'Please, call me Jules.'

'All right, Jules. I know these aren't great photos, but do you recognise the woman in them?' Sally placed the photos on the counter. 'We believe she lives in St. Petersburg area and is a member of the NRA club.'

He studied the photos for a moment, then with an almost look of defeatism, opened a draw and pulled out a pair of reading glasses. 'I hate to use these blasted things.' He looked up at Sally after a moment. 'Can't be hundred percent, but… I'm going to get Fanny over here. She's out on the range at the moment,' Jules spoke over the radio. 'Fanny, can you come give me a hand with something when you get the chance, please, darling.' Jules, went back to looking down at the photographs on the counter and then without looking up at Sally, he walked out from behind the counter and across the room to study a framed photograph hanging on the wall. Sally watched him closely from behind.

'These are from last year's shooting championships,' Jules said, turning to meet Sally's gaze. 'I think this is the woman in your photographs, but I can't be certain,' he said pointing at a photograph on the wall.

Sally walked over dreamily, heart beating fast. A beautiful woman smiled back at her holding a shotgun in her arms across her chest and an award in both hands. The woman wore a wedding band on her third finger, left hand and an NRA members ring on the third finger of her right hand. The hairs on the back of Sally's neck stood up on end as she looked at the ring and then back into those eyes. She had a joyful smile, but the eyes were sad and distant. And yes, she did look as American as apple pie. The engraving on the award read "2016 FLORIDA STATE FEMALE SHOTGUN CHAMPIONSHIPS, 1ST PLACE". And on a golden plaque at the bottom of the wooden frame read the name — "Caroline Joy Wheeler, My Little Friend Shooting Range, ST. Petersburg, Florida".

'What you call me over here for, you big brute?' Sally turned to see a large, heavy-set woman with a slight limp coming through the sliding doors at the other end of the room. 'I hope you're going easy on him today, Dennis,' she said, looking down at the two men playing checkers. 'If you kids get any closer to that television screen your eyes will go square.' She smiled at Malia as she limped on past.

'Fanny, this here is Agent Anderson with the FBI,' Jules said, whispering.

'Is this about that damn tax return, 'cause I swear...'

'No. No tax return,' Sally laughed. 'It's about the woman in this photograph.'

'Who? Carol?' Fanny said, resting her hands on her hips, hunched over slightly, looking at the photograph.

'Would you say the woman in this photograph is Carol?' Sally asked, pointing at the photographs taken from Geeks and Treats, that Jules held in his hand.

'It's not a great photograph, but I would say it's a decent likeness, yes.'

'When was the last time you saw Carol Wheeler?'

'Not for a few months. She just stopped coming round. People go through spells. It's a shame really because she is one hell of a shot — a natural if I ever saw one. Could shoot the wings off a bee.'

'How was her behaviour last time you saw her? Anything out of the norm?'

'I respect the law and all, but I really don't feel comfortable talking about a member without their knowledge,' Fanny said, raising a hand to her neck and pulling the skin around her throat nervously.

'I totally understand. We just want to cross her off our list of suspects.'

'What is it that she's suspected of doing then?' Fanny asked, feeling more uncomfortable now.

'I can't disclose that information, and I'll have to ask that you don't talk about our conversation either. It's a federal matter.'

Fanny sighed and rubbed her eyes. 'Her behaviour was normal, nothing out of the norm,' she said, flatly. 'This is absurd. I don't really know Carol and Franklin that well.'

'Franklin her husband?'

Fanny nodded. 'Quiet guy, bad shot, can't hit shit. The complete opposite of his wife.'

'Anything else you can tell us about them?'

'No. I think you got it all.'

Jules put a hand on Fanny's shoulder. 'They're just doing their job hun.'

'I know,' Fanny said, shaking her head, then looking at

Sally. 'I'm sorry, I just don't like being a tell-tit.'

'Totally understandable. Have you got the Wheeler's details on record?'

'I'll get them printed off for you,' Jules said, and walked back behind the front desk.

Sally looked at Malia who was sitting with the children and watching The Simpsons.

'I know it's something bad. They don't send you guys if it ain't. I hope it's just one big mistake, whatever it is,' Fanny said, frowning and then held out her hand for Sally to shake.

'So do I,' Sally said, and shook her hand.

'Here we go,' Jules said, handing Sally the details of the Wheeler's. 'Everything we have on them. I hope it helps.' Jules watched as Fanny limped on across the room and exited back through the sliding doors.

'Will she be all right?' Sally asked.

'Don't mind Fanny, Agent Anderson. The limp she has, it's cancer, sarcoma. It's gone way too far. She's a dead woman limping. I think she got on well with Carol.'

'I'm sorry.'

'Do we have a name for the face?' Malia asked, as they got back into the car.

'Sure do. Carol Wheeler.'

At a dusty roadside kiosk, they stopped to get some fresh donuts and coffee. Sally phoned headquarters and asked for all the information they had on a Carol and Franklin Wheeler.

# 24

They were sat close to each other, shoulder to shoulder. If you stood by the bar at the back of the room, looking out towards the band at the front, everyone seated in the middle of the dimly lit room seemed connected, as if they were one large group. But each party had their own small circular wooden cocktail table, and the tables were very old and on them people had carved initials and dates of long ago. Everything about Lester's was intimate, an experience, one heart beating.

'You have to feel it, not just hear it,' Franklin explained to his wife.

It was hot inside, and you could smell the mixture of sweat, perfume and booze lingering in the dusky air. Lester's from the outside looked derelict, apart from a small neon light, that shone down upon the lonesome bouncer. Scaffolding stood on the buildings adjacent to Lester's and it looked like the last place in the world you would expect to see a jazz club. Especially one frequented by rich yuppy types. It was a small room that you got to by descending a steep set of stairs in a dimly lit, narrow stairwell, with old pictures of Charles Mingus, John Coltrane, Miles Davis, Thelonious Monk and many more black and white faces, smiling from the wall on the way down. A long bar stood at the bottom of the stairwell — manned by two smartly dressed men, wearing bright yellow bowties, who were totally engrossed in the cocktails they were putting together for the yuppies. The yuppies sat looking up at the musicians on the stage, like they knew something about what was unfolding in front of them. The band was in full jam now, trying to make the magic happen. The pianist was keeping the harmony, dancing his long Hispanic fingers across the keys. The bass player was standing tall, playing simply — he looked totally alone on the packed stage and very sad to look at. Sweat ran down the face and covered the white shirt of the young drummer who appeared to have blood running from one of his hands — he was in a world of total concentration and playing great. The guitarist, who was more than slightly drunk, played just perfectly, never going on an ego trip. The ego trip was taken up by the saxophonist — a large black man, who began solos, never knowing when to stop them, long after peaking. Play loud or go home, that was the motto of the trumpet player — an old school, skinny black man, who hid his dope problem well. The style award went to the trombonist, who played angry and went home with a different woman each night — his daytime job was teaching 5th graders home economics.

No real talking had gone on inside Carmen's Italian restaurant. They both had pizza and Carol had drunk her own weight in shiraz. Franklin had wanted to express himself — tell her his feelings. He wanted to ask her if they were really going to go ahead with this. Carol had sensed her husband's desire to talk, but it was too late for talking now. Alcohol was her way of pushing him away. It always had been, ever since their children's deaths. So, they sat in silence and ate their pizzas and drank and got drunk. There was a miserable, silent tension in the air. The other couples dined and laughed and talked of fond memories from the past, the happy present and their hopes for the future. The Wheelers sat coldly, like two ghosts in a room full of life, not wanting to think of the past and having no future. Only the now counted for them and that was running out.

They had stumbled upon Lester's by chance, after leaving Carmen's. Franklin, who being a massive lover of jazz, had heard of the club before, but never actually been. Carol didn't decline when she saw his eyes light up with joy upon seeing Lester's. The taxi driver pulled up and they went inside. He reached across the table for his wife's hand in the darkness of the room, never taking his eyes of the band. He held her fingers softly, with no more strength than that of a newborn, rolling his forefinger and thumb over her hand. She looked at him with total love. Sorrow and joy were bouncing off the walls, leading the audience on a journey. She watched Franklin and wondered, where did this overwhelming feeling of tenderness come from for her husband. Jazz had done it. She had felt it. Music always had a way of evoking emotions in her. The Manhattan in her hand was also partly responsible. After an applause from the audience, that nearly reached the heights of an ovation, the band decided to take a break.

'You want to hightail it?' Franklin asked, still holding her hand.

'Sure thing.'

'Come on then,' Franklin stood up, necked his martini and then slammed the empty glass back down on the table with slightly more force than he had intended to, like a cowboy in one of those old western movies he liked so much. He took

Carol's coat from the back of her chair and held it open for his wife, who slid into it with ease.

As they were walking out a ruckus broke out at the bar, involving the band and the club owner — a little chubby man, with checked trousers and a tall slender black woman by his side.

'I don't pay you slackers to get drunk,' the owner said, hands on hips.

The band weren't paying much attention to the owner, who looked a lot like a shady car dealer.

'Calm down Jerry,' the drummer said, leaning on the bar, eyeing up some skirt at the other end.

'I don't know if I want you guys back on Tuesday. I might try this new band I've had my eye on,' he said, trying to impose himself.

'What's your deal Jerry?' the saxophonist asked, in a low cool cat voice.

'This here is Monique,' Jerry said, putting an arm around the waist of his female companion. 'She's a vocalist, she's gonna play with you guys next set.'

'You ain't right man,' the guitarists said, slightly slurring his words. 'We don't use vocalists.'

'You dead beat drunk. You'll play with who I tell you to play with. It's my way or the highway buddy.'

Monique sighed, pushed off Jerry's grip and marched back to the wardrobe, behind the stage.

'Hunny bun!' Jerry turned to chase after her then stopped and looked at the band members. 'She sings or you cowboys walk.'

The saxophonist nodded regretfully, and the other members necked their booze.

'Shit, we never play with a vocalist,' the drummer said.

'We do now,' the saxophonist said.

Outside the club, Franklin waved a red, newly polished taxi down. 'Where to?' the cabbie asked.

'Take us home,' Franklin said, settling back.

'Where's home?' the cabbie asked.

'Boca Ciega Drive, St Pete Beach,' Franklin answered, holding a hand over his eyes, hoping they still had some Pepto-Bismol left in the drug cabinet at home.

'Nice,' the cabbie remarked. Rich fuckers he thought.

'Actually driver, scarp that plan,' Carol said, leaning forward. 'Take us to a nice hotel, will you.'

Franklin broke his hand away from his eyes and looked at his wife with startled surprise. A bemused smile appeared on his face.

'Whatever you say lady,' the cabbie said.

The heavens had opened up and the windscreen wipers were working overtime as the taxi cruised through downtown. The downpour, which was sudden and harsh was over by the time they arrived at Zelda's.

'Best hotel I know of,' the cabbie said, looking back at them in the rear-view mirror. 'Most folks I know love it here,' he said, looking up at the symmetrically shaped Art Deco building.

'I love it,' Franklin declared, delighted to be spending the night in a hotel from his favourite era. 'What's the damage?'

'Twenty-two dollars.' The cabbie said, looking at the meter.

Franklin past over two twenties and got out quickly, walking around the taxi to open the door for his wife.

'Such a gentleman.' Carol said, as Franklin gave her his

hand.

'Hey buddy, your change?' the cabbie said, hoping the change was actually his tip.

'All yours. Have a good night,' Franklin said.

'I will now. Thanks.' The cabbie pulled off happily, with an eighteen-dollar tip in his pocket. Nice folks he thought. Too much money for their own good. Rich fuckers. A week later Sam Norris would tell a reporter, that that same couple he dropped off at Zelda's in his taxi had given him the creeps.

'It really came down didn't it,' Carol said, jumping over a little puddle. They walked up the steps to the grand impending hotel that was flanked by palm trees on either side. Rain droplets were running off the leaves, making a splish splash sound as they hit the floor. They entered through the revolving glass doors, under the neon lights of Zelda's and into the foyer. The gleaming marble floor they walked on, that had not changed since 1928, echoed with each footstep up to the high swirling golden ceiling and back down again. At the reception desk, a well-tailored man, who looked to be stuck in time; a time of the jazz age, greeted the Wheeler's with a warm impressive smile.

'Ghastly, isn't it!' The concierge said, looking past them towards the revolving glass doors and the night.

'It's stopped now. Better in here. I love the architecture,' Carol said, looking around at the grandness.

'Have you a reservation?' the concierge asked. He spoke with an upper-class British accent that went well with his look, or act.

'No. On a whim,' Carol said.

'Very good,' the concierge said. 'It appears the only room available is the Queens room, at $130.' The concierge was running his finger across the register that looked itself like it was from the 1920's with its French blue leather cover.

'We'll take it,' Carol said gaily. 'Franklin, pay up.' And she gave her husband a playful slap on the bum, that made Franklin feel good below.

They decided against walking up, even though they both admired the iron spindled staircase. They were both far too tipsy for climbing and Franklin hoped he was going to need all his energy for the bedroom. Better to walk down in the morning, he thought. The elevator looked like a time machine to the unknown, with its bronze floor dial above it. An antique from the time of Al Capone, bootlegging and depression era America. A half-naked strong man was standing next to a bull, with its horns pointed downwards, all in bronze on the doors which pulled apart and disappeared as the doors opened. Inside, Carol pressed the button for the fifth floor and mechanics started up. Something from below started clinking and clanking, above them the elevator began winding and pulling. It was cold inside and Carol wrapped her arms around her man. She was small up against him and he liked it this way. Her hair smelt sweet, and her breasts felt firm pressed against his body. The elevator hummed quietly as they rose and jolted them to a hasty stop on the fifth floor. The hallway was wide and well-lit with its wall lighting. It was dead quiet as well, with not a sound coming from any of the other rooms. To Carol it felt deserted and kind of eerie. Their room was at the far end of the corridor, and they walked harmoniously together towards it. Franklin took the key out of his jacket pocket and opened the door with one quick flick of the wrist and as the door opened Carol slid her hand down the front of his trousers and led him into the room.

'Are you with me?' Carol asked softly, standing naked in front of him, as he lay down on the bed, head sinking into the pillow.

'I'm always with you,' he replied, hypnotised by her beauty. He thought never had she looked so radiant, with her tight body and flushed face. She was breathing fast now, and her breasts moved slowly up and down. She moved towards him, climbing on to the bed and then on top of him.

'We have great work to do.' She moved her hands down from his chest to his stomach. 'Will you enter God's kingdom with me?'

'I will,' he screamed in exasperation, meeting her bewitching green eyes, as she moved up and down, up and down.

Franklin was alone in the room when he awoke, and a ray of sunshine was penetrating through the gap in the curtains. His head was spinning in the familiar way it did after too much alcohol. 'Carol?' He leaned up on his elbows and called out her name, thinking she might be in the shower. After no reply and without even considering where she might have gone, he passed out again. When Carol re-entered the room twenty minutes later, Franklin was chopping down trees in his sleep. She pulled open the curtains, exposing the rising Florida sun upon the room, the room that smelt horribly like last night's booze.

'Wake up sleepy head, we have to be out in an hour.'

Franklin let out a helpless groan from the pillow his face was planted on. A patch of dribble had formed on the pillow, and he wiped his mouth with the back of his hand as he pushed himself on to his side. 'Where have you been devil woman?' He asked, squinting, adjusting his eyes in the now bright room.

She had a plastic bag in one hand, with Wogan's Electronics printed on it. 'Drink this.' She passed him a bottle of Gatorade.

He struggled to open the sports drink, twisting it so hard his biceps were pumping. 'Why do they do these blasted things up so tightly?' When he finally got the lid off, a good portion of the green fluid had spilt on to the bed sheets and his hairy chest. He gulped down the Gatorade at speed, like a man who had just been found wandering hopelessly in the Sahara. Carol thought he looked like a baby, clinging on to his bottle. 'That's done the trick,' he said and wiped his chin, with the back of his hand. 'What's in the bag?'

Carol looked down at the bag and then back at Franklin, smiling. 'We're going to make a video, right here, right now. Then they will know why we did what we did.'

Franklin's head starting to ache now. It was Monday and in two days it would be Wednesday. The day of truth. In two days he would be dead and he would still have the remnants of this hangover when he went. He would leave this world feeling like shit.

'Record me first, then I will record you,' Carol said, taking out the video-recorder. 'The guy at the store already set it up for me.' Franklin sat up and Carol past him the video-recorder. He looked down at the recorder in his hands and a sudden urge to run and jump out the window with it and to his death overtook him, and then the urge dissolved away. Two minutes later he was dressed and pointing the video-recorder at his wife.

'Is it recording yet?'

Franklin's finger hovered over the red button for what seemed to him an age. He pressed it gently down and his heart sank. For him pressing record was like killing the first child. 'Now,' he said, pointing it at his wife.

Standing tall and expressionless, like someone frozen in time, she took one deep breath and began.

'A, you, you...' She had rehearsed what she would say in her head a thousand times, but now she was getting stage fright. 'I'm flustered all of a sudden, stop recording.'

'We don't have to do this now,' Franklin said, putting the recorder down onto the bed.

'Yes, we do!' There was anger and sadness in her voice. She put a hand to her head, as if to compose herself and then shook out her arms. 'Yes, we do,' she said, more softly now and smiled, trying to convince herself.

'When you're ready,' Franklin said, giving his trademark understanding smile, that Carol hated.

'I'm ready,' she announced, looking at the video-recorder and urging him to pick it up and record. 'Delete that last one will you.'

Franklin nodded. 'Ready.'

There was more determination in her now and she spoke like a mother wronged. 'My babies were murdered by an evil drug addicted, Cuban immigrant. A sodomite who fucked everything this country holds dear. His nigger defence team got him off on four years! Four years! Two for each of my babies.' A pause for a second and a quick look at her husband, who now had tears running down his cheeks. 'There was no justice for us. We were mocked by the law. Well, I have news for you.' She pointed at the camera. 'God doesn't take kindly to sinners. Hell waits for shit shifters like Juan Carlo and his nigger defence team.' Then raising her arms with clenched fists. 'God has shown me the light and I will spread his word.'

Now she pointed at the camera. 'Now you will see what it feels like to have injustice, to have your babies snatched away from you. Mothers of America, I say this to you. When justice closes its eyes and an eye for an eye is held away from you, make them listen.' She nodded at Franklin, and he stopped recording. He put down the recorder and embraced his wife, sniffling and sobbing.

'Your turn now,' she said patting him on the back.

'I think you've said it all,' he said, wiping the tears away.

'Go on now,' she said insisting and she picked up the video-recorder and pointed it at her husband.

Franklin stood in front of her, red eyed and dishevelled. 'You may think of us as cruel, but so much was taken away from us. Now we have taken away from you. I leave this world a monster, a monster the legal system created. Take heart in knowing that you had a hand to play in the devastation that we unleashed on your children. This is God's wrath for turning your back on his laws America.'

Carol stopped the recording. 'Bravo my love. Bravo.'

'Was that good?' Franklin asked.

'You reminded me of Gregory Peck just then.'

'Really?'

Carol took off her dress and laid down upon the bed. 'We still have forty minutes before check out.'

# 25

Monday June 5<sup>th</sup>, 2017
Gulf Beach Motel and Apartments, St. Pete Beach, ST. Petersburg, Florida 10:30

Netzer Akerman was lying on a sun lounger, legs crossed, looking up at the blue sky. The top buttons of his shirt were undone exposing his hairy chest to the sun. He had on a ten-dollar pair of sunglasses that he had purchased at the front desk of the motel. In one hand he held a cigarette that was slowly burning itself away over a glass ashtray that rested on his crutch. In the other hand he held a cornetto ice cream and was licking it methodically, excited to get to the end of the cone — the hard chocolate bit that Netzer loved the most. In the swimming pool an old lady was getting her morning laps in, with her sausage dog loyally following her up and down along the edge as she went.

In the corridor on the top floor of the Gulf Beach Motel and Apartments, Sally Anderson stood looking defeated, cursing a vending machine. She was having a hard time trying to get the blasted machine to take her dollar notes so she could get a coke.

They had set themselves up on the top floor and paid the motel manager for a week's stay for two rooms. Rooms 20 and 21 faced out on to Boca Ciega Drive, about one hundred and twenty meters up on the opposite side of the street from the Wheeler's home.

In room 21, Ron Yaffe was standing by the window, hidden behind partly drawn stained curtains, looking down Boca Ciega Drive with a pair of binoculars. In the four hours since they had arrived at the motel and begun the stakeout, he had only put the binoculars down once and that was to take a leak. Although he was focused on the task at hand, Ron had found his mind drifting. He found he was not so much thinking about the people who resided in 7325 Boca Ciega Drive and the trouble that may wait behind the doors. Instead, he was thinking about Rachel and what could have been. He had loved her — still loved her. He hadn't seen her in more than two years now. He was told she had had a child, a little girl. Like Rachel, her husband was a lawyer as well. Well, fuck he thought, didn't they say people in the same profession are more likely to fall in love, or to be together. She had loved him, he was certain of that, but it was the same old excuse. He was never home. She was patient at first and when she got tired of being patient, she became impatient and eventually his side of the bed, that had been lonely, began to get less lonely. He had caught her with their neighbour of all people — a CrossFit coach, a fucking CrossFit coach. He had even brought his fucking protein shake over and left it on the kitchen top, before going into the bedroom. She had wanted to be caught, so it could finally be over. She didn't care for Mr CrossFit, he was just there. Ron didn't kick up much fuss and that pissed her off even more. 'Aren't you even going to get mad, you finally fucking come home and find another man in your bed!' she had said.

That was Ron, never one for hasty decisions, step back,

carefully analyse, pick it apart, then strike. Netzer on the other hand was the complete opposite and that was just one of the reasons why, Ron liked him so much.

In the next room Malia Kimani and Chris Wallace were seated at a desk going through the Wheelers phone records and bank transactions. Chris Wallace hadn't been this happy in a long time, every time he pointed something out, Malia would lean across him and he would catch her scent and it would remind him of flowers on a spring morning.

'What's this one?' Malia said, pointing to a recent transaction at Richardson's chemists.

'$215 at a chemist's, not three miles from here. I think we should check this out,' Agent Chris Wallace said, turning to his new partner.

'What, now?'

'Why the hell not, this could be something?' Chris Wallace said meeting her eager gaze.

Chris and Malia came across a thirsty Sally Anderson down the corridor. She was leaning against the wall and looking at a vending machine with spite.

'We got something worth checking out,' Chris explained, showing Sally the American Express transaction at Richardson's chemists.

'Good work. Keep alert, we may need you back here if the shit hits the fan.'

As Malia and Chris hurried away down the flight of steps, Sally made her way back to the room. She knocked once and entered. She looked admiringly at Ron, who was watching out the window down the street at the Wheelers residence. She crashed out on the bed, staring up at the ceiling. 'Any movement?'

'None,' Ron replied, never taking his eyes away from the Wheeler's. 'What if I sneak over there tonight and take a quick look?' Ron suggested.

Sally sat up. 'This is as close as we get for now. We don't want a repeat of…'

'I know,' Ron interrupted. 'You're right.' They were both thinking of Cadoc Elneny now.

'Have a rest, I'll take over for a bit,' Sally said.

'I'll just grab a coffee and a smoke and come back,' Ron said, handing over the binoculars.

'Have a nap. I'll wake you if we get anything. We have a unit less than a mile away, ready to ramble when we give the word. We got it covered,' Sally said reassuringly.

Just as Ron was about to open the door, Netzer burst through. 'Fucking little shit fuck, low body, long-eared fudge nudger.'

'What's wrong partner?'

'Dog bit me. I only went over to stroke it and the fucking mutt bit me.' Netzer pointed at his calf.

'You mean that little friendly dog down by the pool?' Ron asked.

'Not so friendly, I tell you man. If I had a gun.'

'That's not even a bite, it's more of a scratch, there's not even any blood,' Sally said.

'Ron, have I had my rabies injections?' Netzer asked, looking to his wingman for reassurance.

'How do I know?' Ron replied.

'I think I should maybe go to hospital. What you think?' Netzer said, looking down at the scratch on his calf.

'You'll be fine, you've had the same jabs as me and I'm pretty sure last year we had a bunch of rabies shots.'

'Yeah?' Netzer asked doubtfully.

'And this ain't India,' Ron added.

'Is he always this much of a drama queen?' Sally asked.

'Drama queen, drama queen! I've seen this kind of shit before, give it two weeks and this scratch that you call it will have infected my nervous system. Then lady FBI agent, I will fall into a coma, and wake up an idiot.'

'I think that ships sailed already,' Sally said, laughing and then turning to look out the window with the binoculars.

'Netzer!' Ron said, more seriously now. 'Go downstairs and see if they have any antiseptic cream for that scratch.'

Netzer stood up, with a hurt look on his face and was about to say something, but resisted, realising sympathy didn't exist for him in this room and hobbled away, slamming the door behind him.

'How do you put up with him?' Sally asked.

Ron pulled a cigarette out of a pack of Camels and put it behind his ear. 'This. What we do, is all he knows. I believe after a time you can become fragile.'

'You mean to say he is coming unstuck,' Sally said, with an almost frightened expression on her face.

'No, not exactly. Just having a midlife crisis,' Ron said, seeming unsure himself and putting no importance on it.

'Same thing. Can we count on him?'

'Netzer? Always!' Ron turned, picking up the files on Mustafa Khoury and Carol and Franklin Wheeler, opened the door and left the room to smoke his cigarette and read the files again.

The woman and the dog that bit his partner were nowhere to be seen. Ron sat down on a plastic chair by the pool and lit his Camel. Gavish had sent a detailed file on Mustafa Khoury.

It had his birthplace, age, parents and sibling's names and occupations, his impressive army records, with honours. His enrolment as a medical student in Beirut and then his fantastic reputation as a young and respected doctor and surgeon. Ron read through the file, not for the first time with real admiration. It seemed whatever this man put his mind to he could pull off. Attached to the file was a photograph of Mustafa Khoury with his wife and their two young daughters. In the photograph they were seated at a picnic table by the sea and looking very happy. Looking at the photograph of Mustafa Khoury and his deceased family, made Ron feel sorrow for the man. Sorrow for the man who had once been so kind and now could kill so indiscriminately and with skill when he needed, or wanted to, as in the case of his old friend Adar. The face of the man sitting at the picnic table by the sea with his family, kissing one of the children on the cheek and that of the man in the recent passport photo with the cold eyes, was so very different, yet it was the same person. Gavish had left a side note that read. "Bomb that killed his family was one of our own." Ron put the photograph he was holding of Mustafa Khoury back into the file and then closed it. He tapped at the file of the Wheelers and then decided to go through it once more. Five minutes later he closed their file and lit a new Camel. Ron watched as Netzer strolled on over, smiling and not hobbling any more.

'You look happy,' Ron said. 'You kill that dog, or something?'

'Forget the dog man. That's yesterday's news. You remember that hot blonde piece behind the reception from this morning?'

Ron had remembered seeing a chubby blonde with a lazy eye when they checked in. He hadn't thought of her as being very attractive, but Netzer had always liked his women big. 'I think so.'

'She cleaned my wound up, then asked me out afterwards. Wants me to take her dancing tomorrow night.'

'You can't, we're working.' Ron said, laughing.

'I know, but hopefully this will be wrapped up by tomorrow night and the bad guys will be dead and I will get to go home with the girl,' Netzer said, jokingly.

'Like James Bond.'

'Yes, like James Bond. She thought I sounded Italian.'

'Really?'

'What's troubling you anyway?' Netzer asked, slapping his friend on the arm.

'If you mix grief and injustice together you can create revenge and that's what we have here with the Wheelers and Mustafa Khoury,' Ron said pointing at the files on the table. 'Something is coming and it's going to be soon. I can feel it.'

'Hey good buddy, I wouldn't want to live any other way. We don't do the everyday shit; we live seconds from death.'

Ron nodded at his old friend and smiled, then they both began to laugh.

Two minutes later Malia and Chris Wallace came over to them, walking fast. 'We got news, come upstairs now,' Malia said.

Sally Anderson looked at the list of items purchased at Richardson's chemists with delight and dread. 'Wow. That's a lot of cake mixing equipment,' she said, softly.

'That seals it, it's them,' Chris said, picking up the binoculars to look out the window.

'The girl who worked in Richardson's chemists said Mr Wheeler bought the equipment for his daughter who's a budding scientist, or something like that,' Malia recalled.

'Has anybody seen them yet?' Chris asked.

'There is a car on the drive and the blinds are pulled, but there has been no movement as of yet,' Sally said, worryingly. Worried that they might be watching an empty home, whilst there is a massacre happening somewhere else. And suddenly her stomach tightened.

And like magic, they had been given an answer. 'Oh guys, we have that movement we wanted,' Chris said, looking down the street, with the binoculars.

Sally snatched the binoculars from his hands, as the gang all rushed towards the window to look down the street where there was a taxi parked up outside 7325 Boca Ciega Drive.

# 26

Monday June 5<sup>th</sup>, 2017
The Home of Carol and Franklin Wheeler, ST Pete Beach, ST. Petersburg, Florida 12:18

Carol and Franklin Wheeler didn't feel the many eyes watching them from the motel up the road, as they got out the taxi and walked slowly up the drive to their home, climbing the four steps to the front porch. Carol was about to knock on her own front door, when Franklin opened the door with his key.

'Do you think he will be mad?' Carol asked her husband, as they stood on the porch. She felt like a naughty teenager.

'Mad?'

'Yes. That we stayed out all night.'

Franklin looked at his wife, dumbfounded. 'You kidding? No. It's our fucking home and we are not fucking children,' Franklin said, then spat on one of the porch steps.

'I know, but we should have phoned to tell him.'

'He wouldn't have answered.'

'We could have left a message.'

'Coulda, woulda, shoulda.' And he kissed his wife on the head and then closed the door behind them.

Sally Anderson put the binoculars down to her chest, like a

general watching the field of battle and deciding where to move the troops and how to attack.

'Mustafa Khoury is in that house,' Ron said. 'We all saw her raise her arm to knock on the door.'

'What now?' Malia asked, looking at a deep-thinking Sally Anderson.

'All the players are in that house and whatever happens we can't let them leave. Storming the place is out of the question. Boca Ciega Drive is one of the most prime real estates in Florida, so chancing another fuck up is out of the question. We have to be ready for them. The minute they walk out that door together we will be ready for them. This will be our stand' Sally said, pointing down to the street.

'Our Alamo,' Netzer said.

'Remember the Alamo, that didn't end well,' Ron added.

'It depends which side you were on señor,' Netzer said, attempting his best Mexican accent.

'The next time the three of them leave that house together they will get the surprise of a lifetime,' Sally added.

Chris, who had left the room when the taxi pulled away, came back in. 'We've stopped the taxi a couple blocks away, got a unit with the driver now. Do you want to talk to him yourself?'

'You betcha,' Sally said.

'Mustafa?' Franklin called out, walking down the stairs slowly, feeling like a stranger in his own home. His head was cocked to one side as he descended the stairs, nervously like a first-time burglar. He wanted to get a glance of the man who was now living in his basement, before he reached the bottom. 'You down here pal?' It was quiet, dead quiet and it gave

Franklin the creeps. He wanted out, wanted to be anywhere but down here with this guy. God, he gives me the willies, a term his mother always used to say. Planting both feet on the concrete floor of the basement seemed like stepping into hell, and a cold sweat had begun on Franklin's forehead, as he surveyed the room. Mustafa had enclosed the makeshift lab with heavy duty stretch wrap from floor to ceiling, using adhesive tape to hold it together. He must have found the nail gun, Franklin thought looking up to where the warp was nailed to the ceiling. One of the tube lighting fixtures on the ceiling was flickering rapidly and there was a smell, yes definitely a smelly odour, even with his nasal congestion problems Franklin could smell a sour-ish, fruity smell in the air. He thought the smell must be great for his nose to pick it up. Franklin pulled the adhesive tape apart and slid between two sheets of wrap, entering Mustafa's laboratory. Inside the enclosed space the unique smell was even greater, and Franklin had to stop himself from gagging. Sitting before him on the bed was Mustafa, naked apart from a tight white pair of briefs, or butt-huggers, as Carol would call them. He had on a chemical mask around his face that made him look like Bane from the Batman comics. Beside Mustafa, on the bed, was Carol's Glock G19 9mm handgun, with his hand rested just behind it.

'Mustafa, are you okay?' Franklin asked squinting, his eyes beginning to sting now from the chemical smell in the enclosed laboratory. He was looking at the sickly pale complexion of the naturally dark-skinned man before him. This man has suffered greatly, Franklin thought, not able to take his watering, stinging eyes away from the deep winding scars on Mustafa's legs and torso. A picture of Frankenstein's monster popped into his mind and a childhood memory of waking in terror and crying out for his mother after watching an old black and white monster movie.

'Is it Monday?' Mustafa asked, sounding muffled and far away under the mask, then realising this himself and pulling it off.

'Monday. Yes,' Franklin confirmed. My God, he doesn't even know we've been gone all night. 'Come and eat something, you must be starved?'

Paying no attention to this, Mustafa walked over to the fridge and knelt down and opened the door. The light of the fridge glowed before them. 'Look, come see,' Mustafa gestured for Franklin to kneel beside him. Tentatively Franklin did and before them on a shelve was a baking tin, lined with Paraffin waxed paper and on top of the paper was the crystallised explosive, glittering beautifully, thousands of them. 'This is my best work,' Mustafa said proudly, then let out a nasty cough from the back of his throat.

'Come on, best go upstairs and eat, the air down here is killing us,' Franklin said.

'The smell does take some getting used to,' Mustafa agreed, chuckling to himself. He closed the fridge door and then stood up. 'Another three hours and we can take them out of the fridge,' Mustafa said, as they climbed the stairs.

'Wonderful,' Franklin said, with just a slight hint of sarcasm that didn't go unnoticed to Mustafa.

'Wonderful, yes,' Mustafa said, following behind him, wanting to tell him that he had read his little diary and knew all the nicknames he had been given.

They were sat around the kitchen table, with the sunlight of the day shining upon them through the window. Carol was amazed and Franklin quietly impressed with the amount Mustafa was putting away at lunch. They hadn't seen him eat this much in the whole time he had been with them. Mustafa sank black coffee after black coffee and was polishing off his second plateful of eggs and hash browns, when Carol broke the silence. 'I see your work agrees with you?' Carol said, looking at Mustafa's plate.

'I was famished,' Mustafa said, happily.

'I bet the bomb-making business does that to you,' Franklin added.

'Speaking of that, I will need your help wiring up the detonator later. I have already filled the metal tube with liquid and paste. I just need help with linking the electric wire.' This was not true, he just wanted to test the man sitting at the table next to him, the man who had giving him the nicknames of The Mad Alchemist and Doctor Death.

'Certainly.'

'Franklin is a genius with electrics, he's even helped build a computer before,' Carol said.

'Long time ago,' Franklin said.

'Don't be modest. When he was younger, he was hanging around with some of the guys who started up Apple,' Carol said, putting her hand on Franklin's.

'But you decided on the porno business instead,' Mustafa said, clearly hitting a nerve with Franklin, because the look he was returned was not that of a friend.


'I picked them up at Zelda's. It's an old hotel downtown,' the cabbie explained, leaning against the trunk of the taxi. He had only been a taxi driver for three months and this was now the fifth occasion in that time that he had been pulled over by the police, but never like this before. There was no taillight out and he hadn't run a stop sign today, this was more serious, much more serious. These guys held high powered weapons, not handguns and not one of them was dressed in cop's blues. It made Jun-ho extremely nervous and he was already beginning to despise the taxi business and the long hours, with bad pay and the wife and her mother who were ignoring him when he came home after a long day. Jun-ho, who had never really enjoyed being married to his wife, partly because he had married two women that day, back in 1992. Recently he had started to believe that the two of them were plotting his death and he had got it in his mind that they were poisoning his food.

'Did you talk to them? Overhear anything that they said?' Agent Anderson asked, talking slowly and loudly, like sometimes ignorant people do when talking to people of a different race. Jun-ho was finding this out daily being a taxi driver. They didn't see a man who had lived in the country since he was five, only a yellow noodle eater. Passengers couldn't even insult him right, just last week he was called a stupid Jap. Another time he had picked up a group of drunk college kids and they had asked him about the ladyboys in his country. That time he had snapped back, saying he was Korean and had lived in America practically his whole life.

'No. I. Did. Not. Talk. To. Them,' Jun-ho said, slowly in the best broken English accent he could muster. 'And I didn't hear anything they said,' he added, sounding like any regular American-Joe.

Sally smiled, looking a little embarrassed. 'When you picked them up, were they alone?'

'They were. What's this about? I'm losing money talking to you.'

'I can't divulge into an ongoing police matter at this time. And I am sorry for stopping you, but I can assure you, it is of the upmost importance. So, if you would just bear with me a little longer, then you can be on your way,' Sally said sincerely.

'Okay, okay,' Jun-ho agreed, motioning with his hand for her to hurry up and ask her questions.

'Did you drive them straight here from Zelda's?'

'I did and I can tell you that that man is a good tipper, tipped me nearly the cost of the fair itself.'

'Anything else, can you tell me anything at all?'

Jun-ho looked at Agent Anderson, considering for a moment, he had noticed something. 'Well. I think they had just both been crying, because their eyes were red, and the lady kept cuddling up against the man and sniffling.'

'Okay. Do you know what was in the bag?'

'I do. It was a video camera.'

'You sure?'

'Positive. She took it out to look at quickly, then put it away again. I saw it in the mirror. Yes. Definitely a video camera.'

'Did they mention another person?'

'No. You have everything.'

'Okay, okay, you can go.'


The antics from the previous night had finally caught up with Carol Wheeler and shortly after midday she crashed. She was passed out, snoring on the sofa, whilst the television played an old Sesame Street episode — Big Bird and Elmo were talking about emotions. Meanwhile, downstairs in the basement, Mustafa — The Mad Alchemist had Franklin Wheeler right where he wanted him.

'Finally, some man time,' Mustafa said, giving Franklin an awkward pat on the shoulder.

Franklin let out a nervous laugh. 'Yes, just us men.' Man time. Hell, Franklin thought, this crazy fuck doesn't know what that means. Other fellas might consider it a football game and a pack of nice cold brewskies.

Franklin was put to task. Kneeling on the floor, he drilled a small hole through the side of a lightweight steel container. Carol had purchased a set of them a few years back, with the intention of using them to keep food fresh when they went camping, but they never went camping and they never got used. The container measured twelve centimetres wide and six centimetres tall, perfect for a pot roast, or a bomb Franklin thought to himself, as he blew the metal shavings out from inside the container.

Mustafa was sat at a wooden table, with his back turned to Franklin. He was the picture of concentration. In front of him on the table, under the lamp light, was a small aluminium detonator tube that he had coated in silicone spray the night before. He was now placing the detonator carefully into a copper sleeve and sealing it with glue.

Franklin placed the container onto the bed and then walked up behind Mustafa, to see how he was getting on with the detonator.

'You good?' Franklin asked.

'All done here,' Mustafa replied, then yawned. He was tired and a little agitated. He knew it was a mistake to do this kind of business feeling tired.

'I bet you're wacked,' Franklin said, putting a hand on Mustafa's shoulder.

'We will have plenty of time for sleep soon enough,'

Mustafa said, standing up and stretching out his arms.

'What's next?' Franklin asked.

'The explosive is ready now. We have roughly eight hundred grams of Triacetone Triperoxide, that's just over a pound and a half,' Mustafa said, smugly. Proud of his own achievement.

'Is that a good amount?'

'It's a beautiful amount.'

Mustafa took the baking tin out from the fridge and placed it next to the steel container. The white crystals were glittering beautifully under the flickering tube lighting. Mustafa layered the steel container with paraffin wax paper, then gently poured out the TATP into the container. Franklin wondered how something so insignificant looking could be so deadly. Mustafa then produced a white and red coloured checkered kitchen towel from underneath the bed. The towel was rolled up and thick looking and when Mustafa unrolled it, Franklin gasped in horror.

'Is this necessary?'

'Not really. Not with the amount of explosive we have and detonating inside the school and all, but there is the off chance that I may have to detonate outside. Adding them just ups the casualty rate outside of the kill zone. And the kill zone will be great,' Mustafa declared, teasing his partner.

'Great,' Franklin said, sorrowfully, looking down as Mustafa rerolled the kitchen towel that was compacted with rusty nails and chunky nuts and bolts. He then placed the towel inside the container, lining it along the base in a circle, with the TATP in the middle.

Suddenly feeling his legs go light, Franklin sat down on the bed. Mustafa noticed this and started to whistle happily, as he went about connecting the twenty-dollar Yuasa 12-volt 2.1amp lead-acid battery to the electric wire. Then he placed the detonator into the container, resting the detonator on top of the crystallised explosive. Next, he pulled the electrical wire that connected the battery through the hole in the container that Franklin, his now emotionally wrecked assistant, had made with the drill. Once through the hole, the wire was then connected to the detonator. Afterwards Mustafa stood over the container for a minute, looking down, admiring his work, then he clamped the steel lid back down on top of the container.

'Job done. We've done it,' Mustafa said, holding the battery in his hand. 'If we flick down on this little black switch now, we would take out the whole street. Crazy, isn't it? Here, hold it for a second,' Mustafa held out the battery to Franklin, 'I have to use the little boy's room.' Franklin looked up from his feet and took the device in his hands cautiously. 'Remember don't flick that switch, unless you want to kill us,' Mustafa said tempting his man.

He's baiting me, Franklin thought, testing me. Franklin looked at the switch. I could save the children and blow us up instead, maybe take a few neighbours with us, but nothing as bad as the children. He imagined hearing the click of the switch. Would I feel anything? Maybe a brief burst of heat and a breeze, a great flash of blue.

Franklin was still staring at the device, when Mustafa came back, pulling down part of the wrap from the ceiling, as he entered the makeshift laboratory. He was holding Franklin's diary in one hand. Franklin's mouth dropped open when he saw his most personal secrets in all the world, in the hands of a man he saw as a monster. He's read it, Franklin thought. Franklin knew. A sinking feeling rushed over him, his body seeming to tighten up.

Mustafa was smiling down at him and waving the diary in the air. The monster opened the diary up on a pre-marked page, like a man who knew every word, on every page of what he was about to read. He held the diary close to his face, as he read. This reminded Franklin of a poetry reading he had attended once, many years back, with Carol and another couple that they had been friends with at the time. He had been forced to sit through nearly three hours of utter garbage, listening to pseudo-intellectual's ramble on, one after another.

'I particularly like the part where you refer to me as Doctor Death,' Mustafa said. 'Doctor Death lives in my basement. The man is broken and has hardly any apathy. His only concern is for the kill. He is haunted by the past, like the vampire. I know he will not be satisfied until everyone around him is dead. He haunts my dreams.'

Franklin tried to speak, but the words failed him. He could only muster something incoherent. 'Bu-bu-bu-bu—'

Mustafa raised a finger to stop Franklin's mumbling. 'But we must continue, it's just getting good,' Mustafa said turning the page. 'I have followed my wife this far, but I truly don't know how much further I can follow her. What started out as fantasy, for me anyway, is now fast becoming something real. My wife, my love, she has become unhinged and is at a loss from reality. I too want the establishment to be punished, to suffer for what they've done to our little family, although I fear the course we are taking will only lead to our damnation. We've invited the devil into our home and now our backs are against the wall. It is near the end now and I will probably be following my wife into hell soon. God help me. Forgive me.' Mustafa closed the diary and put it down next to Franklin, who sat snivelling on the bed, with the device now resting on his lap. Mustafa took a step back and waited for a reaction. He wondered if Franklin would flick the switch and kill them, only that wouldn't happen, because Mustafa had not connected the wire to the detonator. Mustafa had considered killing Franklin, only that would bring about more problems. He would then probably have to kill Carol as well and that was no good. The mission didn't really need three people, three was a luxury. It could easily be done with two, but one person alone would bring a high risk of failure. No. This method was more affective. Break the man down, strip him of everything that's holding him back, then build him back up again. He had seen Walid use it many times on new recruits. Only Walid had weeks and months to do such a thing, Mustafa didn't even have forty-eight hours.

'I pr-pr-promise, you, ca-ca-can count on me,' Franklin cried, red faced, a huge snot bubble appearing from one of his nostrils. He stood up, laying the device gently down on the bed. 'Please don't mention this to Carol,' Franklin pleaded grabbing hold of Mustafa's wrists.

'Franklin?' A soft voice spoke from behind Mustafa. Standing at the bottom of the stairwell was his wife, in her pyjamas, arms held out for her husband.

Franklin let go of Mustafa's wrists and staggered over to his wife, like a mummy in a monster movie. 'How much did you hear?' Franklin asked, wiping his eyes with the sleeves of his shirt.

'Everything, my love.'

Franklin started to sob again.

Mustafa had woken Carol from her sleep. He had brought her to see this. To bear witness to Franklin's weakness.

'I'm with you. Til death do us part,' Franklin said, hugging his wife's small frame.

'I know. I always knew and now Mustafa knows. He just wanted to be sure,' Carol said, meeting Mustafa's gaze. She hated him for putting her husband through this.

'Let's get some rest. Tomorrow we will run through our plan one last time,' Mustafa said.

Carol and Franklin held each other as they ascended the stairs. Mustafa watched them with envy, they had lost everything, apart from each other. Mustafa laid down on the bed and closed his eyes.

At about the same time that Mustafa was reading out Franklin's most intimate feelings, Ron was putting on a pair of sneakers. Sneaking on to the Wheeler's property would be far too dangerous, but a jog along Boca Ciega Drive, past their home was not out the question.

Malia and Chris had just come back from Zelda's, where they had questioned the concierge, who had remarked on what a lovely couple the Wheeler's were. They went through security cameras and visited the Queen's room, where the Wheeler's had made love and a confession video. The trip to Zelda's had told them nothing about the Wheeler's.

'Just a couple acting like a couple do. Carol Wheeler went shopping in the morning for an hour and came back with a video camera. Apart from that, the only strange thing was the concierge's accent,' Malia said.

'What was with the accent?' Netzer asked.

'I think he was trying to sound British, but from like the colonial era,' Chris said.

'Go for a run around the block, once or twice before you go past their driveway,' Sally said.

'Like a method actor,' Netzer said.

'It's important you look like you've got a sweat on. You know, just in case they happen to see you from the window or something,' Sally stressed.

'I just want to do a quick flyby. See if there's a chemical smell coming from the property. Don't worry, I'll blend in.'

Netzer began to laugh. 'With those bowlegs. When was the last time you went running?'

'I'm still in excellent shape,' Ron said, opening the door.

Twenty minutes later they watched Ron running along Boca Ciega Drive, huffing and puffing and soaked in sweat.

'He looks like he's been dragged through a carwash,' Sally said.

'Looks like he's gonna have a coronary,' Chris said.

'I bet he regrets smoking now,' Malia added.

As he approached the Wheeler's property he slowed down, it wasn't possible to go any slower. Going no faster than a fast walk Ron glanced quickly in at the home, huffing and puffing in agony, trying to regain his breath and then carried on suffering along the sidewalk. Fifteen minutes later there was a knock at the door and a man who now resembled a drowned rat and went by the name of Ron Yaffe stepped, or rather fell into the room.

'Someone loves his job,' Netzer said, slapping Ron on the back.

'Wat-wat-water,' Ron said, huffing and puffing, eyes red, hands, on knees.

'I thought you Mossad boys were meant to be as fit as lions,' Chris said, passing Ron a bottle of Evian.

'Not these guys,' Malia said. 'These guys snuck in the backdoor.'

'Anything?' Sally asked.

Ron gulped down a mouthful of water and then caught his breath. 'It may have been my senses fucking with me, but I'm sure I got a faint whiff of a bleach like smell coming from that garage.'

'You hear anything?' Sally asked.

'Nothing. But there is a light on in the garage.'

'That's good. We have them right where we want them,' Sally said. 'Go get showered up.'

'I'll order pizza,' Chris said.

'Could we get sushi instead?' Malia asked. 'I'm sick of pizza.'

'Definitely. I love sushi,' Chris said. He hated sushi.

'So. What now boss, we just sit back, wait and watch?' Netzer asked.

'Exactly,' Sally Anderson said, pointing at the map on the wall. 'We have them covered in every direction. We have a unit four blocks away at the Community Centre and another waiting at Egan Park. These guys are crack shots, they don't mess about. The next time the Wheeler's and their special guest come out of that house, we'll be ready and waiting for them.'

'Simple,' Chris added, picking up the phone to order sushi.

Netzer smiled. 'This is normally around the time the ground starts to fall out from underneath your feet.'

'Have some faith Mr Akerman,' Sally said.

Netzer took his cigarettes and lighter from the table and walked towards the door. 'Faith is for small children and the deluded in mind.' He closed the door and went down the corridor, whistling Spanish Harlem.

# 27

Tuesday June 6th, 2017
The Home of Carol and Franklin Wheeler, St. Pete Beach, St. Petersburg, Florida 13:56

Heavy rain wasn't forecast, but in the night, whilst the residents of Boca Ciega Drive slept safely in their beds, it came. By the afternoon the storm drains were struggling to cope, and Boca Ciega Drive began to resemble a small river and the cars that past slowly along the road made small waves, that hit the sidewalk. Franklin was sat out on the back porch, drinking a cappuccino and looking out at the rain lash down on the bay. He watched the many boats on the bay, bob up and down. Looking at his own boat, he wished he had taken the old girl out more. Grey clouds were making way for greyer clouds and behind them darker ones were looming. The heavy rain had cancelled out his morning run and instead he had had to listen to Mustafa go over repeatedly tomorrow's game plan, play by play, like his old college football coach, Mr Shelly. I wonder if that old grisly bastard is still alive, I doubt it, he thought.

Laughter came from inside the kitchen, where Carol and Mustafa were seated, cleaning their weapons of choice. Franklin took a sip of his cappuccino. That's about right, ladies and gents. You wouldn't want your victims to see that you're about to blow them away with an unpolished firearm. Whatever would they think. I'm going to have a T-bone steak tonight, Franklin decided, still looking out over the bay. Inside the radio came on, volume turned up high, pumping out Bowie, singing This Is Not America. Oh, but it is David, it is. Franklin stood, flung the remnants of his cappuccino out, aiming for the shrubs, missing the shrubs and soaking the wooden decking. Taking one last look at the boat, regretting again not taking her out more and not naming her. That's bad luck he thought, not naming a boat. 'I name you, Cleopatra,' he said aloud. 'Cleopatra, I hope you find a good home and an owner who appreciates you better than myself.'

On the radio Bowie had made way for Kool & The Gang. Kool & The Gang were singing about a girl named Joanna. Carol was reminiscing, telling Mustafa about the time she saw Kool & The Gang in concert with her then best friend, Wendy Daniels. Mustafa had tuned out. He was hearing her noise, without actually listening. Occasionally he would look up, nod and smile.

Carol gave Franklin a great smile when she saw her husband standing by the kitchen entrance. Her smile was false, he thought. She was gone now, broken, totally taken by the devil and in less than twenty-four hours, the devil will collect. 'What weapon you going with tomorrow, hun?'

He restrained himself from laughing at the absurdity of the relaxed manner, in which she asked the question, as if it was a matter of little importance and not really significant. The red, or white wine? How was your day at work? Same, same, oh Ted from next door said he was thinking about taking the family to Hawaii this year. I said we wouldn't be going on holiday this year. Told Ted we're thinking about staying home and massacring a bunch of infants, then spending eternity in hell. Franklin smiled 'I'll go with the Uzi.'

After a long hot soak in the bath and a few too many neat whiskeys, Franklin fell asleep on his lazy boy in his den. Carol spent most of that afternoon deciding what she was going to wear for the big day. 'Can you believe I use to be a size six,' she told Mustafa, twirling in front of him.

'I think you might find it hard to run in a cocktail dress,' he responded.

'Yes, quite right,' she said, looking in the mirror, 'I'll go with joggers and sneakers.'

'It's biblical out there,' Chris said, looking out the window on to Boca Ciega Drive, as the rain pelted down.

'When I was younger, I used to love sitting in my room being all cosy, watching the rain fall outside, listening to the pitter-patter on the window,' Sally said.

'I hate waiting for something to happen,' Malia added, pacing the room. 'What if they don't leave the house for a month? How long will we wait?'

'Right now, we have them right where we want them. They will leave soon enough; we just have to be patient,' Sally said.

'This one time, Ron, Adar, Gavish and I did a stakeout for almost three months... three months!' Netzer said, holding up three fingers.

'Prague, wasn't it?' Ron remembered. 'That place is a fucking KGB hot spot, spies everywhere.'

'The KGB doesn't exist any more,' Sally said.

'Haven't you heard; Putin has resurrected it.' Netzer said.

'It's just got a different name,' Ron added. 'And Prague is

full of KGB agents. They are everywhere you turn, maids, waiters and waitresses, taxi drivers, teachers, they are everywhere.'

'Even in the soup,' Netzer added, smiling.

'Don't,' Ron smiled, shamefully back at him. Silently between them they were recollecting the time they had poisoned a suspected female double agent's soup, with Ricinus Communis. Ron and Netzer watched across the restaurant from the bar where they were drinking cocktails, with two escorts they had picked up for the evening. Fifteen minutes after slipping the poison into the double agent's red beetroot soup, the young woman started to cough and sweat. Then, just as the waiter came to collect the starter the young woman straightened, bolting upright in her chair, like a clown in a Jack-in-a-box. She then made a desperate grab for her chest with her hands, eyes bulging upwards, realising she had been had. She let out one last squeal of life and then her death face fell forward, planting into her soup.

'Why Prague, why not Berlin, or France?' Chris asked.

'They are there too, but not like in Prague. In Prague, it is safer for them to exchange information, meet other spies, closer to home,' Netzer said.

'Who were you staking out in Prague?' Sally asked.

'Ibrahimović' Netzer said.

'Who?' Chris asked.

Ron slapped his knee and threw his head back laughing. 'Ibrahimović, good old Zlatan.'

'What's so funny?' Sally asked the two laughing men, who were sharing an inside joke.

'No, no,' Ron said, trying to compose himself, as Netzer slid off his chair laughing so hard he had turned the colour of beetroot. 'The guy. The guy we were watching looked like the footballer Zlatan Ibrahimović.'

'Looked like! No way, it was him, or a twin, he was a dead ringer, same nose, same hair, same height and the arrogance, everything. I'm telling you, if it was not Zlatan, it was his brother from another mother,' Netzer declared in delight, climbing back on to his chair.

'What happened to Zlatan?' Chris asked.

'Gavish killed him,' Netzer said, looking at Malia, who sat looking embarrassed. She did not like the way they were openly talking about past operations.

'Why?' Chris enquired.

'Forging travel documents for the bad guys, people we didn't want travelling freely,' Netzer said. 'Every other weekend he would leave the city and stay in his cottage and go carp fishing in Panský rybnik. A shitty little pond southeast of Prague. Once it was decided he was to go, Gavish was the obvious one to dispose of him.'

'Why Gavish?' Chris asked.

'Why? Because he was the best fisherman out of the four of us.'

'How did he do it?' Chris asked, excitedly, like a child hearing a spooky story sitting around the campfire.

'Aren't we the morbid enquirer,' Sally said, flashing a glance at Chris.

'He befriended him, asked him what he fly fishes with, general fishing shit, sharing stories of places they've fished. They talked for a good hour before Gavish garrotted the guy with fishing wire. Poor bastard was rummaging through his cool box for a sandwich, when Gavish went up behind him. I think that was the last time Gavish actually killed someone,'

Netzer said, thoughtfully. 'I remember Adar telling us later on that the guy's left eye had popped out and that he was still holding the sandwich clenched in his hand and there was a fish biting on the line.'

'Adar was there too?' Sally asked.

'A couple of minutes afterwards, when Gavish left, Adar went through the crime scene, erasing any evidence Gavish was there. That was Adar's specialty,' Netzer explained. 'You see, when you kill someone, the adrenaline is pumping through your body and you're not always thinking correctly. You touch things you wouldn't normally touch, you drop something, you leave something, you're more likely to just fuck up. That's where a clear mind comes in, it only takes a minute or two, but that guy will sort everything out.'

'That's fucking cold, man,' Chris said.

'Okay, that's enough chitchat,' Sally said, looking at Malia, who was not at all impressed with Netzer dropping names and dates of murders.


Franklin awoke, as the last hours of daylight were vanishing through the Parisian blinds. Making his way from the den to the kitchen, he smelt his T-bone steak that Carol had started cooking for him. I hope she's seasoned it the way I like, with lots of black pepper. He was starved and knew a juicy T-bone would hit the spot. He didn't hear the sizzle of the pan as he approached the kitchen, instead he heard Carol talking, sounding muffled, as if she had food in her mouth and the sound of knifes cutting on plates.

'There you are sleepyhead, we thought you would never get up,' Carol said.

Franklin was watching Mustafa tuck into his T-bone. The

T-bone steak looked perfectly cooked, red, rare and juicy. Franklin's mouth began to water, and he had to swallow before speaking. 'Why didn't you wake me? You could have woken me?'

'We tried,' Carol said, sounding a bit hurt. 'I sent Mustafa to wake you half an hour ago, but he said you were in a coma.'

Mustafa was nodding, with a mouthful of T-bone. 'A whiskey coma.'

Franklin looked from his wife to Mustafa, who was devouring his steak. 'You tried to wake me?' Franklin asked, in an I don't believe you way, you lying bastard.

'I tried. I really did, you weren't going to wake up, not without me slapping you awake,' Mustafa said, giving a chuckle. 'And I wouldn't want to do that.' He lied.

'We can't help that you got so drunk you passed out,' Carol said, sounding defensive now. She looked away from him and carried on cutting and chewing and swallowing her half of the T-bone that they were sharing.

Franklin watched Mustafa wash down his steak with coffee. 'What have I got to eat?' he asked, walking to the fridge and opening the door.

'I'll rustle you up some corned beef sandwiches and some eggs in a second, hun,' Carol said.

Franklin poured himself a coffee and sat down at the kitchen table. He wondered how many condemned prisoners on death row had requested a corned beef sandwich as their last meal, before being injected with poison, shot by firing squad, or sent to the electric chair. Burgers yes, fried chicken most definitely, steaks obviously, a shitty corned beef fucking sandwich, hell no. He knew damn well Mustafa never even made an effort to wake him. Heck he thought, I bet he doesn't even like steak.

After two corned beef sandwiches and a plateful of scrambled eggs, Mustafa ran through tomorrow's game plan (massacre) one last time. Franklin was to be the driver and they would arrive and park outside the St. Petersburg Mercy Gospel Church at around 11:50. Carol would set off first at 12:00, with her 12-gauge, cutting through the grassy knoll and jumping a small brick wall that separated the back of the school and the church. Franklin and Mustafa would set off three minutes later, walking around to the main entrance of the Young Palms Fundamental Elementary School. Once inside they would split up. Mustafa, armed with a Glock and a Ruger, would take the bomb down to the basement, where the boiler room is located and Franklin, armed with his Uzi, would make his way to the north end of the building, where the main hall/canteen is located. At 12:15 and only earlier if absolutely necessary, Mustafa would detonate the bomb and according to Mustafa, flatten the school and destroy a good portion of the nearby neighbourhood, and with a bit of luck, God willing, level the St. Petersburg Mercy Gospel Church.

Mustafa went to bed early and Franklin's advances towards his wife were brushed away. Carol, telling him that she felt a migraine coming and that she was going to run a hot bath and have a soak in the dark.

Franklin resigned to sitting in his den, drinking whiskey and listening to jazz, his old friends Coltrane, Davis and Monk, keeping him company. At around midnight he fell asleep. He woke up two hours later, still hungry and needing to piss, and saw that the storm outside had subsided.

# 28

Wednesday June 7<sup>th</sup>, 2017
Young Palms Fundamental Elementary School, St. Petersburg, Florida 06:45

Noah Templeton Jr. cherished his position as the janitor of Young Palms Fundamental Elementary School. A position the thirty-six-year-old, had held for the last seven years. Standing, holding his mop with the bucket at his feet, he looked proudly across the gleaming floor, that the sun was now kissing, through the windows of the main entrance. Today was a big day. The last day before the summer break. Some of the children would not be coming back next year and he would miss them. Today was also a big day because the mayor was coming to visit.

Originally from Dayton Ohio, "Birthplaces of aviation, hometown of the Wright Brothers" he would say, when someone new would ask him where he was from. Dayton Ohio where he spent a happy childhood, up until that fateful morning, when fourteen-year-old Noah woke up feeling different, something was very different indeed, on that beautiful summer morning. The birds on the maple tree outside his bedroom window sounded the same, singing blissfully in a new dawn. Likewise, so did the brown Volkswagen Beetle that his neighbour, Mr Hockstetter, drove and swore at and occasionally kicked in the mornings when the engine refused to start and the exhaust ticked over loud enough to wake the whole state. Listening to Mr Hockstetter berate and kick at that old relic brought endless amounts of laughter to Noah, his two brothers, sister and mother. But not this morning, because something felt different. His mother knocked on his bedroom door, as she always did in the mornings, holding a glass of milk for her special little man. He was the youngest and he suspected her favourite. 'He always gets away with everything.' His brother Mikey would say often, sounding frustrated. And it was true, he did. Typically, the youngest always does.

'Get up sleepy head, you got a whole new day of adventure ahead of you.' He loved the way his mother was always positive, greeting every day with a smile. He still misses that smile, her reassurance that everything happens for a reason and that God has a plan for all of us. Pancreatic cancer finally took her away from him in the spring of 2009.

'I can't mum,' Noah remembered saying, then suddenly breaking into a coughing fit, head pounding hard, eyes aching.

'What's wrong, darling?' she had asked, placing a hand on his head. 'My, you got yourself a temperature.' But it wasn't the temperature she was worried about at that moment. What she was more disturbed about was his left eye, that seemed to be blinking rapidly and performing its own kind of morse-code. 'What's with the blinking?' she had asked, looking worried.

'I can't stop it.'

An hour later he needed to pee. The bathroom was just down the hall, but it might as well have been on the moon. He swung his legs out of bed easily enough, but the muscles in his legs refused to work properly and he found himself falling to his knees. Some seconds later his mother, holding a family medical encyclopaedia in her hands entered his room.

'Noah, what is it?' she asked, looking down at him whilst he held on to his desk drawer.

'My legs, mum, they have cramp.'

With the help of his two elder brothers, they got Noah to his feet and to the toilet. As that sunny summer's day wore on, Noah's symptoms worsened. Although he was able to walk, he felt that he was not in total control of his movements. He seemed to be walking at times on tiptoe and making little jumps in the air and throwing his arms up. His mother phoned her best friend Thelma, whose ex-husband was a retired neurologist and asked her for advice and if he could maybe come over. Thelma phoned her ex, who still came over to her house every Thursday night for dinner and occasionally dessert, but not the kind you eat. Later that afternoon Fred, Thelma's ex, pulled up outside the Templeton residence on his Harley-Davidson. Noah had never met Fred before, but he had heard his mother and Thelma talk about him many times in the kitchen, whilst they smoked a packet of Lucky's between themselves and shared a bottle of red wine, or two.

'How ya doin kido?' Fred asked, holding out a hand to Noah, who was sitting nervously on the sofa, sweating from all the strain his muscles were under. Noah thought he looked more like a criminal, than a man of medicine. This was Fred, who one day five years before, at the age of fifty woke up one morning and decided he was done with work and family responsibilities. He grew a beard, swapped his suit and briefcase for some biker gear, purchased a pair of sunglasses and a Harley, left his wife, Thelma, giving her everything and set off on the open road for three years, before he finally ran out of money. These days he does odd jobs here and there and lives above a laundrette, underneath a comic store and next door to a dominatrix called Mistress Clara. He normally falls asleep to the sound of the whip against the skin and other sadomasochistic activities, where mostly middle-aged male professionals scream out safe words in agony or cry out pretending to be babies.

'I'm not sure how I'm doing,' Noah replied, shaking Fred's hand.

'Let's take a look at ya. Can I get you to stand up and walk over to the window and back?' Fred asked kneeling on the floor.

Noah stood up slowly, then jumped up on his tiptoes, as he did this his neck made a forward jerking movement and his mother thought he looked like a chicken when he did that. His mother put her hands to her mouth as he struggled across the room jumping uncontrollably, like he was being given little jolts of electricity, with a grimace on his face and his blinking it reminded her of morse-code. Fred noticed her pain and gave her a comforting smile. He also knew what was happening to the youngster he saw before him.

'Outstanding kido, you can take a seat now and rest, don't worry I won't get you to do that again,' Fred said, putting a hand on Noah's wrist and looking at him and his pale complexion and tired eyes from the strain and blinking. He will have to get used to that tired feeling, Fred thought, feeling sorry for the kid. Hopefully he doesn't develop the vocal tics and it's just the motor. It's the Tourette's that kills their soul and isolates them more than anything else.

'What's wro-wron-wrong with me?' Noah asked, tears

rolling down his face and then his mother had her arms around him, kissing his face.

'Nothing's wrong with you,' she cried, still kissing him. 'Is there?' she asked looking back over at Fred.

'Could I get a cup of coffee please, Mrs Templeton?' Fred asked, not really wanting a coffee.

They went into the kitchen and left Noah watching cartoons. 'How bad is it?'

'It's not life threatening, but if I'm right it's definitely life changing. Mrs Templeton, I want you to go see an old friend of mine to get a second opinion and'

'What's he got!?' she asked bluntly, cutting him off. There was anger and dread in her voice.

'Motor tics, maybe Tourette's as well, it's too early to say,' Fred said.

'Like those people who swear and shout uncontrollably?'

'Like I said, Mrs Templeton, it's way too early to jump to conclusions.'

'Call me Mae and it's not Mrs any more, my husband's been dead now twelve years,' she said, and lowered her head. 'He was fine yesterday.'

'Mae,' Fred spoke calmly. 'I'm going to phone my old friend, Dan Fraser. You won't find a better neurologist in the state of Ohio, heck this side of the Mississippi even.'

Mae was crying softly now, head down feeling defeated. Fred put his cup of coffee down and walked over to Mae and put his hands on her shoulders. 'Look at me.' Mae was shaking her head in disbelief at the floor. 'Everything is going to be okay.' Mae looked up, with that don't bullshit me look, I'm a single mother to four monsters. Then from the living room, where Noah was watching cartoons, they heard repetitive grunting and coughing.

'I haven't got that kind of money. Charles didn't exactly leave us with a fortune.' Her watery eyes moved over the ceiling.

Fred had noticed, when he had pulled up that the house was in need of a few repairs. 'Don't worry, Dan owes me a few thousand favours. And the dirt I've got on him would make the Nixon administration blush,' he said, hoping to make her laugh and it worked, she did, with eyes full of tears as well.

'How can this be!? He was fine yesterday,' she asked with clinched fits, then hitting them against her thighs.

'It can come on like this. I've seen it many times. Let me get in touch with Dan and get him to see Noah this week.'

'How much will it cost?'

'He will do this for free and I'll come by once a week to help with some useful techniques.'

'Thank you.'

'No problem.' And from the living room came more grunting and coughing.

Two days later Fred's diagnosis was confirmed by Dr Dan, as he liked to be called. A kind man with the whitest teeth Noah had ever seen. 'Technically we cannot diagnose Noah until he's had the symptoms for a year or more, but it's what he has. I don't always play by the rules,' Dr Dan had said.

'Will it go away?' Noah asked.

'No. I'm sorry son,' Dr Dan said, leaning back in his chair. 'It's important that you know that there is no cure, but it can be controlled, and we are advancing in medicine all the time.'

'What's brought this on, did I do something wrong?' Noah asked.

'No, you did nothing wrong, honey.' His mother reassured

him reaching out for his hand from the seat next to his.

Dr Dan laughed. 'You did nothing wrong. The simple truth is, we don't really know what causes it. With Tourette's we are a little in the unknown, but I have a belief that genes play a role. We're still finding out the science behind it. Lollipop?' Dr Dan asked, unscrewing the lid from a jar and taking one out for himself and popping it in his mouth.

So that was that, and just like that Noah's world was different. One day he was playing soccer with his friends, climbing trees and building bike ramps the next struggling with the basic motor functions, like peeing; managing to piss everywhere except the fucking toilet bowl. By his sixteenth birthday, his only real friend, if you could call him a friend was Fred, who came by twice a week to help with behavioural therapy and relaxation techniques and who stunk of bourbon and cigarettes. Most importantly, Fred was someone to talk to about grownup stuff, which he couldn't talk to about with his mother. Guy stuff. Girls mainly.

Fred felt for the kid and in a way had grown to love him. Even thought he had two children of his own, they had never really forgiven him for walking out on them, or riding out (on his Harley) to be more exact, all those years before. His ex-wife had sort of forgiven him, but even she was dating again now — a plastic surgeon named Andy, who had persuaded her in to having breast enlargements. Fred loathed fake tits and especially on her, they just didn't seem to fit the rest of her body. He also loathed Andy, whose own face looked like that of a porcelain doll because of one too many facelifts. He had only met Andy twice and even though he was pleasant and charming towards Fred, Fred loathed him. It was the way his children spoke fondly of Andy, and the way he put his arm around his ex-wife's waist when they talked, pulling her close to him. It was even the way the fucking cat, who always spat and clawed at Fred, rubbed up against Andy's legs and purred in affection at him. But mainly it was because Andy was balling his ex-wife in his old home, that was a palace compared to where he was living.

Fred had seen Noah deteriorate over the last two years and he knew relationships, with the opposite sex would be difficult for the kid. Also, Noah's complexion was not great, he looked pale and ashy and for a black kid, that isn't a good look. The tics had worsened and Fred had thought he had never seen a case this bad before. Noah had also developed OCD and a mild form of Tourette's, but that was probably because he was only sixteen and he hadn't learned all the bad vocabulary that there was out there in the world just yet. He did however pick things up quickly and his mother had told his brothers, who liked to swear, to be extra careful around him. One night, Noah over heard his brother Mikey on the phone telling Veronica Finney, a girl who was breaking up with him, that she was a "Clap Havin Jezebel." Noah then kept repeating this for weeks at the dinner table like a parrot and Mikey had got that look from his mother — the look that said you're not too old for a slap around the back of the head. To make things super awkward, Mikey and Veronica got back together and every time when Veronica would come over to the house, she would get called a "Clap Havin Jezebel" to the amusement of both his brothers and sister and the embarrassment of his mother and Veronica.

'Veronica Finney! You're a Clap Havin Jezebel! Jezebel! I'm sorry, I'm sorry! Veronica, I'm sorry! Jezebel!' After a while Veronica Finney stopped coming over to the house.

Noah had also developed some rather frightening habits

as a result of his tics. One of these involved pointing a sharp kitchen knife towards his own eyes, sometimes brushing the eyelid with the point. Seeing this action would always cause his mother to stumble back and flush a little.

'Don't worry! I won't do it!' Then pushing the knife closer to his own eyeball. 'I won't do it! I'm just joking! Don't be scared mum! Mum don't be scared! I love you!' Then lowering the knife, before raising it to his eye again and wincing at the same time, as if he was battling with another part of him, a part of him that wanted to kill him. 'Don't worry! Just joking!'

When this regular dance with death was completed, his mother always looked like she had aged a few more years. 'I need a cigarette,' she would say, reaching for her smokes and lightning up a Lucky with shaking hands. Her hair had started to turn white, a colour she secretly blamed on Noah.

But the behavioural therapy was working. Fred and Noah were making small steps together, using a technique called a competing response. For example, whenever Noah was sitting down and felt the urge to throw his arms up in the air, he would instead push his hands gently against his legs. Similarly, if he was standing up, he would fold his arms together. The key, Fred would say, was to delay the urge and break the compulsive ritual.

By the time Noah's eighteenth birthday rolled around he was already familiar with all the Tourette's drugs knocking about. Fred would joke and say he rattled when he jumped. His mother would say her cupboards had more medication in them than food and that her house was a junkie's dream. In truth none of the medication worked, or the ones that did gave out equally shit side-effects. It was years of trial and error, or just error.

Clonidine — a drug sometimes used to treat attention deficit hyperactivity disorder, was used to help ease Noah's anxiety and lower his blood pressure. And it worked. A little anyway. In a mad swap deal that would leave him feeling a little less anxious and in return he would get painful headaches that would last hours, diarrhoea, loss of appetite and insomnia.

Aripiprazole — an antipsychotic to help combat the severity and frequency of his tics, by altering the chemicals in the brain. This wonderful drug did help with the severity and frequency of Noah's tics, if by helping, you mean replace them with daily vomiting, constipation, an unbelievable hunger resulting in weight gain, drooling like a little idiot and nightmares. The nightmares were the worst. They seemed so very real and very unpleasant, and Noah started to dread sleeping. It was as if H.P. Lovecraft himself was the caretaker of his dreams.

These were just two examples in a long line of head fucks that nobody, no so-called expert, really had any idea about. The list was long, sometimes combining two medicines to try and counteract the others side effects — Haloperidol, Risperidone, Pimozide, Dopamine, Fluphenazine and many, many more. And the list of side effects was longer, much longer.

The best progress had been made working with Fred, who didn't much care for the medicines that were being thrown Noah's way. Fred had become a firm believer in natural medicines and a regular user himself of marijuana. Fred had seen first-hand the benefits marijuana had on people who had full blown AIDS, down at the support clinic he volunteered at every Thursday night. Del and Georgia McGee who ran the clinic and who themselves had lost a son to AIDS in 1985, promoted its use. Vitamins and marijuana was their motto. They had become sick to the teeth (Georgia's words) of seeing people deteriorate both physically and mentally before their very eyes. One day a young man named Ricky walked into their support clinic. Ricky looked a picture of health with a slight tummy and fat cheeks, which for a person with full blown AIDS was an unusual look. Also, he showed no sign of anxiety or depression, a common trait with people who had the disease and only a matter of time to live. The depression was the real kicker. Suicide also seemed to be a common trait when you had the disease and nothing to look forward to. And Ricky took no prescription drugs.

'How are you doing this?' Georgia asked, handing Ricky a coffee, when they were alone after everyone had left the support clinic.

'Canadian Marvel,' he said, smiling at her, sipping his coffee and taking a biscuit from the snack table.

'What's that?'

'Marijuana, weed, pot, Mary Jane. I have a guy who gets me the best stuff from Canada.'

'Are you saying you look this good because of' — Georgia whispered, — 'weed.'

'Yes,' Ricky whispered back.

'Really?' Georgia said, sounding dumbstruck.

Ricky nodded. 'I still suffer, but not like I was before I started smoking pot. I'm going to die soon, that's a given, the clock don't stop, won't stop. But I'm going to go out my way, not wasting away, looking like a skeleton with flappy skin and inward sinking eyes.'

Georgia suddenly remembered her own son and sitting by his bed in New York's Mount Sinai hospital and holding his hand when he died on the hospital bed in the summer of 1985. She remembered what he looked like and how she didn't recognise the feeble skeleton with the black eyes laying on the bed. She remembered his suffering, him telling her before he died, "mum, I don't want to die", and crying little tears. She remembered the nurse saying sorry and marking down the time of death. She remembered the drive back to Ohio and how powerless she felt.

'Let's do it,' Del replied instantly, when Georgia suggested they could try giving out marijuana to the people who came into the clinic, who had AIDS.

At first, the majority of people who came to the clinic were sceptical about taking marijuana. It was, after all, illegal and in a way disapproved of with Ohio being a mainly Republican state and all. However, a handful of people did decide to start taking it. The improvements were remarkable, even after just one month. Patients reported improvements in mood, reduced anxiety, chronic pain relief and weight gain. Within two months everyone who came into the clinic was taking marijuana. After a year the suicide rate of people suffering from AIDS had declined to more than seventy percent on previous years. Every month, Del and Fred disguised as two Catholic priests would cross the border into Canada, and smuggle back as much of the stuff, as they could, in Del's camper van. It was risky, but as Del always used to say, Catholic priests are untouchable and that they could have ten children tied up naked in the back of the camper and no one would butt an eyelid. And it worked.

Mae's face dropped when Fred suggested Noah start smoking marijuana as a form of medicine.

'Have you lost your mind!?'

'Face it, Mae, nothing is working.'

'The relaxation therapy is?' Mae said, already looking defeated.

'It helps,' Fred agreed. 'And I believe the marijuana can help him so much more.'

The habit reversal techniques, the weekly massages, the deep breathing techniques, had all calmed the tics down a little. Noah was at his best, feeling calm and relaxed when listening to soft rock bands like Chicago, 10cc and The Eagles. Baseball and basketball also had a calming influence on him and although he would still tic whilst watching the Cleveland Indians and Cleveland Cavaliers play on television, it was far less frequent. Fred, Mae and Noah even went to an Indians game, but the car journey and Noah's Tourette's was a big strain on him, and he got a lot of the unwelcoming glances from a lot of people who didn't understand in the stadium, and they never went again. They opted instead to watch the games at home on television. Mae, even though she didn't much care for sports in general would regularly bake cookies and try to look like she was interested and having a good time when the games were on, and Fred would bring round the root beer. Fred and Noah would also go for walks in the nearby woodland some days and just talk.

'I don't know,' Mae said, not happy with the idea of putting her son on to a gateway drug. 'What next? Heroin, crack?'

Fred laughed and got daggers from Mae. 'Marijuana is far better than the crap the doctors have been giving him up until now. The shit in those drugs is crazy, this is a herb, we're talking about a plant.'

'Oh, I don't know,' Mae was anguishing like only a

mother could.

'Let's ask Noah,' Fred said.

And without any reluctance Noah agreed, to the envy of his two brothers, who were forbidden to even mention drugs. A week later Fred brought over a joint. He rolled the joint sitting on the porch step, the porch he had fixed up last spring. Mae stood watching over him, disapprovingly, with her arms folded. Noah watched, sitting next him, transfixed.

'It smells funny,' Noah remarked, leaning forward.

'Sweetish?' Fred suggested, closing his eyes and holding up the joint to his own nose.

Noah's morning had been a bad one, he had vomited twice already and was frightened to eat anything in case he brought it straight back up again.

Fred put the joint between his lips and lit it up. He took two drags and held them for a few seconds and then exhaled the thick, sweet-smelling smoke up into the air.

'Just like that, Noah,' Fred said, passing him the joint.

Noah grasped the joint between his thumb and middle finger, just like Fred had. He was excited and a little nervous and his arms were jolting up and down and his head was jerking, that horrible chicken movement his mother hated so much. 'Nothing ventured, nothing gained,' Noah said, hoping for a miracle.

Mae looked down at her boy, her boy who had suffered so much. She saw the hope in his eyes and hated it. She had seen that hope too many times in his eyes over the last few years. She had seen it every time the doctors wrote out a new prescription, for a different wonder drug, that simply never worked. But deep down she was asking God, to please let this work.

Noah put the joint to his lips and took one small drag on it and then started coughing almost instantly. Fred gave him a gentle pat on the back and laughed.

'Coughing is good, it opens up the lungs,' Fred said.

'I'll get a glass of water,' Mae said, and ran back into the house. When she came back Noah was taking a second drag. She held the glass in her hand, looking down helplessly at her son. He took the second drag much better and only coughed slightly after.

'That will do for now, champ,' Fred said, taking the joint from between Noah's thumb and middle finger. 'You may feel a little light-headed at first, but that will pass.' Fred took a long drag on the joint, then sighed, blowing a plume of smoke into the air. He seemed to go somewhere far away for a second and Noah looked at him and thought wherever it was he went must be nice, judging by the smile on his face. Fred came back, wet his finger and thumb with his tongue and put the joint out by pressing on the end of it.

'Drink this, Noah?' Mae said, passing her son, whom she had just watched take a gateway drug on her porch with a man dressed in biker gear, who looked like a murderer, a glass of water. I'm going to hell she thought and could almost sense another grey hair coming through.

Noah took a sip of the water and a huge smile appeared on his face. He touched his face, smiling. 'It feels numb, is this normal?'

'Is it normal?' Mae spoke accusingly. 'Will he be all right?' she demanded to know.

'He's doing just fine,' Fred assured her.

Just then Noah started to laugh a little. He tried to take another sip of water, but couldn't because he was laughing too much and the water spilled on to his shorts.

'Do you want to lay down inside on the sofa?' Mae asked.

'Good idea,' Noah said, still laughing.

Mae helped him on his feet, then noticed that his eyes were slightly bloodshot. 'Your eyes, Noah, they're red?'

'Are they?' he said, still smiling.

'What have you done to him?' Mae shouted at Fred.

'It's all perfectly normal,' Fred said softly.

'Mum, I feel great,' Noah said, the new owner of a big grin.

'The worm has turned for you then,' Fred said, patting Noah on the back.

'Help me get him inside,' she told Fred.

Noah laid down on the sofa. The brand-new owner of a powerful smile. Mae and Fred sat opposite him, waiting and watching.

'I can't believe I let you talk me into this,' she said, holding her head in her hands. Fred didn't speak, he just sat there silently next to her.

Five minutes later Noah sat up, eyes a little bloodshot. Mae raised her head, then knew what Fred had already suspected. 'Mum, my tics have gone,' He sat in front of her for the first time in years, not jolting, not jumping, not blinking, not swearing, not shouting. He sat looking at his mum, like her normal little boy. 'Mum look?' he gasped and held out his arms, that were steady.

A minute later Noah was on his feet and walking without trying to push off like a chicken.

'No urge to tic?' Mae asked him.

'None, but I sure could eat a horse.'

'That's called the munchies,' Fred said laughing and Mae

and Noah joined him.

'I'll cook pork chops,' Mae said. 'This calls for a celebration.'

'How long will this last?' Noah asked. 'You know, before it goes back to normal.'

Fred shrugged his shoulders. 'Hard to say, an hour, maybe two, maybe three, but it will come back.'

About an hour after Fred had left for home and after Noah had destroyed three pork chops and Fred two, his tics reappeared like that aunt you try to stay away from at weddings. "I'm back, you didn't think you could fuck me off forever did ya." Fred had explained that Noah should only take the marijuana when his tics were really bad and when he was having a hard time with them and never more than two or three times a day.

That night after her prayers, Mae Templeton went to bed and cried herself to sleep, but for the first time in a long time they were happy tears. Life for the Templeton's got a little easier after that and Mae found herself cooking a lot more pork chops. After a while Fred's visits became less frequent, first weekly, then monthly, then a random phone call out of the blue, then nothing at all. He had met a woman, a botanist who lived in a cabin in The Wayne National Forest, an area that covers a quarter million acres of Appalachian foothills. The last time Noah ever spoke to him, Fred said he was doing fine and very much in love.

Mae died from pancreatic cancer in the spring of 2009, she was surrounded by her children and their families, that included three grandchildren. That same day in the hospital cafeteria, Noah's sister Janet asked Noah if he wanted to come and live with her and her husband and their young son in

Florida.

'It will be a fresh start, the sun always shines and the air is clean and crisp down there,' Janet said, holding an arm around Noah, who had taken it bad. Looking at his red cheeks, Janet thought he must have cried half a pint in tears.

'I've never been out of Ohio.'

'Well, it's about bloody time you had an adventure,' Janet said, planting a kiss on one of her brothers red cheeks.

'You really want me?' Noah said, wiping his sore eyes.

'You kidding? I miss you down there. Plus, you can help with Theo, that kid is a handful and he seems to love you.'

Noah smiled and just like that he was to be a resident of St. Petersburg, Florida. It was a match made in heaven. Weed was just as easy to get hold of and slightly cheaper. He did however have to smoke it in the tool shed so that Theo wouldn't smell it. Above all else Florida had something that Dayton Ohio didn't at that time — A Tourette's support group, or the club as his fellow sufferers called it. Also, he loved the name of the club — The MisFits.

Noah smoked more than usual that first summer in Florida. The humidity played havoc with his body, and he struggled to get a good night's sleep and keep food down. It got so bad Janet finally got Leon, her husband, to replace the AC unit that had broken the summer before.

Noah's confidence grew with The MisFits, finally finding people just like him. His small world became considerably bigger and much brighter. New avenues were opening that he had never even dreamed of. For starters many of the MisFits had jobs, one of them was even a stand-up comedian. Most of them had their own apartments and were in relationships too and not just with fellow sufferers. And nearly all of them smoked pot, not to the extent Noah did, but then again none of them had it as bad as Noah. Also, there was a wonderful rumour going around that marijuana was going to be made legal for medical use soon.

In the supermarket one autumn morning, as Noah was leaving with a loaf of bread in one hand and a jar of chocolate spread in the other, his eye caught the bulletin board. Advertised on the bulletin board was a vacancy for a janitorial position at Young Palms Fundamental Elementary School, not two miles from his home. When he told his sister that he was thinking about applying for the position, she was fully supportive, not thinking that he would actually get the job. A week later, Leon drove Noah to Young Palms Fundamental Elementary School for his interview. Noah wore a red suit, white shirt, red bow tie and red shoes to his interview and looked more like game show host, than someone going for an interview to be a janitor. Dream big his mother always said. Janet and Leon had tried to persuade him into wearing a normal coloured suit, but Noah didn't want to know. Red it was for him.

Noah sat in a waiting room, a black man in a red suit, sweating buckets. He glanced down at the palms of his hands, and they were dripping wet. He was fighting his urge to tic, remembering the competing responses he had learned with Fred all those years before. He wished he had smoked this morning before Leon gave him a lift on his way to work. Every worry in the world was floating through his mind now. He was just at the point of getting up and walking out, when the door to the principal's office opened in front of him and a tiny lady with old fashioned glasses and a head of white curly hair stood in front of him.

'Noah Templeton Jr?' She asked softly with a radiant smile. Her smile put him at ease at once.

Noah nodded slowly at first, then stood up quickly. 'Noah Templeton Jr, that's me, yes ma'am.' He held out his hand and walked towards her and jerked forward once, then jolted up in the air in his red suit.

She didn't laugh at him or show any expression of surprise in his appearance. 'Lovely to meet you dear. I'm Gilda Coleman the Principal of Young Palms. Please come in and take a seat.'

Noah sat down by the desk with his hands clenched together. The walls were filled with colour. The colour of children's drawing and paintings and there was hardly any free space on the wall.

Gilda hadn't even sat down in her chair when Noah said, 'I have Tourette's, but I'm really good at keeping it under control.'

'Noah? Do you mind if I call you Noah? I like to use first names. I find it less formal and more relaxing.'

'Not at all,' he replied and then after a pause he added 'Gilda.' And smiled.

Gilda smiled, leaned forward and whispered. 'Would you like a cookie?'

'Okay.'

Gilda opened one of her desk drawers and pulled out a plate of chocolate chip cookies wrapped in clingfilm. 'I always keep these handy for the children when they've been sent here for being naughty or have a problem. Even the teachers love them. If one of them is having a rotten day, I sit them down, give them a cookie and let them talk.'

They talked and ate cookies together for twenty minutes

or more. Gilda talked about the children and school and how she thinks learning should always be made fun. Noah talked about the home he grew up in back in Dayton Ohio. They both found a common love for basketball and had a disagreement on who was the best ever player. Noah refusing to believe that anyone could ever better Michael Jordan and Gilda wishing Noah had seen Magic Johnson work his magic. By the time Gilda brought up her first real interview question, Noah was so at ease he had forgotten that he was there for a job interview.

'Do you like children, Noah?'

'I do and they seem to like me for some reason, well Theo, my nephew and his friends find me funny.'

'I bet you are good with children and that's important here. They are going to be seeing you around the school every day and a grumpy person is a no no here.'

'Wait, I have the job?'

'If you would like it. The current janitor, Mr Morton, a truly lovely man, is retiring at the end of the year and we need someone very special to fill his shoes. You would work with him and learn from him from now until the end of the school year and then be on your own.'

'I would love this job and I promise to be the best I can be.'

Gilda laughed. 'I know. But we haven't even talked salary yet.'

'I don't care. I have a job.'

'We will need to do the usual, a background check, but once that is done, you'll be free to start,' Gilda paused for a moment. 'Is there anything I should know before we go ahead?'

'Like what?' Noah asked.

'Any conviction? Any special medication? Anything you think I should know?'

Noah's heart suddenly sank. He didn't want to tell Gilda about the marijuana, but he couldn't lie to her. She was someone he thought he had to be completely honest with. He was looking down at his feet now. 'I take marijuana sometimes to control my tics.' He confessed and let out a deep breath.

'I hear it's going to be made legal soon anyway,' she said.

Noah looked up, astonished at her reply. 'I thought you wouldn't give me the job once you knew.'

'You were brave for being honest, Noah. I admire that immensely. Although you must promise me one thing?'

'Anything,' he said, leaning forward with both hands on the edge of the desk.

'You never bring it to school, and you never tell anyone that you smoke. Other than that, welcome to Young Palms Fundamental Elementary School.'

'Do they know you dabble in drugs?' Janet asked, folding a pair of Theo's little trousers. It was laundry day and Janet was nearly always prickly on laundry day. Still, Noah thought she might have been pleased for him, instead of not pleased.

'I told Ms Gilda, that I sometimes smoke a joint to ease my tics. She didn't mind, just as long as I don't bring it to school.'

'She said that?'

'Yes. I thought you would be happy for me.'

'I am. I just don't want you putting too much pressure on yourself and getting sick.'

'I won't,' he said and gave his sister a hug. She smiled, but he thought it was false. She didn't think I would get it, he thought. Worse, he thought, she didn't want me to get it.

When Leon came home from work, he declared it a celebration and went straight back out and brought a bottle of bubbly and a small cake. Leon clearly didn't see a problem with Noah getting a job, in fact he was thrilled about it. Later that night, lying in bed, Noah heard them arguing.

Noah didn't see his work as a job. Often waking up before his five a.m. alarm. He didn't mind the two short bus rides to work, in fact he rather liked them. He liked seeing the same tired faces making their morning commute to wherever they were heading and the same bus drivers and exchanging pleasantries with them. Always arriving at school early and with a big smile. Pleased to learn everything Mr Morton showed him. Mr Morton even remarked over a cup coffee with Earl Barnes, one of the teachers at the school, that he had never seen anyone clean a shitter with a smile on his face like Noah. And the children loved him. Noah had a remarkable gift for remembering the names of all the children at the school. The children would often high-five him, or exchange fist bumps as they passed. And the teachers and parents all liked him.

Shortly after Mr Morton retired, Noah took another huge step, moving out of his sister's house and into a one-bedroom apartment, which was only a ten-minute walk away from the school.

Gilda Coleman was the first person to enter through the doors of the main entrance on the same morning Mayor Kellerman, Mustafa Khoury and the Wheelers were planning to make a visit.

'Noah, the floor looks beautiful. I hope you didn't get here too early?' Gilda asked.

'Just a little earlier than normal,' he replied.

'You shouldn't of.'

'I want the mayor to be impressed,' he said.

'You are too good,' she said and gave him a kiss on the cheek. 'Now come to the teacher's lounge and I'll make you a cup of coffee and you can rest a little.'

# 29

Wednesday June 7<sup>th</sup>, 2017
Boca Ciega Drive, ST Pete Beach, St. Petersburg, Florida
11:00

Franklin shut the door to his den for the last time, saying goodbye to his favourite room, where he would retreat in deep thoughtfulness. He had spent the last hours playing sudoku from an old magazine on men's health that he had found and finished it. Above the number placement puzzle, he wrote these words, "forgive me".

Franklin reached up in the kitchen cupboard and found the box of pop tarts. He smiled when he saw there were two left. He wasn't smiling two minutes later, when his wife walked into the kitchen, just as the pop tarts jumped out the toaster.

'What in holy fuck have you done?' he asked.

'You don't like the new hairdo?' She replied, doing a little twirl.

'No. Who would. You look like Robert DeNiro.' What he meant was, Carol looked like Travis Bickle.

'It feels liberating,' she said, running her hands along her mohawk. 'Your pop tarts are up.'

'Suddenly, I don't feel hungry any more.'

'Pre-match nerves?'

'Something like that,' he replied to the woman he used to

recognise as his wife.

The door to the basement opened and Mustafa walked through carrying blue rucksacks. Carol had given Mustafa, Billy's old school rucksacks to use to put the container full of explosive in. Franklin wanted to shout out and tell the bastard to get his filthy hands off his boy's rucksack.

'Are we ready to go?' Mustafa asked.

'Ready as I'll ever be,' Franklin said.

'You like my new hairdo?' Carol asked.

Mustafa raised his eyebrows. 'I love it. Wear a baseball cap, until we get to the school, we don't want people seeing you looking like that, it will draw suspicion.'

'You have a shaved head?'

'Yes. Yes, I do Carol, but I am a man, not a woman,' Mustafa replied.

'I'll get the car started,' Franklin said, opening the front door.

The very second Franklin opened the front door, a Sully and Sons removal van pulled up, two houses down, blocking the view of the Wheelers residence, from the Gulf Beach Motel.

'Aargh, bat-zonna, fuck you, stupid moving van.' Netzer moaned, his view of the Wheelers now blocked by the Sully and Sons removal van.

'What's wrong?' Sally Anderson asked.

'We are blind. There's a fucking removal van in the way.'

'We need to get eyes on the house,' Sally said.

'I'll go, I need a smoke anyway,' Netzer said.

'I'll join you,' Ron said.

'Take a radio and keep out of sight,' Sally said.

'We are the ghost and the darkness, they'll never see us,'

Netzer said, leaving the room.

'What the fuck does that mean?' Sally asked, but it was too late, they were gone.

'He's not all there, that one,' Chris said.


Franklin started up the Buick and some song by a popular, pretty faced boyband came on the radio. Another break-up song, Franklin thought. 'No wonder the kids are all killing themselves these days,' Franklin said, aloud. He switched the station over and Gerry Rafferty came on telling him he'll get it right next time. Playing the drums with his hands on the steering wheel of the Buick, Franklin's eyes fell upon two fellows, further up on the other side of the street. They looked a long way from Kansas, he thought. One of the men was smoking a cigarette and the other one had something in his hand. A radio, that's a two-way radio in his hand. Worst of all, the men were looking right at him. Franklin's hands dropped from the steering wheel, his legs began to shake and his heartbeat faster. He jumped and almost screamed when he noticed movement in the rear-view mirror. He turned and saw that Carol was looking in at him on the driver's side, wearing a baseball cap.

She knocked on the window and he wound it down. 'Get out and open the passenger door, Franklin?'

He turned his head to look back at the two men further on up the street, but they were gone. 'Where are they?'

'Who?'

'Two men. There were two men.' He was pointing, on up across the street.

Carol glanced in the direction that he was pointing. 'I see nobody. Probably removal men. What the fuck, Franklin, don't freak out on me now. It's game day.'

Franklin nodded, got out slowly and pushed forward the driver's seat. 'They were looking right at me,' he said, looking back on up the street.

'What a fine day,' Mustafa said, emerging from the house for the first time in days. He was holding the blue rucksack by the straps. He placed it gently on the backseat of the Buick. 'Carol, you go in the back, I'll ride up front with Franklin. What's with you, Franklin, you look like you've seen a ghost?' Mustafa asked.

'He thought he saw two men on up the street,' Carol said, rolling her eyes.

'I did see them, and they were looking right at me. I'm not mad.'

Without saying anything, Mustafa walked calmly towards the end of the drive. At the end of the drive, he looked up and then down the street. It was quiet. There was the sound of traffic way off in the distance, but nothing on this street, apart from the removal guys, who were carrying furniture out and talking about last night's game. Still, he didn't like it. Franklin was edgy, but not delusional.

He turned and walked back towards the car. 'It's time to go.'

'I'll just go get my shotgun,' Carol said, and ran back inside.

'What did they look like, these two men?' Mustafa asked.

'Not from around here, tanned looking, scruffy. One of them had a walkie-talkie.'

'A walkie-talkie?'

'You know, a two-way radio.'

'Okay.'

'You believe me, right?'

Mustafa nodded, surveying the street. 'I believe you.'

Carol came back out. She now had on a black raincoat and looked excited, like a child about to go on holiday. 'I got your Uzi under here as well, Franklin. You forgot it.'

She was about to get in the back, when Mrs Wesley caught her eye. She was waving across at Carol and looked like she wanted to come on over and say goodbye.

'Fuck me,' Carol said, waving back at the Wesley woman. 'In all these years, only spoken to the ugly bitch twice and now she's moving, she wants to come on over and say farewell.'

'Just get rid of her,' Mustafa said.

Just for a second, for a single moment, Carol Wheeler, thought he meant shoot the bitch, kill her.

'We're moving to Georgia. Gonna start up a guest house.'

'Can't talk Shelly, we gotta run.' Then turning to Franklin and Mustafa. 'Quick get in the car, let's go.'

'It's Shelia, not Shelly,' Shelia Wesley said, stopping in her tracks on the lawn, face dropping, watching as her neighbours and their guest all climbed into the Buick and pulled away fast.


If the residents who lived across the street from the Wheeler's were at home and had witnessed Ron and Netzer hurdle their hedge, they would have said the two men looked more like Laurel and Hardy, than two of Mossad's finest.

'He made us,' Netzer said, holding his buttocks. He had landed nastily on a rock, hurdling the hedge. 'The rat is coming out the hole.'

'Looks like the whole gang is out now,' Ron said, looking through a gap in the hedge. 'I even see our man, Mustafa, and he's holding a rucksack. Call it in, tell Sally, it's happening now.'

'Would you believe it?' Netzer said, showing Ron the broken radio. 'Must have got damaged when I landed on that fucking rock.'

'We can't let them leave,' Ron said, turning back to look at the driveway of the Wheeler's. Mustafa Khoury was now meters away, standing, scanning the neighbourhood. 'Crawl round the back, stay low and get back to the motel,' Ron whispered.

'What you gonna do, stop them with harsh words?' Netzer asked.

'Just go, and stay low.'

Carol Wheeler didn't see the man who was holding something large in his hands charge the Buick, as it was about to pull out the driveway. She was in hysterics, laughing at Shelia Wesley, who was standing on the lawn, looking dejected. Carol was just about to give her old neighbour the bird, as a parting gift, when Franklin slammed hard on the breaks and let out a piercing scream. Carol — seat belt free and laughing, face planted the back headrest of the front passenger seat. The 12-Gauge, that was resting across her lap flew up then back down, then went off blowing out the passenger window, narrowly missing Franklin's head and her sons old rucksack and sending them all to hell.

'No, no. Drive through him, Franklin!' Mustafa cried, as Franklin's foot slammed down on the brakes. Mustafa, who in all the excitement had not had time to put on his seat belt, hit the dashboard face first, thanks to the force of Carol's head from the backseat. His nose made a crunching sound, smashing against the Buick's clean mahogany dash, spraying red up the windscreen. Then his body catapulted back against the seat, and he slumped down low, blood running down his mouth and chin, disorientated, unable to focus on the mad man outside, eyes filled with a mixture of tears and blood.

Franklin, who had been wearing his seat belt, felt something hot and sharp burn into him. Fragments of glass from the window the 12-Gauge had blown in and shrapnel from the shotgun itself, had grazed the back of his neck. He was the only one in the car who saw the rocky boulder fly into the windscreen. He sat in a hellish silence as the windscreen was attacked, caving in, with thousands of little cracks appearing and forming a huge glass spiderweb. Blood was seeping out from his ears, thanks to the 12-Gauge going off right next to his head. Unable to hear the screams coming from his wife's mouth, or the piano intro to Bruce Hornsby's The way it is coming from the radio. Franklin in a state of shock, put the Buick into reverse and flawed it fast, crashing with speed into his garage. The car disappeared into the darkness and then the garage ceiling collapsed, sending a dust cloud up into the air.

'This is some fucked up shit.' A normally reserved Shelia Wesley, said to no one in particular.

Other everyday folk were standing on their drives now, watching the excitement unfold. The removal men had run over to where Shelia was standing. They watched as the man who had just thrown the boulder at Wheeler's Buick's windscreen, marched on towards the garage.

'Hey buddy, what's your deal?' one of the removal men said.

'Police are on their way, fella.' The other removal man

said, hoping this would scare the madman into stopping his rampage.

Ron paid the men no attention. He had to get to the people inside the car, before it was too late. Ron hesitated for a moment, then climbed in through a gap, where the garage ceiling had collapsed onto the hood of the car.

Inside the cool, dark garage, Carol Wheeler's fight instincts kicked in. She pulled herself out the blown-out passenger side window, cutting her hands, arms and legs on jagged strips of glass. Reaching back inside the Buick and taking the 12-Gauge, Carol Wheeler went around to the back of the car and knelt down low next to the bed that Mustafa had been sleeping on the past few nights and waited like a hunter for her prey, which she suspected would be arriving shortly.

Netzer Ackerman began to bang down the motel room door at about the same time Franklin Wheeler was reversing his beloved 1979 Buick Century Turbo Coupe back into his own garage.

'The fuckers are leaving; we have to go now!'

Malia opened the door and Sally Anderson and Chris unholstered their weapons.

'Why didn't you call it in?' Sally asked.

'Crappy radio's fucked.'

'Where's Ron?' Chris asked.

'Improvising.'

'What the fuck?' Sally shouted.

The four of them ran down the motel steps and out on to the normally peaceful Boca Ciega Drive. The street was filling with spectators and just off in the distance came the sounds of police sirens. Malia was a good twenty yards in front of her teammates and she got to the driveway of the Wheeler's first, where there was a small crowd gathered. The crowd were doing what all good crowds do in 2017 — filming the action and dreaming of all the views that they might get on their social media accounts. And that's when the 12-Gauge began to sing, firing rapidly from inside the garage, the breaching slugs sounded like an explosion outside on the street.

'FBI, everybody, get back, get back and down, now!' Sally Anderson screamed, holding her gun down low. Residents ran back into the relative safety of their homes, tripping over the curb and bumping into one another on their way. A police cruiser came round the corner further on up and Chris went to meet it holding his badge out. Netzer kicked in the front door and made his way in, Malia flanked the house going round the back.

The firing that had come from the garage had ceased now. Slowly Netzer made his way down to the basement, with a meat-cleaver he had taken from the Wheeler's kitchen. Malia who had come in from the back porch, made it to the top of the stairwell just in time to see the basement door open in front of cleaver clad Netzer. A dazed looking man, with blood running from his ears and a dark wet patch, presumably urine, covering his trousers, stumbled through. The man was Franklin Wheeler, and his expression was stupefied. His eyes rose and watched, in what Malia thought at the time looked a like relief, as Netzer swung back, then down, burying the cleaver a good way into Franklin's skull. Franklin eyes did not move from the top of his head, as blood ran down from the cleaver like a fountain, covering his face red. Franklin began to stumble backwards, back to where he had just come, cleaver like

Excalibur, unmoving.

'Franklin? What? Who?' Carol whispered from behind him, then Franklin stopped, still looking up, flapped his arms around, doing one last boogie and collapsed in a heap, like a puppet.

Carol snarled and marched towards the stairwell, stepping over her dearly beloved, 12-Gauge ready to sing again.

Netzer, who was now unarmed, had taken one step backwards up on to the first step of the stairwell, when he locked eyes with Carol Wheeler, who now had him fixed in her sights.

'Netzer?' Malia cried out, looking down on him and his last seconds.

Netzer turned, looked up, then winked. A bang was followed, by the back of Netzer's scull rupturing the front of his face. Maila screamed and jumped in terror, and she backed away leaning against the wall, then tripped over her own feet and fell over on to her backside. She kicked the door to the basement closed with her feet, got up and ran up the stairs. She knelt behind a wardrobe in one of the bedrooms and waited. She could still hear the echo from the 12-Gauge ringing in her ears. She could still see the mess that the breaching slug had made of Netzer's face.

Carol Wheeler walked through the smoke of the 12-Gauge and looked down upon the remains of the man, who had planted a meat-cleaver into her husband's head, like it was a coconut. There was a hole where there had once been a face, teeth stuck out, like broken pegs. Yellow stuff was mixed with blood and bone. One eye ball was still visible, but the nose was mash now.

'You look like mincemeat, you do. That's what you get for

killing Frankie.' Then she spat on him, on his blended-up hole and walked back into the basement. Mustafa was leaning against the bonnet, wiping the blood away from his face, with an old rag.

'Look what they did to my Frankie?' She said, snivelling.

'We have to get out of here.' Mustafa said, listening to the screams and sirens coming from outside the garage, where there was a little sunlight creeping in. He looked down at the man. The first man Carol had put down. She had shot him twice, with the 12-Gauge. One in the leg and one in the neck. There was a pool of blood on the floor. His arms had cramped up and his hands curved over, and he looked like some sort of man-penguin. But it was his eyes. His eyes were staring out, bulging out of his face, as if they were trying to escape his face.

'The boat? We have the boat?' Carol said.

Agent Sally Anderson was the first one to come upon Ron Yaffe, laying in a puddle of his own blood. The gunshot wound that had ripped his neck apart, had killed him almost instantly. From the look on his face and ridged body, he had suffered a catastrophic seizure on impact. Sally knelt beside him and closed his eye lids, getting some of the frothy blood from his mouth on her shirt sleeve.

'Agent Anderson?' Chris called out from the stairwell.

'All clear,' Sally returned.

A moment later, Sally and the Chris were looking down on the butchered remains of Franklin Wheeler and the mess, which once resembled Netzer Akerman.

'Malia?' Sally called out, fearing the worst.

'I'm okay. Up here.' Malia called back.

Sally and Chris found Malia leaning on a washing basket, with a distant look on her face — what veterans of bloody conflicts might refer to as the hundred-mile stare. 'Where are they?' Sally asked.

'I think they've left. I heard a boat start up.'

'I'll get a call out, see if we have any marine patrols in the area,' Chris said.

'Let's get eyes in the sky, as well. We have to find out where they're heading,' Sally said.

'They killed Netzer,' Malia closed her eyes. 'I saw his face disappear.'

'They got Ron, too,' Sally said.

'Ron, as well?' Malia's voice seemed to come from somewhere far away now.

'Did you hear them say where they were going?' Sally asked, grabbing hold of Malia's arms and giving her a little shake, trying to bring her back from the place she was now hiding in.

There was a momentary pause and then Malia's, eyes lit up and she came back from where she temporarily went. 'No, but there's a video recorder on the bed, in there.' Malia, motioned with her eyes to the Wheeler's master bedroom.

By the time a police helicopter was up in the air and flying over the bay, Carol Wheeler and Mustafa Khoury had already made it the short distance across the bay in Franklin's 2009 Sea Fox 236 Centre Console to the Aquarius Marina.

The yard manager for the day, Raymond Machen and head of security Troy Patrick, watched from the port of entry office, where they had a chess game going, as the Sea Fox cruised in down the row.

'It's going a tad fast, don't ya think?' Raymond said, bothered by its approaching speed.

'Woman driver?' Troy asked, before getting up himself to take a better look.

'Slow down, you there, damn it,' Raymond shouted, banging on the window, even though there was no way anyone outside the office could have heard him. He stumbled across the table for the tannoy, but it was too late.

'This is going to be a rough one,' Carol said, as the Sea Fox entered the slip and rammed the dock, cutting the mooring line of the boat in the slip next to them.

'Best we get down there, see these idiots,' Troy said, putting his Security Cap on.

'Fucking a—' Raymond snarled, biting his lower lip in anger. 'These shit-bags are gonna get a piece of my mind.'

Raymond Machen was a big man, with fingers the size of bananas. Welsh by birth, with fiery red hair, and a temper to match. No one fucked with Raymond, no one. Married three times, lived at sea most of his life. His biggest loves in life; the sea, the Lord Jesus Christ, beer and giving people a piece of his mind and beatings. The beatings normally belonged to his wife, who was practically a human punching bag.

The strange couple disembarked the Sea Fox, with their rucksack and weapons of choice hidden from view and made their way along the wooden dock.

'Those fuck-wits have disembarked already, old buddy,' Troy said, marching a few paces in front of Raymond.

'Looks like we got company?' Carol said laughing, gripping the trigger of the 12-Gauge under her raincoat.

'Hey, idiots!' Raymond shouted, pushing past Troy.

'Oh, no. Looks like these amateurs are gonna get the full

Raymondo treatment today,' Troy said, giggling, taking his cap off and slapping his thigh with it.

'You don't enter my boatyard like that,' Raymond said, pointing a thumb at his chest. 'And you never disembark before being properly cleared.'

Raymondo must have been no more than ten feet away from Carol and Mustafa, when Mustafa said. 'Let's not make a scene.' But it was too late. Carol had already raised the 12-Gauge up from under her raincoat. She pressed the butt firmly into her shoulder, keeping it tight not wanting a kick. Raymond Machen was a big target and at this range it would be harder to miss. With the glare of the afternoon sun in his face, Raymondo didn't even have time to fully comprehend what was happening, when Carol squeezed the trigger.

'Home run,' Carol screamed, as Raymondo was struck dead centre, just above the bellybutton. His beer-barrel, as he so often liked to call it, when drinking with his fellow sea dogs, erupted like a volcano, spraying blood and innards into the warm sea air.

Troy Patrick, who was a good three feet behind Raymondo, before Carol Wheeler blew a hole in his stomach killing him instantly, watched as the big man flew past him, guts hanging out, leaving his sandals where he last stood. Suddenly Troy Patrick, wanted to get away, to turn and run, but his legs felt like lead. Warm water ran down his legs, for the first time since he was seven, and butterflies flew around in his stomach. He was aware of a sinking feeling, that familiar one right after take-off, when the plane drops.

As the big guy went flying back, leaving a trail of blood across the jetty, Mustafa screamed and clasped his ears with his hands, pulling at them in agony. He was having a rough morning, and he could now add perforated eardrums, to a broken nose and smashed teeth.

Carol took little notice of her deaf companion and calmly reloaded her 12-Gauge, as she walked towards the squirming Troy Patrick, through the blood trail, that looked oddly like a red carpet at a world premiere on the jetty.

'No, no, no, no!' Troy Patrick cried, pitifully, hands held out rolling around in Raymondo's blood and his own piss.

'Well, it's off to the next life for you, my friend,' Carol said, aiming the 12-Gauge a breaths whisker away from Troy Patrick's thick Irish head.

'Oh, God no, please, oh God no, please, I have kids!' he cried out in desperation. A truth yes. Troy Patrick did in fact have two children. A father, maybe not. He had walked out on them three years before and had not seen them since. The child maintenance money that he should have been paying, always found its way to the strip clubs and hookers who roamed dazedly along 34th Street. Instead of paying for little Alex and Gabby's education expenses, he was funding Starr's coke habit and Crystal's love of meth.

'You don't, no more,' Carol said and squeezed the trigger.

Mustafa saw Carol swing around from the recoil and the man's flailing arms drop down to the floor, and a mist of blood hijack the air. Carol turned to Mustafa, with the 12-Gauge swung over her shoulder. She said something, but all Mustafa could hear was a high-pitched buzzing. She walked over to him and this time he could read her lips.

'We have to get going, we can get a taxi outside the Marina.'

'I can't hear you,' Mustafa shouted, pointing to his ears.

'Why, you've gone deaf, haven't you? How unpleasant

that must be for you.' He saw her say. She turned away from him. 'I will be your ears now,' she said, but he didn't get it.

They walked around the two dead men lying next to each other. Mustafa yelled out, nearly slipping in their combined blood. The right side of Troy Patrick's head was blown completely off, just above his right eyebrow. The smell of blood, mixed with the sea air and heat was sweet. Flies were already starting to gather on the two dead moist bodies. They walked fast along the jetty, past the peering eyes of the scared people hiding in their boats. They climbed a set of steps, past the port of entry office, where only five minutes earlier there were sat two men playing chess and drinking cokes. A picturesque picnic park, which overlooked the bay, was all that now separated them from the road and a taxi, which would take them to their final destination.

A young family, who had been picnicking under the shade of an old oak tree when the gunfire started to go off, now hid behind a small island of shrubs. The father watched as the mother held her two young children tight against her breasts, telling them to keep still and quiet. The father witnessed two people, one of whom was carrying a rucksack emerge from the Aquarius Marina gate and walk fast across the green grass. They came to where the family had been picnicking and stopped. One of them; a woman, took off a black raincoat and dropped it on to the red and white blanket, that the family had just been picnicking on. The woman was holding a shotgun and she laid it down on the blanket. She then emptied the contents of the picnic basket on to the blanket, discarding everything apart from an apple and a bottle of water. The woman drank some of the water, then took off her baseball cap, revealing a mohawk. She poured some of the water over her head, then put the baseball cap back on. The woman's companion, a man with a bloodied face, was then given the bottle and he did the same. The woman took a couple of bites of the apple then offered it to the man who waved it away. The woman took another bite and then threw the apple in a bush. The woman put her shotgun into the picnic basket and the two of them strolled out the park, holding hands. The father got his phone and took a picture of the couple, as they got to the road and waved down a taxi. He was about to phone the police, when he heard the sirens of approaching police cars. He saw a police car pull in, not a minute and ten feet away from where the strange couple had just left in a taxi.

While Boca Ciega Drive was being evacuated, and the bomb disposal squad were searching high and low at the Wheeler's residence, Agent Anderson and her final remaining Israeli counterpart, Malia Kimani drove fast through the early afternoon traffic. The four-minute video they had just watched had made both of them feel sick to the stomach. On the video recording, Carol and Franklin Wheeler, had both spoken of the murder of babies, children. Revenge. They had a destination. A target. Only, the four-minute recording gave no indication of where the target was to be. Sally and Malia raced into the city, hoping for a miracle. Chris had stayed back at the Wheeler's, looking for clues on their computer to where the target might be. Tim Baines had been informed and he had made the decision to tell Washington and call in all the other authorities.

'We have two crazies running around St. Petersburg armed with god knows what and we just let them slip right through our hands,' Sally said, gripping the steering wheel so tightly that her knuckles were going white.

'Can't we just evacuate all the schools?' Malia asked.

'There are close to five thousand schools in Florida.'

'Disney World?'

'We have extra units heading there now. But it's not there. It's closer than that. Disney World is ninety miles away. It's a school, close by.'

The car phone rang once before Sally answered it on speaker phone.

'Go ahead, Chris?' Sally answered.

'We found a map, a lay out of Young Palms Fundamental Elementary School. That's their target. It looks grim.'

'Address, Chris?'

'2229, 25th Street. Units are already on the way there. Looks like they might be in a taxi. Two people matching their descriptions got into a taxi outside the Aquarius Marina, five minutes ago. Reports of shots fired and several fatalities.'

'We're only a few blocks away from 25th Street,' Sally said.

'Jesus Christ, an elementary school,' Malia said. 'How far away is that?'

'Five minutes, max.' Sally glanced over at Malia, who was looking straight ahead at the road and nodding. 'Listen,' Sally said. 'There should be a shotgun in the trunk, you'll need it when we get there.'

Malia drew in a deep breath and blew out. 'Let's go clean them up.'

Ethan Shiherlis dropped off his fare, a strange looking couple, outside the St. Petersburg Mercy Gospel Church. He would go on to tell later, that he thought they might have had children that went to the school. Both passengers sat apart from each other, looking dazedly out the window. The man had a child size rucksack resting on his lap and the woman had a picnic basket at her feet. They gave him the creeps, yes, but so did many of the people who got in his taxi. He had seen it all. Odd maybe, but at least they were not trying to shoot up, or have sex, like so many of his fares. The woman paid with cash and tipped generously. A block and two minutes later, Ethan Shiherlis pulled into a gas station, and saw another cabbie, Zack Hanna.

'You haven't seen them, have you?' Zack shouted, from the row across from Ethan, where he was standing at the pump and filling up his tank.

'Who you on about, Zack?' Ethan shouted back across.

Zack closed the cap and walked across to Ethan. 'Did you not hear the controller say to be on the lookout for a couple carrying a rucksack and weapons. Apparently, these jokers wasted some people at the Aquarius Marina and then jumped into one of our cabs.'

Ethan's face dropped, 'I think I just dropped them off.'

'You kidding? Didn't you hear control say?'

'Ear-piece is fucked, keep getting static. Reported it yesterday, but no one gave a shit and two cents.'

'Where did you drop them?'

'Young Palms Elementary,' They both turned to look down the street, in the direction of the school. 'They tipped me good.'

Mustafa watched the taxi pull away and drive on up the street, where heat waves from the sun were bouncing off the tarmac. He looked at his wristwatch, 12:02. They had made it, a few minutes late, but they had made it. Somehow, they had escaped. He opened the rucksack and checked the bomb for the last time. He took the detonator in his hand. Not long to live now, he thought. The doors to the St. Petersburg Mercy Gospel Church were open, letting in the sunshine. It was rehearsals day, and the choir were belting out "He's got the whole world" in a stirring harmony. Across the street, a man was mowing his lawn, and somewhere off in the distance a dog was barking, maybe sensing something coming.

'A beautiful day for a massacre, wouldn't you say?' Carol said, kneeling by the picnic basket and checking her 12-Gauge. Mustafa who couldn't hear her, said nothing. He was looking on down the street.

Carol stood up, kicking the picnic basket into the road. She tapped Mustafa on the shoulder, and he turned to face her. 'It's-time-to-go,' she said, speaking slowly so he could understand. This irritated him, but he was glad he would not have to see her again. He nodded and held out his hand and they shook. Carol started off across the green towards the wall. Her shadow danced on the grass as the branches above swayed in the breeze, breaking the sunlight.

As the St. Petersburg Mercy Gospel Church choir sang "He's got the whole world in his hands" Carol Wheeler joined in, changing the words, as she strolled across the green with her 12-Gauge flung over her shoulder.

'I've got a 12-Gauge in my hands, I've got a 12-Gauge in my hands, I've got a 12-Gauge in my hands, I've got a 12-Gauge in my hands.'

Carol rested her 12-Gauge on top of the wall, then clumsily scaled it, throwing one leg over and then pushing her body up, before swinging the other leg over and sliding down.

Mustafa watched as Carol disappeared over the wall. He walked to the corner and turned on to 25th Street. He was ten feet from the main entrance, when he saw a car racing up the street. Mustafa unzipped his hoodie and grabbed hold of the Ruger, unclipping it from his shoulder holster. He walked on, holding the weapon in one hand down by his side and the detonator in the other hand, a simple press away from oblivion.

Sally Anderson turned onto 25th Street at speed, skidding across the road, the car's rear swinging out, narrowly missing a sign that read "School Zone 15 MPH".

'Young Palms, there it is on the left up ahead,' Malia said, holding on to the passenger's side grab handle for dear life.

'I see it.'

They pulled up level with Mayor Jake Kellerman's dark limousine that was facing them. The driver's window was down, a young dude of no years whatsoever had his earphones in and was listening to some young teenage boyband sing about how love really, really hurts. He was bobbing his head to the noise coming from his earphones, oblivious to the world outside. On his lap was a newspaper that he had no intention of ever reading, and inside the newspaper was a Playboy magazine, that he had every intention of using again and again.

Malia wound down her window. 'Hey kid? Hey kid?' He didn't notice her. The kid was in a titty trance. She got out, and banged on the roof of the limousine, looking in at him at the same time. 'Jesus, kid,' Malia said, looking down at the Playboy.

'Argh,' he screamed with fright, newspaper and Playboy flying up in the air.

'I'm with the mayor, the mayor,' he screamed with

embarrassment, as if saying this gave him a license to look at Playboy.

'The mayor's in there?' Sally Anderson asked, getting out the driver's side.

'You seen anyone strange go inside that building?' Malia asked.

'What? What?' The kid snapped, his face red, but not with embarrassment now, but with anger. These fuckers had interrupted him. 'You don't come up on someone like that lady,' he snarled.

'Calm down, jerk-off,' Malia responded.

Parked behind the limousine was a four-wheel drive. Neither Sally Anderson, Malia, or the young jerk-off driver noticed Mustafa Khoury standing the other side of it, holding a hand cannon in one hand and a detonator in the other.

'It's Billy, and you can't call me that.'

A shadow fell across the limousine's roof. Malia looked up and saw a man, holding a gun. The man was smiling at her, with dark expressionless eyes and she knew all at once that he was insane. From behind her, she heard Sally Anderson shout something inaudible. Then time seemed to slow down for her. She watched the man, whom she realised now was Mustafa Khoury, pull the trigger. A loud thumping noise as the bullet broke the sound barrier. She saw the gun recoiled back. Something hot, whizzed past the side of her face and she felt her cheek warm. Instinctively she rolled her head to the side and dropped to the floor, letting her legs give out and falling flat on her face. Suddenly she was aware that she was screaming and not for the first time today. Overhead, three more cracking thumps, as more bullets broke the sound barrier. All at once her cover was broken. Jerk-Off Billy turned on the ignition and floored the limousine, with his head down.

'Mommy!' he screamed.

Malia Kimani watched as the limousine mounted the pavement and then crashed, dead on into an oak tree. She turned her head to the right and saw that Mustafa Khoury was lying face down in a pool of his own blood, with a small blue rucksack on his back and detonator resting in his hand.

'You got him,' Malia said, victoriously and got to her knees. Silence. Malia got to her feet and began to walk around the car. 'Oh, no,' she sighed. Sally Anderson was leaning forward in a sitting position, still holding on to her gun, that was now resting on her left thigh. There was an entry wound in her temple, a perfect in and out and she looked like she had been scalped by an Indian. Her hair was damp and soaked with blood that ran down and covered her face. 'Oh, Sally,' Malia said, kneeling down next to her. She hardly had time to mourn her friend. More firecrackers, cracking, screaming, children screaming. She turned her head towards the school. Carol Wheeler? She had forgotten all about that crazy bitch. Malia took the gun from Sally Anderson's lifeless hand and ran towards the school, stepping over the lifeless body of Mustafa Khoury. She heard approaching police sirens, then saw the limousine driver's door open. Jerk-Off Billy got out, after a struggle with his airbag. He looked at Malia, who was holding a gun.

'Don't kill me,' he moaned, tears rolling down his spotty face. 'Please, look, I'm not worth it,' Malia ignored him and he ran down the street towards the police sirens, screaming.

Carol Wheeler walked along the passage that led all the way down the back of the school and ended at the playground. She peered into the first window and saw that the classroom was empty. A sudden fear crept into her crazy mind, a mind now void of all rational, and moral logic. Where are the little fuckers? Please tell me, school's not out already. Then from the next classroom along, where the window was slightly ajar, came the innocent laughter of the pure. She peered in and saw little hands waving up in the air, little legs swinging, not yet long enough to touch the floor. One child was picking his nose, and two others were giggling at each other, the beautiful way that only children can. Carol saw something move out the corner of her eye and she jumped with fright, hiding up back against the wall. A black cat had walked along the wall and was now looking down at her. It hissed at her, not once but twice. She wanted to shoot it. It knows what I'm here to do, she thought. It knows my business. Carol remembered her aunt telling her, when she was very little on a trip to the zoo, that animals know things, they know the good and they know the bad people. Carol got on to her hands and knees and crawled like one of the devil's imps under the window and along to the next classroom. She peered in. Empty. There was one more classroom, before the playground. This is the one she thought.

Carol Wheeler took in a deep breath and exhaled. She smiled and began to caress her weapon. She began to sing. 'Run children, run children, run, run, run, here comes Carol with her gun, gun, gu…'

Crack, crack, crack, crack, the unmistakable sound of gunfire. He's started without me? Carol Wheeler thought. Carol Wheeler stepped out, 12-Gauge aiming at the window.

Noah Templeton Jr. was standing next to Gilda Coleman, by the classroom door. They watched on as Mayor Jake

Kellerman sat on a chair, that was far too small for him. The children sat around him in a semicircle on the floor. He was reading, The Tiger Who Came To Tea, with his back to the window. He read with purpose and seemed to genuinely love the book. Gilda was impressed with him, and the children were engrossed in the tale. Gilda had mentioned to Noah earlier in the morning, over coffee, that she believed Jake Kellerman could one day become the governor and maybe one day even higher, because he had a wide appeal. 'He's the only politician, I've met who doesn't act like one, he's got the JFK thing going on. Most of them these days are like psychopathic robots, like LBJ, and that maniac we've got now, with the ridiculous combover. I think our current one probably played too much Lego as a child. He would have been better off being a bricklayer than a president.'

Annie Garrett was sitting with the children on the floor. Gilda's glaze was on her future President, but Noah's eyes kept wandering to Miss Garrett. Noah thought that glory rose in her face when she smiled at him, and the sun set when her eyes fell upon him. She had only been teaching at Young Palms a year, but in that year, Noah had found himself daydreaming about her frequently. In his dreams he wasn't the janitor, but a modern-day knight. A hero. But when do dreams ever come true? He glanced at her, he folded his arms, he wanted to tic, to jump around like an idiot. How unfair, how unfair he thought, then jumped a little.

The other adult in the room was Glen DeCroce. He was the mayor's personal assistant and he was going around the classroom taking photos, as the mayor sat like a giant in one of the children's chair, reading.

When Agent Anderson and Mustafa Khoury, started

exchanging bullets, Mayor Jake Kellerman looked up from the book with fear in his eyes. Some of the children, who had never heard the sound of gunfire before, began to giggle and look around the room at each other with curiosity. It sounded like firecrackers, it sounded like fun. Looks of anguish were exchanged between the adults, Gilda to the mayor, Annie to Noah, the mayor to his assistant. Gilda nodded at the mayor and she opened the classroom door to leave the room.

'Lock the door behind me will you, Noah,' Gilda Coleman instructed.

'I'll come with you.'

'No. Stay here with the children, don't let anyone in, you don't know.'

The mayor kept on reading, the children turned back to the mayor, whatever it was, it was over for now.

'Lady,' one of the children said, pointing to the window, directly behind, where the mayor was sitting.

Mayor Jake Kellerman, turned around just in time to see thousands of glass shards explode into his face. Annie Garrett screamed and got up and ran to the front of the window, to shield the children with her body. Children screamed and started to run around the classroom aimlessly. Mayor Jake Kellerman was laid out, rolling in agony on the floor, holding both hands to his bloody face. Glen DeCroce dropped his top of the range Nikon camera on the floor and turned around to jump behind the teacher's desk. He was flying in mid-air when Carol Wheeler caught him with a shot to the thigh, spinning him around and snapping his right femur like kindling. The gunshot echoed monstrously in the classroom, deafening the screams of the little ones who cried out helplessly for their mothers. Annie Garrett, looked towards Noah, like a princess in jeopardy.

Carol Wheeler began to climb through the broken window, like a troll, who has found a porthole to the land of easy chewing children.

'Here I come children. Here's Carol, with her, gun, gun, gun.'

Noah, never one for sprinting anywhere, ran across the classroom with such speed that Annie Garrett said later that she could have been watching Usain Bolt run across that classroom.

Carol Wheeler had just put both feet down onto the classroom floor, when she noticed a man racing towards her. She lifted her 12-Gauge up towards him and before she had a chance to pull the trigger, the man kicked out. The 12-Gauge flew out of her hands and across the room hitting a whiteboard.

A look of dumb horror was in her eyes. 'Hey, you can't do that,' she said vaguely.

Noah picked the woman, the troll, up, wrapping both his hands tightly around her neck. Carol Wheeler's legs dangled, kicking out at him, her face turned red. Carol grabbed a hold of his arms, but it was of no use, he was superiorly stronger. Noah, span Carol Wheeler around like a shot putter and launched her across the room. Carol Wheeler flew, like a rag doll across the room, smashing face first into the far wall, knocking down some drawings that the children had done. She staggered back up to her feet, blood streaming from her nose, head pounding and dazed. The classroom door flew open and Carol Wheeler turned towards it.

Malia Kimani had kicked the door open, and all at once, she was face to face with Carol Wheeler. Malia Kimani had not noticed that the Wheeler woman was unarmed, she didn't much care either.

'Well, fuck,' Carol Wheeler, snarled, shrugging her shoulders.

Malia Kimani squeezed the trigger and put a bullet into Carol Wheeler's memory bank, sending her straight to hell.

# 30

Wednesday June 14th 2017
Jerusalem, Israel 19:33

'You did well. You know that, right?' Ayala Gazit said, leaning forward in her chair, in her newly furnished office.

'Still,' Malia paused. 'Many people died.'

'True. But in Florida there are mothers reading their children bedtime stories and fathers who are pushing them on swings. Generations have been saved,' Ayala smiled. 'Do you know the president himself thanked us for our part in stopping this disaster. Of course, not publicly,' Ayala said regrettably.

You, ambitious ladder climbing bitch. 'Aces,' Malia said.

'Shame about that Mayor losing sight in one of his eyes. But I hear his popularity ratings have skyrocketed. You watch,' Ayala laughed. 'He'll be running for president next.'

'Ron and Netzer and Sally Anderson died. Sally was a good Agent. Very young.'

'So I've been told. As for Ron and Netzer, they will be missed.'

'They were solid, right to the end.'

'Take some time off, visit some friends and come back when you're fresh. I want you working closely with me. I have big plans for you girl,' said Ayala Gazit, lighting a cigarette. The two women were looking out over the city now, from the balcony of a government building.

The sun was going down over Jerusalem, blood glory. The same way it had done for thousands of years, whilst numerous clans fought over it and would continue to fight over it forever.

Malai Kimani, who had only two days before been to the funerals of both Ron Yaffe and Netzer Ackerman, said nothing.

In the car park, Gavish Molcho was waiting for her. 'I will miss them. They were unique,' Gavish said, resting on the hood of the car. Up ahead, coming towards them, a group of small children were walking and laughing the evening away.

Malia Kimani, nodded. 'I think they were the last of their kind. They really cared. For them it wasn't about ambition.'

'Can I give you a ride back to Tel Aviv? Shazamat are playing later tonight, I have a spare ticket. I'm good friends with the bassist.'

'Nope, I'm gonna visit some friends here in J-town,' she lied.

Malia Kimani walked down to East Jerusalem and brought a shawarma from a street vendor, amidst the array of taxis and shuttle buses coming and going from the West Bank and airport. She sat down on an old brick wall to eat. Three stray cats waited impatiently at her feet, rubbing themselves up against her legs, eyeing up her shawarma. Malia took in the hustle and bustle, the aromas. She watched as a small tour group, of mostly Americans, hurried their way through keeping their hands in their pockets and on their fanny packs. She watched them dissolve into the crowd, their long white socks disappearing on their way to the Garden Tomb for an evening musical concert. Two young Arab men, holding hands, crossed the street to talk to another young man, who had just finished loading a cart with cardboard and was now fastening it down with a worn strap. Her gaze wandered to a nearby cafe. Inside Arab men sat at tables smoking hookah whilst watching a football match on a small television. She walked through an ally past more stray cats and an Arab woman sweeping the floor. She climbed a set of stone stairs and checked into to a cheap hostel opposite the Damascus Gate. She asked for a single room. The manager of the hostel was named Faisal. He told her that this was his hostel, and she was most welcome. He was missing a hand and in its place was a hook and he was blind in one eye. Faisal made Malia sit down in the lounge with the other guests, whilst her room was being prepared. A boy brought her over a cup of mint tea, and she thanked him. In her room she pulled the curtains, took off her clothes and laid down naked on the bed and began to cry. When she was done crying, she went to sleep. She awoke a few hours later and switched on the bedside lamp. She went over to where her jacket was flung over a chair and took out a copy of the report from one of the inside pockets and read it over again. She skipped down to the part that read, the bomb, that was found on the deceased Mustafa Khoury, had the potential to blow up the school and much of the surrounding area. Mustafa Khoury's thumb was resting on the detonator when he was killed.

It bothered her. Malia was sure Agent Anderson died a hero and Ron and Netzer didn't die in vain. But it bothered her, nonetheless. Mustafa Khoury had enough time to detonate, and he didn't.

'Why didn't you detonate? Why? Had you second thoughts? Was it a moment of hesitation? You had time.'

Questions that would never be answered. Malia crunched up the report in her hands and dropped it on the floor. She switched the light off and laid back down on the bed. She thought of Sally Anderson. She thought of Netzer Ackerman. She thought of Ron Yaffe. 'So much violence. So much violence.' She closed her eyes and went back to sleep.

# 31

A Spring Day In 2018

In a cafe in Maryville, Tennessee, two lovers sat side-by-side. Winona Rieves put down the dessert menu she was holding in her hands. 'No, no, it's impossible, I couldn't possibly eat another thing, but I won't say no to another coffee. There is nothing in this world that makes you appreciate a good coffee, like three weeks of hiking.'

'You can say that again,' Fred said, picking up the dessert menu.

'And appreciate a nice dessert as well!' Winona said, smiling at him, as he studied the dessert menu, deciding on what delightful sugary treat he was going to indulge in.

'That's the winner,' Fred said, smacking a finger down on his choice.

Winona looked to where his finger lay. 'Homemade apple cobbler, with vanilla ice cream. Good choice.'

The waitress came over and took their orders. Afterwards Fred declared that that was the best apple cobbler he had ever eaten. 'I think I'm turning into a dessert aficionado.'

'I don't know how you managed it, after the catfish.'

'I'm afraid you fell for a gourmand,' Fred said, smacking both his hands down on his stomach, that really wasn't that big at all.

'Let's get back to the motel before you pop,' Winona said, giving him a wink.

'Like the Frenchman, in that Monty Python film? The one you don't like.'

'Meaning of Life.'

'That's the one.'

They strolled hand in hand the short distance up the road, and back to the motel, with no great urgency. The remnants of the day were fading, and a wonderful red sky lay over the Great Smoky Mountains National Park.

Shortly before midnight, Fred was awoken. Winona was tapping at his shoulder. 'What's wrong, darling?'

'It's my darned head.'

'Migraine?'

'Bad one, feels like I got pins digging in my eyes.'

'Have you got any painkillers left?'

'I used the last of the painkillers the night before last.'

'Okey-dokey. There's a seven-eleven down the road. Just let me put my jeans on and find my wallet.'

Fred went to turn the bedside lamp on and Winona pulled his arm away, stopping him. 'Don't, please, no lights.'

Fred kissed her on the head. 'Sorry hun, nearly forgot. Luckily yours truly has excellent night vision.'

Fred stumbled around in the dark, putting his clothes on, almost tripping over a few times. Once he was finally dressed, he made his way to the door, opened it and went outside. There was a chill in the air, and he could see his breath, but the air smelt good, crisp and springy. All the stars were out, and Fred thought that they would be impossible to count up. He saw not another soul on the short walk down to the seven-eleven, only hearing a barn owl off in the distance. He gave the clerk, a young kid, a nod as he entered the seven-eleven and the clerk gave one back, then went back to watching the television and eating chips. Fred picked up a pack of Tylenol and then took a long hard look at the array of candy bars but decided against getting one. On the way to the counter, he glanced quickly at the shelves with the magazines on, trying not to look up at the dirty ones. He stopped just before the counter, dead in his tracks. He had to turn around and walk back to look at the picture on the front of Time magazine. 'What is this?' He picked the Time magazine up in both hands and brought it closer to his face, to make sure there was no mistake. There wasn't. Fred smiled. 'Noah!!' he shouted in delight. The picture showed Noah grinning, holding a mop and a bucket and wearing sneakers. Behind him, in what appeared to be a classroom, was a bunch of little children smiling. In the middle of the picture, written in bold white capital letters:

NOAH TEMPLETON JR

HERO OF YOUNG PALMS ELEMENTARY

Fred paid for the magazine and sat down on a bench outside and read the article. He read about how Noah had helped stop a domestic terrorist from killing the children in the classroom. The article also told how a brave female FBI Agent, had killed another one of the terrorists, but subsequently lost her own life, doing so. No children were killed, but both the mayor, who was visiting the school and his assistant, suffered severe life changing injuries in the attack.

Ms Annie Garrett, who was witness to the classroom attack, recalls the events on the 7th June 2017. "It happened so quick. The mayor and his assistant were shot and the noise was just incredible, deafening. The little ones were running around screaming. I saw the woman with the shotgun climb through the window, and I remember looking towards Noah. That's when it all turned to slow motion. I can still see Noah running towards the woman with the shotgun. She was ready to fire again, but Noah kicked the shotgun out of her hands. Then I saw the woman fly through the air. I've never seen strength like it, and probably never will again. If not for his quick actions, it would have been a massacre, and I would not be here talking to you."

When asked by Time what his plans for the future were? Noah tells Time "I'm happy to stay here, with the people I love. I love being the janitor of Young Palms."

Fred closed the magazine, folded it and put it in his back jean pocket. He walked slowly back to the motel smiling and weeping. He had never felt so proud in all his life. Fred wiped away his tears just before entering the motel room, he didn't want Winona to see he had been crying. He shouldn't have worried, because the room was dark when he entered.

'Medicine man is back,' Fred declared, sitting down on the bed and passing Winona the Tylenol.

'Thank you, my love,' Winona said. She swallowed the Tylenol down with a glass of water.

'Isn't it a funny old world,' Fred said, lying down, hands behind his head, and looking up at the ceiling.

'Sure is,' Winona said, cuddling up against him. 'Sure is.'